THE REAL DEAL

— A ST9 THRILLER —

C. M. CONNEY

Published by
Ace Lyon Books
June 2017

Published by
Ace Lyon Books
Acelyonbooks.com
First Edition
Cover Design by S. M. Savoy
C. M. Conney *The Real Deal*
ISBN 978-1-947122-29-1
eBook ISBN 978-1-947122-01-7

Dedication

To the amazing women in my life who are too numerous to name here— thank you for your fine examples.

To my mother, Lynn, who imbued in me a love of books.

(Mom, you might want to skim the racy bits!)

To my grandmothers who were all amazing women in their own ways.

To my mother-in-law, Joan, whose marriage has been an inspiration for true love that neither time nor death can wither.

To my 'Aunt' Anita Nysik, who published her first book in her seventies and inspired me never to give up a dream. A woman who lived a life worth emulating with strength and grace. She is sorely missed.

And lastly, to my beautiful daughter, Natalie, who is a dream come true.

CONTENTS

THE REAL DEAL

ONE

———◆———

I SURE DID PICK A GOOD ONE

GLASS shattered under Lena's feet, and she sobbed, stifling the sound behind a clenched fist. A man yelled, but the pounding of blood in her ears drowned him out. Lena stumbled and caught herself before she fell. Unsteady in her heels, she cursed herself for venturing out alone in such a rundown section of town.

A dim streetlight beckoned, an oasis of hope in the dark alleyway. Legs trembling with fatigue and fear, Lena put on a surge of speed and chanced a glance backward. Only murky darkness and indistinct shapes met her terrified gaze.

Rapid footsteps thudded, smashing through the glass bottle she'd broken moments earlier.

Unbidden, a scream burst from her lips as she collided hard with a man, so intent on the men

1

chasing her, she hadn't noticed the man in front until she'd bumped into him. Fear caused her knees to buckle, and only the man's tight grip kept her upright.

"Lena?"

"Daniel, thank God!" Lena grabbed her husband's shirt in two trembling hands as she craned over her shoulder, peering back the way she'd come.

"Run, Lena. Get to the hotel!" Dan pushed her behind him.

Lena hesitated, biting her lower lip as she tried to force the darkness to reveal her husband's expression.

"Go!" he barked, already running toward the advancing men.

She spun on her heel and ran as fast as her four-inch stilettos would let her.

What the hell was she doing in this dark alleyway? Dan glanced back at his wife, then turned his attention to the approaching assailants.

Thank God he'd decided to check on her. The fool should've known better than to try this shortcut to the hotel. No part of Tijuana was safe, but some parts even a trained soldier would be wary of entering.

A hard smile crossed Dan's lips. He was more than a trained soldier; he was a trained killer. The two men chasing his wife had picked the wrong target. With natural grace, Dan ran into the dark alley toward the sound of the approaching men.

"When I get my hands on that little bitch—" the man speaking cut off abruptly as Dan grabbed him by the throat with one hand and pulled him close.

Without giving the man a chance to react, Dan punched him as hard as he could in the stomach.

2

The man wheezed and sagged in Dan's grip. Dan shifted his hold, placing an arm around the man's neck, turning him away, and dragging him backward.

"Carlos?" another man yelled.

"Carlos is busy now!" Dan shouted as he tightened his grasp, not letting Carlos speak.

"Whoever the fuck you are, this don't concern you. Let Carlos go and you get to live."

"The fuck it doesn't!" Dan squeezed tighter as Carlos tried to pull away.

Carlos gagged as he clawed at the arm holding him.

Dan punched him in the kidney. A streetlight loomed out of the darkness, illuminating a real road, not another alleyway. *Few people were abroad, but someone would be bound to see this altercation and likely call the police.*

The man in the alley seemed to reach the same conclusion.

"Take one more step, and I'll blow your fucking head off! Let Carlos go!"

Standing in the weak light cast by the streetlamp in the mouth of the alley, the man facing Dan held a gun in both hands. Slicked back black hair with a pair of sunglasses resting on top and an angry scowl were all Dan had time to notice before the man fired.

The bullet came nowhere near him but did cause him to jump back. Carlos struggled in his grasp.

Dan's gaze flitted around the nearly empty street, landing on a woman standing under the streetlight with a shocked expression on her face. Long blond hair caught up in a high ponytail trailed across a black sweatshirt.

Dressed in black jeans and boots, she appeared to

be a cat-burglar caught in the act. Hands raised and backing away, her horrified gaze locked on the scene unfolding before her.

"Run!" Dan gestured with his chin.

The woman stared at him for a moment.

"Or don't." Dan rolled his eyes, shrugged at the woman, hit Carlos in the side of the head and pushed him at the gunman.

Carlos landed on his hands and knees. The gunman hesitated. Dan didn't. He headed at his top speed to a nearby street corner, opposite the woman.

"Stop!" The gunman yelled, then fired.

A man screamed, the scream turning into a gasping moan and dull thud.

"Fuck— Carlos— what the fuck?"

Dan glanced back. The gunman had shot his partner who'd apparently leaped up to give chase right as he shot. Dan put some extra oomph in his step. He didn't want to be anywhere near this alley when the police arrived. Time in a Tijuana jail wasn't on his to-do list.

Within five minutes, he reached the hotel. Lena threw herself into his arms as he opened the door. Tears had tracked through her makeup, and her hands shook as she ran them over his chest and then stood back to inspect him.

"Oh, thank God you're okay."

"Who were those men?"

"No idea," Lena said as she turned away and wobbled to her suitcase where she took out a bottle of tequila with hands that still trembled.

Dan absently accepted the drink she handed him. "Are you okay? They didn't hurt you, did they?"

"No, I'm fine, just a bit shaken."

She drank her glass in one gulp and poured herself another. This one she sipped as she headed to the bathroom. After a moment, the shower ran.

Dan followed her.

"Lena..."

Lena gave him a coy smile over her shoulder as she unbuttoned her white silk blouse. Underneath was nothing but woman. Surgically firm breasts tipped with dark-rose nipples reflected in the mirror over the sink. She dropped the light-gray skirt she wore to the floor. Naked, she trailed her hands over her body as she leaned down to remove her heels.

"I shouldn't have tried that shortcut. Let me thank you for rescuing me." A seductive smile on her full lips, Lena stepped into the shower and lifted her face to the warm spray. Steam filled the small room, obscuring the dated fixtures and cracked linoleum floor.

Dan chuckled, downed his drink, and placed the empty glass on the counter before joining his wife in the shower.

"Remind me to re-tape the shower-head," Dan said as he adjusted the angle of the spray. "Why the hell are we staying in this pit anyway? Much nicer hotels are just a few miles away."

"Don't complain, lover boy. Let Lena make you real happy."

Dan laughed as she slid down his body and took him in her mouth. Eyes closed and head tipped back, he rested his hands lightly on her head as she used her tongue and mouth to get him off. With practiced efficiency, she made him come in minutes. Dan sighed hard when she twisted away from his embrace.

"Give me a few minutes to clean up," she said.

Dan sighed again and left her alone to finish her shower, knowing if he pursued physical contact she'd become angry.

His discontent faded as he spied the bottle of tequila. A few drinks and they would be relaxed and happy. The real Lena would emerge past the practiced seductress, the Lena he liked with the bold laugh and devil-may-care attitude. While he appreciated her bedroom skills, he liked her better when she forgot to try so hard.

Thirty minutes later, he slouched on the bed with his arms behind his head as his wife dressed. An almost empty glass of tequila sat on the bedside table beside him.

Damp blond hair caught up in a twist on the back of her neck, she dropped the threadbare towel, stretched out one long leg, and leaned over to pull on a sock. Every move she made was calculated to provoke a male response. Pointed toes and breasts outthrust, she made putting on socks a sexual show.

Dan laughed and patted the bed beside him. "C'mere and I'll keep you warm."

Lena glanced at him and straightened, letting the silk robe in her hand fall to the floor. Her gaze traveled his body as her cheeks flushed. "I sure did pick a good one, didn't I?" she murmured as she climbed onto the bed on her hands and knees.

"Me too." Dan ran a palm over her generous curves. "I could get used to this."

Lena giggled and straightened as he attempted to kiss her.

Dan scowled and dropped his hands. His new wife

hadn't ever kissed him on the lips and slept as far from him as she could get on her side of the bed.

"Don't frown, lover boy. I'm going to make you real happy." Her hands wandered over him as she kissed his neck and then worked her way down his body.

When she had him panting for her, she stood and strutted to her suitcase where she poured him a shot of tequila.

"Lena," he groaned.

She giggled and poured herself a glass. Brown eyes examined him over the rim, a wicked smile on her face. "It's too dark in here, lover boy. I want to see your face."

She headed to the curtained balcony and opened the drapes, letting silvery moonlight into the room. Across the street, another hotel's neon sign threw colored light into their room and over her body.

With deliberately seductive movements she turned from him and loosened her hair, running her fingers through the damp strands. One hand fluffed her hair as the other traveled over her naked breasts.

"Like what you see?"

"I like to touch it more." Dan placed his drink on the small nightstand and rose.

Two steps from her, the glass on the patio door exploded. Instinctively, he rose an arm before his eyes as he reached for her with the other, knowing he was too late.

Warm stickiness coated his face and chest. Lena's body crumpled to the floor in slow motion. He hadn't heard the gunshot. A roaring filled his ears as if he stood atop a waterfall.

Without thought, he jerked to the side of the patio

doors, training saving his life as another bullet passed
through the space he'd occupied just moments before.
This shot punched a twelve-inch hole in the concrete
wall.

Fifty-cal, he thought, as he dropped to his knees
and felt for Lena's pulse, knowing there would be
none. Blood oozed from the jagged edges of the
remains of her skull. The first shot had blown her
head off.

A violent wave of nausea burned his gut. Crouched
naked on the floor beside his dead wife, he vomited
until only dry, aching heaves remained.

The sight and smell of death were familiar to him.
In his career, he'd seen and caused more gruesome
sights, but this was his wife, now a bloody corpse, her
face eradicated. The smell of her blood lingered on his
body, replacing the scent of her perfume. A few
minutes later a police officer found him there still
trembling and retching.

The officer let him bathe for which he was grateful.
In the shower, he kept his eyes closed and head tipped
back, trying not to see his wife's brains and blood
swirling down the drain. Officers crowded the bedroom
when he exited the bathroom, and a blood-stained
sheet covered the corpse. Numb, he followed an officer
from the room.

This couldn't be happening, Dan thought as he
gazed out the window of the police car over the dark
and tawdry streets. *Why the hell did they come here?*
For the life of him, he couldn't remember. She must
have told him, but he hadn't cared where they went, so
didn't object when she'd picked here to honeymoon.

Dan put his head back on the seat rubbed his

cheekbones with the heels of his hands.

The nausea had passed, replaced by numb disbelief. An hour ago he was looking forward to a future with her, seriously considering talking her into staying with him. Now she was dead, and he'd never have a chance to fall in love with her or make her fall in love with him.

"Sir?"

Dan realized they'd arrived at the police station and the officer had been speaking to him for a few moments.

"Sorry, I'm a bit shocked," Dan said as he climbed from the car on unsteady legs, following the police officer into the building.

"Yes, sir. I'm sorry, sir, but we need a statement."

The officer's voice reverberated, suddenly loud before resuming a more normal tone. Shock was doing weird things to his hearing.

"Yes, of course." Inside the police station, Dan sat in the indicated chair and answered every question asked of him.

A haze of disbelief became augmented by exhaustion as new people arrived and asked the same questions over and over. By noon the next day, he was bleary with fatigue. Dan held an untouched cup of coffee in his trembling hand, scanning the face of the new detective before him with bloodshot eyes.

"Are we finished here? I've answered these questions a million times."

"I'm Detective Torres, and I'll be taking over this investigation, Mr. Barstow. This case is something of a puzzle." Detective Torres placed a file on the table as he sat and then slid it to Dan. "You see, we found your wife trying to cross the border this morning. While we know you didn't kill the woman in the hotel, the fact remains you're lying about her identity."

Dan frowned as he set the coffee down and opened the folder. In the folder, lay a mugshot of a blond woman. *Naturally blond,* Dan noted, her coloring too delicate to be achieved through makeup. Blue eyed and fair skinned. Five-feet, five-inches, a hundred and forty pounds. The name on the banner beneath the picture read Angelina Morrow. There was something vaguely familiar about her.

"That isn't my Angelina. My wife had brown eyes and dyed her hair. The resemblance is there, same height and weight, but—"

The detective tapped the picture with one stubby finger. "I assure you, this is Angelina Morrow. Ms. Morrow works for the IRS. Her fingerprints are on file."

"Fine, then there's two of them. It's not like that's an unusual name."

The detective leaned back in his seat and narrowed his eyes. He passed a hand over his bald skull, then smoothed his mustache. "While that could be the case— it isn't. The document's in your room match her ID's, her social security number, her credit cards, her everything." Each her was empathized by a finger stabbing the picture of Angelina.

Dan opened his mouth, then closed it. "I can only tell you what I know. Maybe I should speak to a lawyer. That woman," –Dan tapped the picture before the detective— "isn't my Lena."

Another officer banged on the door. Detective Torres rose and stepped outside.

Dan picked up the file and leafed through it. This

Angelina lived in Washington. She was twenty-six and had worked for the IRS since interning there in college.

Stunned, Dan set the folder on the worn, metal tabletop.

A few minutes later, the detective returned with another file. "The woman in your bedroom has been identified by fingerprints," the detective said as he slid the new folder across the table. This one was much thicker than the two pages in Angelina's file.

Dan's hand trembled as he picked up the first mugshot of a brown-haired Lena arrested for shoplifting at seventeen and again at eighteen. At twenty-two, her hair was blond, and she was arrested for petty theft and solicitation. By twenty-six, she'd added identity theft, bad checks, and public drunkenness. In the next photo, her hair was red and her eyes green, the arrest was for prostitution. Dan had thought she was twenty-six, two years younger than him when in reality she was six years older.

"Who did I marry?"

Dan had to clear his throat. His eyes narrowed when Detective Torres smiled for a moment before the detective coughed and tapped the nameplate beneath the most recent mugshot of Lena.

"Candice Brooks Conti is the woman in these photos. A lawyer might be a good idea."

Dan glanced up from the pictures spread on the table before him. "I swear I had no idea what... who she was... I mean, I thought I did." A headache throbbed in his temple. "We met a week ago, in Vegas."

"Yes, so you said. The fact remains you married Angelina Morrow." The detective tapped the picture of Angelina. "This woman. This name, consistent with the information for Angelina Morrow, is on your marriage license. As far as the world is concerned, you married Angelina, not Candice." He stabbed the photo of Candice with a finger.

"Oh, dear God." Dan leaned back in the chair and rubbed both eyes.

The detective snorted.

Dan said nothing. For the first time, he considered the full implications of the situation. The fog surrounding him melted away as adrenaline pumped. Someone had put a hit out on her— or him? But why shoot her if the hit was for him? Besides, she'd picked the destination. He hadn't known nor gave a damn where they'd go, content to go wherever she wished. Nobody on Earth knew or cared where he was.

How could he prove he wasn't involved with whatever Candice was up too? And good Lord, if the hit was for him, was the real Angelina in danger now? Thoughts whirling in his head, he straightened in his seat. A Mexican jail was looking more and more likely.

His shoulders tightened as he remembered the man in the alley. That wasn't a mugging. It was definitely an attempt on his wife. No, not his wife— Candice. His wife was still alive.

Dan hesitated. The incident in the alleyway was likely connected, but if he mentioned it, he'd be asked a million more questions, including the hard one— why hadn't he reported it. The simple answer was he didn't want to get involved with a police matter. He'd thought it was nothing, petty criminals looking to mug a tourist. It was so much easier to ignore it than go through the hassle of reporting. And there was always the chance the police would think he'd shot Carlos.

"Can I speak with Angelina?"

The rhythmic drumming of fingertips on the metal table stopped as the detective rose. "Yes, I'm interested to see how your wife explains this situation."

TWO

━━━━━ ◆ ━━━━━

MR. BARSTOW, YOUR WIFE, ANGELINA

Angie huddled under the blanket the police officer had given her. *This had been a dumb idea, foolish, reckless, and utterly with merit. What did I think I could've done when I confronted the woman? Demand she return the money and identity she stole and go home as if nothing had happened?*

So stupid to come here! Angie dashed the tears from her cheeks and sat straighter. The worst decision she'd ever made was to leave the country chasing a criminal. Since being in Mexico, she'd seen a shooting and been informed of another. No one answered her repeated requests for a lawyer. *God, I hope Parker arrives soon.*

At least the police officers here believed I am who I say I am. Never again will I use an unsecured credit card. How the hell am I going to fix the mess my life has become?

A glance at her watch showed she'd been in this room for twelve hours now. A shiver traveled her as she contemplated her predicament. She didn't know what her rights were here, or what could happen to her alone in a foreign country where violent crime was rampant. Horror stories of corrupt foreign police swirled through her thoughts. The shiver escalated to a shudder.

The door to the small holding room opened, and a police officer gestured her to exit. Angie stood and tightened the blanket around her. No matter what she did, she couldn't get warm. The man at the door glared and beckoned impatiently.

Apparently, he didn't speak English and didn't care if she understood Spanish. She licked her lips, straightened her shoulders and exited the room. The blanket dropped to the floor when she spied Parker seated beside another man on a thin, metal bench. Parker appeared tired and disgruntled. The blue suit he wore was wrinkle-free and spotless and not a hair on his head was out of place but circles ringed his eyes.

He must've come as soon as I called, she thought gratefully.

"Parker!" The glad cry escaped her as she rushed to him and fell into his arms.

"Angelina, what in the world?" Parker drew back and examined her, a frown growing on his face. An angry light in his eyes, he pulled her closer and turned to the police officer. "Has Ms. Morrow been charged with anything?"

The officer glanced from Angelina to Parker and smirked. Another officer seated at the desk nearby laughed, pushed back his metal desk chair and stood.

"Mrs. Barstow hasn't been charged with any crimes, but is wanted for questioning in the death of Candice Br—"

The man on the bench beside Parker surged to his feet and grabbed at Angie. "You killed my wife?"

Black eyes glared at her from a florid face. Heavy, unshaven jowls vibrated with the clenching of the man's jaw as he shouted at her.

Angie hunched back as Parker pushed her aside and spun to face the man. "Angelina isn't Mrs. Barstow. If you'd be so kind—"

Another officer grabbed the angry man's arm as he swore at Angie and demanded information. "Come with me, Mr. Conti, and we can get this straightened out," the officer said.

Angie and Parker stared after the officer as Mr. Conti continued to rave, yelling threats over his shoulder as the police officer dragged him from the room.

Detective Torres approached and held out his hand. "Ms. Morrow," he hesitated, "or, Mrs. Barstow, I suppose, if you'd come with me and speak to your husband?"

Parker jerked back. "What?"

"What?" Angie repeated, feeling as if she was in a comedy act and didn't know her lines.

The detective turned to Parker. "Sir, we can clear this up, but I need to speak with Ms.— Mrs.— Angelina," he finally finished with a grimace.

"Did you get married?" Parker turned to Angie, his brown eyes wide.

"No, of course not," she said as the detective

nodded and said, "I'm afraid she has."

Parker released Angie's arm and stepped back, his expression cold. "What game are you playing?"

"No game. I don't know what he's talking about." Angie's gaze darted between the men as she wrapped her arms around herself, wishing she hadn't dropped the blanket.

"Sir, Ma'am, you two can work this out later. Right now, we need to resolve a murder." Without waiting for Parker to reply, Detective Torres placed a hand on Angie's back and ushered her from the room.

Angie glanced back in time to see Parker turn to the officer who had snickered.

———— ◆ ————

Detective Torres opened the door of another small integration room and gestured Angelina to enter. "Mr. Barstow, your wife, Angelina." A smile flitted across the detective's lips before he cleared his throat and sat at the table.

Angelina sat weakly. Eyes wide in a pale face, she stared at Dan and hunched as far from him as she could get.

Dan sat straighter. *The girl by the lamppost.* She still wore all black, and her expression remained horrified and afraid.

"I'm sorry, you've confused me with someone else," Angelina said and licked her lips as her gaze darted between the two men.

The detective opened the folder he'd brought in earlier and pointed to the copy of the marriage license.

"This man is your husband. I'm sure you'll have no problem getting the marriage annulled if it was entered into fraudulently, but as it stands right now, you're married."

Angelina blanched and picked up the paper with a trembling hand. "How can that be? I've never even met the man."

The detective sighed. "Look, I understand this is hard to take in, but you, yourself, told us Candice Conti stole your identity. While pretending to be you, she married him. In effect, you married him."

"But, I didn't..."

Dan took the folders and closed them, placing both hands on top. "Can we clear that up later? What's happening about my wife? I mean Candice. Jesus, this is confusing. Regardless of her name, she was murdered right in front of me."

"Did he kill her?" Angelina asked the detective in a voice that cracked. She hugged herself with both arms as if she were cold.

Detective Torres sighed and rubbed the bridge of his nose. "No, he didn't. Like you, he was a victim of identity theft. So far, his story has checked out. Are either of you aware of anyone who had motive?"

"Oh God, you think I did it?" Angelina jumped to her feet and clutched the table edge.

"Well, I hadn't considered that." The detective stroked his mustache a moment. "Tell me— why did you leave so quickly? Your hotel was booked for another day. I believe you came to find Candice as you claim. Did you find her?"

Angelina stared from Dan to the detective and bit her lip. Slowly, she sank into her seat and laid her hands in her lap. "Yes, I found her. Well, Parker located her for me, and I was on my way to her hotel when I saw a man get shot."

The detective straightened. "What? Where? Why didn't you say anything?"

"Because I was afraid and just wanted to go home. I returned to my hotel, packed, and headed to the border. The entire plan to confront her was stupid. What did I think Candice would do, tell me how sorry she was and give me my life back?"

Angelina rubbed her eyes with the heels of her hands, then ran her fingers roughly through her hair, pulling it over her shoulder. The blond mass almost reached her waist.

"Crime isn't something I'm prepared to deal with. That became abundantly clear when I witnessed the shooting."

"Can you tell me details?"

Angelina clasped her fingers in her lap and stared at them. "Nanos Verdes Street at ten-thirty or so across from a closed cafe. I didn't see any of the men involved. I heard one addressed as Carlos, but it was dark, and they were in the alleyway while I was on the street."

Dan sat back in his seat. She'd seen him clearly. He was sure of that. *Why didn't she tell the officer? Jesus, she must believe I was involved. Fuck— I was involved.*

"I was there too," he heard himself say and wanted to smack himself. But if he said nothing, she'd be afraid for her life. He practically felt the waves of terror rolling off her.

The detective stood and leaned forward, both hands braced on the tabletop. "Care to elaborate."

"No, like Angelina, all I wanted was to go home. But I guess I have to. My wife..." Dan rubbed his temples, closed his eyes, and sighed hard. He took a deep breath, lowered his hands, and started again. "Yesterday evening, after we'd eaten, Candice left to buy liquor. At least that's where she said she was going. When she didn't return in an hour, I became concerned and headed to the store, taking a shortcut through a back alley. Candice ran from the alley with two men chasing her. I stayed to make sure she got away. I saw a woman" –Dan turned to Angelina– "you, I presume, by the streetlamp and told her to run. As soon as she did, I ran. A gunshot went off behind me, and I kept going." To Dan's relief Angelina no longer appeared terrified, only confused.

An eyebrow elevated, Detective Torres glanced between them. "And you never considered reporting that?"

Dan said, "And end up in a Mexican jail? Are you crazy?"

The detective snorted and straightened, one hand fussing with his tie. "So, then your, err, Candice is murdered, and you never thought there might be a connection?"

"No, all the man said was, 'when I get my hands on that little bitch.' I thought he was a mugger and a really stupid one as he shot his own friend. The gun used to kill Candice was a fifty-cal, not a twenty-two."

"And how do you know that." Eyes narrowed, the detective leaned forward again.

"My job. Which I'm sure you already know, seeing as you have Candice's paperwork, you must have mine as well."

"That we do, Petty Officer Barstow."

Dan lifted an eyebrow.

"Right, so the two of you, who've never met before and just happen to be married, witness the same murder?"

Dan nodded and tried not to grimace. Every word he spoke made him and Angelina seem guiltier.

"I saw the shooter, but it was dark, so I'm afraid my description won't help much," he said.

The detective held up a hand, interrupting him before he gave details. "Would you recognize him if you saw him again?"

Dan heaved another sigh. "Yes."

"Great, we have some albums for you to go through."

"Well, I'm willing and all, but he was American."

Eyes narrowed, Detective Torres drummed his fingertips on the table. "And how do you know that?"

Unexpectedly, Angelina spoke. "Accent."

The detective glanced at her, a frown on his face, and his fingers tapped the tabletop again.

Angelina wrapped strands of her long blond hair around her thumb as she spoke. "When he yelled, 'Stop, or I'll shoot,' I was running away, but I heard him." From lowered lashes, she peeked at Dan for a moment before returning her gaze to her lap.

"Okay, I'll need statements from both of you privately. It looks like you'll be staying longer. Ms. Morrow, please come with me. Mr. Barstow, start writing your statement. Tell me again from the top and leave nothing out."

Dan stood. "Fine, but please, Ms. Morrow, don't leave without speaking to me again. I'm afraid we have details to work out."

Angelina nodded as she headed to the door.

THREE

━━━━━━◆━━━━━━

I Was an Idiot

WHEN Dan exited the interrogation room, Angelina was curled into the corner of a bench with her arms around her body and both legs pulled up. Her blond hair covered her face as she dozed against the wall.

Dan wanted a nap too. It had been a long thirty-six hours. *Fuck, it had been a long week.* He needed a vacation. A snort of laughter escaped him. This was supposed to be his vacation. *With only three weeks left I better make the most of it.* Another bitter snort of laughter escaped him. *Sure, I'll just pretend my wife wasn't killed in front of me. No, my wife is alive and sleeping in the chair. Candice was killed, and she'd already been married.*

Detective Torres joined him as he stared down at Angelina.

"You and your wife are free to go after you speak to

the desk sergeant and pay the, um, bond. If you remember anything that could help us in our investigation, or change addresses, please contact us."

"Thank you." Dan ran a hand through his close-cropped, blond hair and sighed hard. "What do I do with her?"

Detective Torres laughed. "The usual things one does with a wife, I suppose." He slapped Dan on the back and sauntered off, whistling.

Dan sighed again and shook Angelina's shoulder.

She jerked away and pushed her hair behind her ears with both hands, then rubbed her eyes a moment before standing.

"Can we go?"

"Yep." Dan pointed to her suitcase sitting beside the bench. "Is that all your stuff? Do you need to stop anywhere?"

"No. I guess I can fly home from here now."

"About that." Dan gestured her to the door as he spoke. "Even though you didn't marry me, you and I are legally married, so we need to talk about that."

"Yeah, okay. Um..."

Dan glanced at her from the corner of his eye. She looked as overwhelmed as he felt.

"Right, I don't know where to start either. We both need sleep and..." He sighed in frustration. They needed to talk, but he wanted to get out of the country before the police changed their mind.

"How about this? I'll come home with you, and we can speak on the plane. The police in Washington need to be told if you want to clear up the identity theft. I'll stay a few days while we get this sorted out."

"What about your work?"

23

"I'm on leave until February eighteenth."

"Okay, I guess," she said uncertainly as she bit a thumbnail.

"Let's talk to the sergeant and get out of here before they change their mind. The sooner we're back on American soil, the happier I'll be."

At the desk, the sergeant handed them a form to fill out." Dan glanced at it, and his eyes widened.

"Three thousand dollars?"

"Well, you don't have to pay— you could stay here." A smug smile on his face, the sergeant leaned back in his seat and crossed his arms over his chest. "That's each of you. But don't worry, if you can't afford the bond we can make you real comfortable." The sergeant's smile changed to a leer as he let his gaze travel over Angelina, lingering on her breasts. "The money will be returned to you once this case is closed if you attend all mandatory hearings."

Angelina paled and stepped back. Dan grabbed her hand and pulled her closer. "Fine, do you accept credit cards or have an ATM?"

"Both." The sergeant pointed to the right at a cash machine bolted to the floor.

Angelina clutched his arm with both hands as she leaned over and whispered, "Dan, I don't have a credit card. All of mine are maxed. There's only three dollars in my ATM account. I only have a little over a thousand dollars on me, and I need it to get home. I have enough at home, but no way to access it here."

"We're getting out of here now." Dan slid his debit card into the machine. "Son of a bitch," he hissed.

His ATM account was empty. He should've expected that once he'd seen Candice's rap sheet. She'd had this card for a week. His face tight, he returned to the desk. "Is there a computer here I can use to access my bank and transfer funds?"

The sergeant chuckled and pointed to the left. "Come on back. I'll buzz you in, and you can use mine."

The hands clutching his arm tightened as Angelina tried to yank him back. "If you use his computer, he'll have access," she whispered as he dragged her to the door.

"Only one of you can come in," the sergeant said as he peered through the window at them.

"Wait right here." Dan disengaged her hands. Five minutes later, he returned. "Let's go before he changes his mind."

Angelina glanced back at the sergeant. A dazed, scared expression on her face, she followed Dan.

Outside of the police station, bright sunlight hit him like a slap. By her wince and hand held shading her eyes it did the same to her. Dan felt hungover and tired, worn out not just from lack of sleep, but the shocks.

A cab waited, engine idling, while the cabby read a paper. He glanced up as they exited and jumped from the cab. "Need a lift? Fair rates and speedy service."

Dan nodded, got in the back with Angelina, and gave the cabby the address of the hotel.

"That policeman can access your bank accounts now," Angelina said as soon as she sat.

"Relax, I turned off all access. I have to go in person to the bank to reinstate online use. I took a chance and put two thousand dollars back in my ATM account. When I get a second, I need to see if my cards are maxed too."

"Candice maxed every single source of credit I have and took out a loan against my car, which I found out when they repossessed it. My retirement fund and bank accounts have been emptied. I'm sure she would've taken a mortgage on my house if I had one." Low and bitter, Angelina's voice quaked.

Dan felt like a shit. While Candice was partying it up, spending Angelina's money buying him drinks and shopping, Angelina was going broke.

"I'm sorry. But I really had no idea," he said.

"Oh, I'm not blaming you, I'm blaming myself. I never checked the status of any of my accounts. Hell, I didn't even realize I had so many open ones. She maxed everything from furniture stores to Macy's. Now I owe over a hundred thousand dollars, and my entire life's savings is gone just like that."

Dan didn't know what to say. He settled for giving her a quick, one-armed hug. They were both quiet for the remainder of the ride to Dan's hotel.

"Wait here. I'll be down in a few minutes," he said as he opened the door.

Angelina stared after him, her eyes wide, biting her bottom lip with her front teeth. By the time he returned with his duffle bag, she'd bitten her thumbnail to the quick.

"What about your, um, wife?" Low and nervous, her voice stuttered. "Don't you need to make arrangements for her?"

Dan leaned his head against the seat back. "Candice's husband had her body shipped to New York. You're my wife."

Angelina winced. "I'm sorry for your loss."

Dan straightened and laughed a bitter laugh. "I never really had anything to lose. Man, you must think I'm an idiot."

Angelina stared out the side window without answering.

"I was an idiot. There's no denying that."

His head resting on the seat back, Dan spoke with his eyes closed, "I knew her for two hours before we got married. Yeah, I was drunk, but that isn't why I did it..."

"Why did you do it?" Angelina asked a few minutes later.

"For the company." A flush rose from his neck and settled onto his cheeks. "No, for the permanence. Damn it, I just wanted to leave someone behind. To be missed."

He glanced over at Angelina, but her hair shadowed her face as she stared from the window.

"On my last mission, my best friend died, and I'm the only one who really mourns him. He had no wife or parents just like me. Yeah, our buddies miss him, but only I loved him. I wanted someone to miss me— Pathetic, right?"

"Sad. And I can relate. Did you love her?"

Dan shrugged and half-smiled. "I liked her. Maybe I could've fallen in love with her. Well, not her, she wasn't real, she was you."

Angelina turned to him and frowned. "No, I'm me, Angie. Your Lena was nothing like me. Detective Torres showed me her rap sheet. I've never considered doing any of the things she did. Candice wasn't pretending to be me. Don't confuse us. None of her actions were mine. It was only my name she stole."

"No, she was nothing like you."

A flush reddened Angie's cheeks as Dan inspected her.

Dan reached out and ran his fingers lightly over her hair, then turned away and stared from his window. The rest of the ride to the airport passed in silence.

FOUR

---◆---

HOME-SWEET-HOME

ANGIE reached into the bright-blue bookbag hanging over her shoulder and rummaged around one-handed, holding her long blond hair out of the way with the other.

"Ah, home-sweet-home," she said with such relief in her voice Dan grinned.

"Need a hand?" Dan gestured to the bookbag.

"Nope, I got it, thanks."

A half-smile on her lips, she waved a set of keys triumphantly at Dan. At the door, she inserted her key, withdrew it, and frowned.

"That's funny? I would've sworn I locked this." She tilted her head to one side and examined the keys in her hand.

Dan dropped his duffle bag, grabbed her shoulder and pulled her to the side of the door. Adrenaline

29

washed away his fatigue, energizing him. A finger before his lips asking for quiet, he mouthed, 'stay here,' and eased the door open, ducking low as he entered and immediately moving to the left.

Angie's apartment was trashed. Drywall dust, from holes gouged in the walls, floated in the air, sparkling in the sunlight streaming through the wide windows.

Light-blue curtains dangled from broken rods. Open cans surrounded a mound of rotting food beside the overturned refrigerator. Stuffing and padding from the furniture lay in a heap beside the bare windows. Someone had searched every inch of the place, going so far as to rip out overhead light fixtures.

Dan snatched a knife from the pile of dumped cutlery lying in a heap beside the torn-up kitchen cabinets. Knife in hand, he checked the apartment, ensuring whoever did this was long gone. Three minutes later he returned to the hallway and Angie.

"Someone ransacked your house. Call the police."

"What?" She bit her bottom lip and pushed by him. In the doorway, she stopped and lifted a hand to her face. "Oh, my God. Who would do this?" Angie's wide-eyed gaze traveled the wreckage. "Thank God I left Tiger with the vet."

"Tiger?"

"My cat. God knows what they would've done to him. They destroyed everything. Who does this?" She rubbed her cheek absently as she fumbled for her cell phone.

Dan pulled her back from the door when she took a step inside. "Don't go in until the police check it. With this level of vandalism, they'll probably want to dust for prints. Did you have insurance?"

Angie nodded and returned to the hallway. She slid down the wall across from her open door and hugged her knees. "Is this Candice?" Her chin jutted in the direction of her ruined home.

"Maybe. It's a hell of a coincidence if it isn't."

She nodded and rubbed her face again with both hands.

Dan returned to the doorway and examined the mess. *Poor Angie, Candice was ruining her life.* Even though he had nothing to do with Candice's crimes he felt guilty.

The police arrived ten minutes later.

"Holy shit!" the officer exclaimed as he took in the mess from the doorway. "Is the entire apartment like this?"

"Yes. I did a quick check when we arrived, but I didn't touch anything except this." Dan held up the knife he'd taken. He glanced at Angie who'd risen and was biting her lip again.

Dan said, "This might be more complicated than just a crazy vandal. Ms. Morrow and I had a run in with an identity thief." Dan blushed and winced. "I sort of married her." Dan shrugged, trying to loosen his tense shoulders. "I'm sorry, this is confusing. The identity thief, Candice Brooks Conti, pretended to be Angelina. I mean, I thought she was Angelina when I married her."

Dan sighed and squeezed the bridge of his nose, then rubbed the stubble along his chin. Two days since he'd shaved, the stubble made a deep rasping noise. For the first time, Dan considered what a wreck he must appear.

His gaze flitted to Angie. She didn't look much

better. The black clothes she wore were wrinkled and traveled stained from the day and a half in the police station in Tijuana followed by eighteen hours to return to Washington. They'd taken the very first flight going their way, not caring about the time as long as they got out of Mexico. Limp blond hair, pushed behind her ears, framed bloodshot, darkly circled eyes. An almost greenish pallor overlaid her skin. Exhaustion and dismay showed in every line of her body.

They hadn't yet spoken of their marriage. Dan thought they were both dreading dealing with it. Mostly, they'd dozed on the plane. Her low-voiced comments on the movie they'd watched had amused and distracted him from his worries. She was a surprisingly good traveling companion, easy to get along with, laughing instead of complaining about the delays. The detective speaking jerked Dan back from his musings.

"Well, I'll get pictures and write up a report Ms. Morrow can send to her insurance company," the officer said as he removed a notebook from his pocket.

"Um, it's a bit more complicated than that. You see, Candice was murdered two days ago, and if that is related to this..."Dan gestured at the mess before them.

The officer lowered his pad and placed a hand on his gun. "Murdered?"

"Assassinated. A sniper with a fifty-caliber shot her right in front of me."

Dan shivered and rubbed his arms. Angie placed a hand on his shoulder, the small warmth comforting. Dan absently patted her hand.

"Before Candice was shot, she was chased by two

men. One of whom killed the other."

"Two murders?" The officer's brows lowered, and he pursed his lips. "I haven't heard of even one, and that seems like something that would be hard to forget."

"It didn't happen here. Candice and I were in Tijuana. We'd just gotten married. Hell, we'd just met. Look, it's a long story and complicated. Angie went there searching for the woman who stole her identity, and we found out we were married.

"Detective Torres in Tijuana gave me copies of the police report for the police here, in my bag there." Dan nodded toward his duffle bag, took a deep breath, and exhaled loudly. "We planned on going to the police station after we'd rested and spoken, but.... I just think you should take prints in case this vandalism is related. We don't know why Candice was killed. Angelina could be in danger."

"Right. Give me a minute to call this in. Wait here please." The officer returned to his car. In fifteen minutes, three more officers and a detective were on scene.

The detective offered his hand. "I'm Detective Reed; Officer Mathis filled me in. Can you come to the precinct and we'll get this straightened out? The officers here will do a comprehensive investigation. Believe me, we aren't taking this lightly. Identity theft is a growing problem; one we're trying to handle, but since the criminal is usually nowhere near the victim it makes it difficult."

The detective motioned for them to follow him.

Angie stopped by the front door to her home. "What am I going to do? Candice stole all my money. My credit cards are maxed, and now I don't even have a place to live. Dear God, I can't even get my cat out of hock. All the money I had left in the world was in this apartment. I'm sure whoever did this found it and took it."

Dan plucked the book bag from Angie's limp grasp and hugged her. "Once we speak to the police, I'll get Tiger. No wife of mine will be homeless or hungry."

Angie choked back a laughing sob.

"Angelina?" a man said in a harsh, disapproving tone.

Angie pushed away from Dan, her body rigid.

"Parker! Why didn't you return my calls? Where did you go? I can't believe you just left me there." Angie took two steps toward the man and put her hands on her hips.

The man in the hallway wore an immaculate, navy-blue suit and a black, wool greatcoat. The black wingtips on his feet were so shiny they reflected light. Not a hair on his gelled head was out of place.

Clean cut, handsome, and cold, Dan thought as his gaze traveled the man.

"Who is this?" Parker jutted his chiseled chin at Dan.

Dan wanted to hit him. The spurious tone grated on his nerves. By the tight line of Angie's shoulders, she didn't like the tone either.

"This is my friend Dan Barstow."

A sneer curled Parker's lips "Your husband, you mean. That police officer told me you married and after only knowing him for days. This is ridiculous, Angelina. Why call me and make me go all the way there? Why leave me all those messages?"

"Didn't you listen to them?" Angie sounded

incredulous. "Parker... I don't even know where to start. I still can't believe you left me there. You didn't even talk to me when you knew Candice stole my identity. She married him. I didn't."

For the first time, Parker seemed to realize police surrounded them. His sneer deepened as he gazed at the police officers. "Is he a criminal too?" Parker's blue eyes narrowed, and his thin lips thinned even more. "What's going on here?"

"My apartment was broken into and vandalized." Angie sounded disgusted.

Dan didn't know if the disgust was for the vandalism or Parker.

Parker strode forward and gaped at the mess. One hand brushed his immaculate suit jacket as if the sight contaminated him.

Dan bit back a laugh.

"Vandalized," Parker repeated faintly.

"Excuse me," Detective Reed interrupted. "Ms. Morrow needs to come down to the precinct and straighten things out. Could she contact you afterward and the two of you could discuss this then?"

"Yes, of course." Parker turned back to Angie. "Call me when you're finished with the police. Obviously, you can't stay here. Come to my apartment. You can stay with me until you get this," –one hand waved vaguely at her open apartment door–"cleaned up."

Angie opened her mouth then closed it as if she didn't know what to say. She finally said, "Parker, I... Dan and I need to stay together and straighten this out. And we have to get Tiger—"

"Tiger, yes, I'd forgotten. Leave him at the vets. You know I'm allergic."

Angie tipped her head to the side and pursed her lips. "You aren't allergic. You just don't like him."

Parker smiled, a supermodel smile, handsome and debonair. "True. I'm sorry, but I really detest cats. Or more specifically, cat fur. Angelina, you're welcome to stay with me, but your menagerie has to stay somewhere else. You can't expect me to host your husband."

Angie exhaled loudly. "Dan is my friend, not my menagerie. I didn't marry him." She raised her hands and dropped them. "Never mind. We can talk about this later. I'll call you when we're done with the police. Please answer my calls this time."

Parker kissed Angie's cheek and spun away. His greatcoat flared behind him in graceful folds.

Angie sighed again. "He always manages to make me feel gauche and graceless."

"He does have flare," Dan agreed and pulled her hair lightly. "Let's go get this over with and rescue Tiger."

Angie gave him her first real smile. Dan grinned back and put an arm around her shoulder. Together they followed the detective to his car.

FIVE

---◆---

A SMALL CABIN IN VERMONT

A PLUMP woman with graying hair and a kind smile approached Dan as he dithered in the pet aisle.

"Try the feather chaser. My two cats love it. And all cats enjoy a catnip mouse."

Dan stopped tapping his chin with one finger and smiled at the woman. She reached in front of him and took the two items she suggested from the shelf and handed them to him.

"First cat?" she asked.

"My wife's cat." The small happy thrill from saying *my wife* surprised him.

The woman glanced into his cart. "The covered litter boxes are better and get liners. Believe me, you'll thank me."

The woman helped Dan pick out everything Tiger

needed. Dan thanked her and headed to the luggage section where he picked up two duffle bags. A pink bag for Angie and a smaller, dark-green one for Tiger. On a whim, he threw a roll of pink, camouflage duct tape in the cart so she'd have her own. He always carried a roll. The stuff had a million uses. His duffle bag was practically fashioned from tape he'd repaired it so often.

After a quick stop in the men's department, he headed to women's wear where he found Angie debating between two shirts, one long sleeve, the other short. He plucked them both from her hand and dropped them into his cart.

Angie sighed, and her bottom lip curved down as she turned away.

"Hey, it's no big deal. What're a few shirts between friends?" Dan reached into her cart and pulled out the pair of jeans she'd picked to check the size. "You're going to need a few more things than this. Most of your clothing was ruined. Tomorrow, we can go back to your apartment to pack up what's salvageable, but you need enough for a few days at least."

Dan headed to the racks of sweat clothes and picked out two sets. A heavy jacket, a long heavy sweater, and flannel lined jeans went into his cart next. Angie still hunched as if she were cold. The sweater she wore, while good enough for an airline or the balmy nights of Tijuana, wasn't enough for the Washington winter.

"As soon as I can, I'll pay you back," she said.

Tight lipped and blushing, Angie followed him as he picked out clothing for her.

"Don't worry about it. I feel guilty your life is so

screwed up and I'm partially responsible. Let me help and I'll stop feeling so bad."

Angie snorted and ran her fingers through her hair, twisting it into a bun. "We were both victims—"

Dan stopped with his back to Angie and interrupted, "No, you were a victim. I was a willing dupe. Candice took advantage, but I let her. I wasn't a good guy in this, not really caring, using her to ease my loneliness." He frowned as he turned to face her. "My behavior embarrasses me. I'm usually a much better judge of character."

Dan glanced away as a blush flushed his cheeks. "The truth is; I didn't care what she was up too. Granted, I had no idea what it was, but all I cared about was company in my binge. I never even asked her why she wanted to marry me. When she disappeared 'shopping' for hours at a time, I was happy to let her take my card because she came back with booze and a willing attitude."

Angie blushed and turned away, flipping through a rack of scrubs.

"So, let me help. I don't know what else to do to make it up. It's too late for me to help Candice, so let me help you."

A determined expression on her face, Angie turned back to him. "Just so you know, this is a loan. I don't want to take advantage either." She met his eyes for a moment before glancing away. "This has taught me a lot about myself, and frankly, I don't love what I've learned. Do you realize I've never been out of the United States before? Hell, I've barely left this town. I had this big plan to do better than my parents did. Not that they were bad parents, far from it, but they were so caught up in work and paying the bills they didn't have time for me. So, I planned on saving enough money so when I have kids I could stay home with them and be a full-time mother and wife. My career was picked with that in mind. A job I can do from home part-time."

"Nothing wrong with that," Dan said as he absently placed another sweater into the cart.

Angie smiled and removed the sweater, replacing it with a light-blue one. "Sure, a great plan, but I was so busy building my nest egg that I made no friends. No close ones anyways. I was always too busy working to go out. Before I knew it, I was twenty-five, and I realized I hadn't had a boyfriend in four years and there was Parker."

"If you want to stay with him, I can keep Tiger at the hotel with me."

"No thanks. Parker and I are through. What kind of man leaves his girlfriend in a Mexican jail and goes home? I left him ten messages explaining what happened and he didn't listen to any of them." Angie rolled the cart to the sock aisle as she spoke. "I was doing the same thing with Parker that you were with Candice."

Dan stifled a laugh and busied himself examining the wool socks as she continued speaking, appearing oblivious to his mirth.

"Parker was company," Angie continued as she examined the socks. "On paper, he's a great catch. Handsome, with a good job, and he wasn't mean or anything, he just has to have everything his way. It drove me crazy, but I was overlooking it so I wouldn't be alone. If Candice hadn't come along, I probably would've moved in with him like he wanted, and maybe even married him."

"What about Tiger?"

A small giggle escaped her. "Tiger saved me. Parker hates cats. No way would I get rid of Tiger. See that should've told me right there. What kind of man won't accept a beloved pet?

"One who hates cats...."

Angie snorted. "See. Told ya I was desperate. Normally, I wouldn't give a guy a second date if they don't pass the Tiger test."

"The Tiger test?" Dan lifted an eyebrow.

He held up two pairs of thick wool socks, and she pointed to the dark-blue ones. Dan dropped two pairs into the cart.

"When a date picks me up, if Tiger hates him, he's out," Angie said.

"Ahh, I assume Tiger hated Parker?"

She giggled again. "Tiger actually hissed."

"So why did you give him the second date?" Dan laughed when she flushed. "Never mind. None of my business."

Forearms crossed, leaning on the cart handle, Angie rolled her eyes. "Not what you're thinking. I told you, I was getting desperate and he was a good catch."

"Handsome and rich."

"Handsome with a job," she corrected dryly. "Usually, the good-looking ones are taken or looking for a mother. I should've known he had major issues to still be single in his thirties.

"Hey," Dan said in mock outrage. "Some of us are happy in our careers. Or we haven't found the right person yet."

"Uhhh huh."

"Go pick out your underwear. I'll meet you in shoes after I get boxes and packing tape."

Angie laughed and rolled her cart away.

By noon the next day, they were on the way back to her apartment. Dan fumbled in the pocket of his shirt while he drove and handed her a small, digital camera. "Take pictures of everything for insurance. The police report will be proof, but I'm sure your insurance company will want pictures, and I'm not sure you can get copies from the police."

"Thanks." Angie took the small camera and examined it.

"Once you remove everything salvageable, let the insurance company handle clean up and repair. Do you have a place to stay meanwhile?"

"Not really." A sad smile crossed her face. "My family has a small cabin in Vermont. I can go there, but I'll have to take more time off work, and I can't afford too."

"Can you stay with family?" Dan glanced at her from the corner of his eye. She looked sad and worried.

"It's just me left."

"So, it's your cabin?"

"I guess. I just hate to think of it that way. Some of the best days of my life were spent there with my grandparents. My parents would send me there in the summer. I haven't been back since my grandparents died. The taxes aren't much, so I haven't sold it."

"Damn."

"What?" The worry on her face deepened.

"It's in your name then. I was hoping it wouldn't be. Sorry, Ang, but Candice might have stolen that too. Or whoever did this to your apartment might try there."

"Oh jeez. That settles it, I'm going there. Um, if I can take the car that is."

"I'm coming too. Just in case it's wrecked and you need to speak to the police."

"I can't ask you to do all this for me."

"You didn't ask; I offered."

The mess in Angie's apartment appeared even worse on the second examination. The food was beginning to smell, and even though it was thirty-five degrees outside, flies had found their way inside. Dan carried in the stack of unmade boxes.

Her lips compressed, Angie examined her living area and kitchen.

"Start in your room. I'll go through the kitchen and see what's salvageable." Dan ran a hand over her bright hair when she hesitated. The mess was daunting; he didn't blame her for looking overwhelmed.

Four hours later, a small stack of boxes sat in the back of the car. Dan had put a garbage bag in the trunk full of dirty, but still usable kitchen items. Anything that offered a place to hide had been destroyed, leaving only some light clothing untouched. The vandal hadn't cared where they dropped things, and a bottle of bleach had been poured on one of the piles of otherwise usable clothing.

Angie sat in the front seat, lines of strain framing her eyes. Tears had left tracks across her dirty cheeks although Dan hadn't seen her cry. While speaking with the insurance company, she'd sounded calm. After she'd hung up, she'd asked Dan to drop her at her office.

Dan's worried gaze followed her into the building. He didn't like her leaving his sight. The destruction of her home had shown a level of violent disregard he found troubling. If she'd been home, she might be dead now. *Thank god, she'd gone to Tijuana when she had.*

His shoulders tightened, and he wished he brought a gun with him.

———————◆———————

Windshield wipers whisked off the light coating of lacy snow. A coating that reappeared in moments. Another snow plow passed them, sending up a rooster tail of dirty snow from the highway ahead. For two hours now it had been snowing. The flakes gradually grew bigger and fell harder until they drove through a curtain of white.

"Almost there." Angie leaned forward, peering out the front window.

"How can you tell? Everything looks the same." Dan slowed the car even more, not wanting to miss the turnoff.

Angie shrugged but didn't glance at him. Her attention remained on the road. "Nope, not this one," she said as Dan slowed and put his blinker on for a wide turn off. "The next one. Half a mile from here."

Dan paused before turning off. A narrow, unplowed lane lay before them. Snow almost obscured a rickety sign announcing Pigeon Hole Lane. A good six inches of snow covered the road.

"How far down this road?"

"About five miles." Angie bit her lip and glanced at

44

him with troubled, blue eyes. "Electricity and running water, I promise."

"Until there's a power outage. Ang, we could get stuck there, and the place might be falling down or vandalized. You haven't been there in eight years."

"My parents were there six years ago, and it was fine then. Dad boarded up the windows and left a cord of wood, so even if the power goes, I'll have heat."

"Ang...." Dan turned into the narrow lane, both hands gripping the wheel. "If it's bad, I can't leave you here."

Bottom lip pinched between two fingers, she nodded.

"Your apartment should be restored within a week. If your cabin is uninhabitable, I'll rent you a room wherever you like for that week." Dan spoke without taking his eyes off the road.

Trees shaded the narrow lane on both sides making the already gray day deep twilight. A mile in, they passed a brightly lit house between the trees. A truck with a plow hooked to the front sat in the plowed driveway. Dan was relieved. If she had a problem, at least there were neighbors.

"Do you know them?" Dan gestured with his chin at the lighted house.

"Mr. and Mrs. Schaffer used to own it, but I have no idea if they still do." Angie glanced away from him and smoothed her hands over the knees of the flannel jeans she wore.

"What?" he asked.

"Nothing." She cleared her throat. "Mr. Schaffer is a criminal. Granddad used to warn me not to go anywhere near them, but I'm sure it's safe now."

The hesitant, choked way she said the name Schaffer worried him. "Hmm, what kind of a criminal."

"A pedophile. He did ten years, and his wife stood by him. Claimed he was innocent and they moved out here to get away from nosy neighbors."

"Nice," Dan said in disgust.

"Could be someone new there now," Angie said with laughter in her voice.

"Let's hope," Dan mumbled.

He slowed even more as he glanced in the rear-view mirror to check on Tiger who'd made the ride sitting in the back window. The orange cat still slept curled in a blanket Angie had placed.

When they finally reached the cabin, true night had fallen. Dark and dismal, the boarded-up house greeted them.

"I can't leave you here, Ang. Look at this place.

"Stay tonight. You'll see, once the lights are on and the windows unboarded, it's real nice."

Dan stepped from the car and peered into the sky. Already a light dusting coated the vehicle. "If we stay the night, we aren't getting out of here until the storm clears."

Angie hurried to the front door and unlocked it. An alarm keypad began to beep. Without her doing anything, the keypad fell silent.

Angie giggled at Dan's disgusted snort. "It's not real. Granddad said there wasn't any point as no one was around to hear it and by the time police arrived the thief could be long gone. Besides, we have nothing worth stealing inside."

Dan had to take her word for it as the room was too dark to make anything out. Angie flicked a switch beside the door and sighed hard when nothing happened.

"Wait here." She followed the dim radiance of her cellphone into the room. A moment later, a light came on, illuminating the room with a soft glow. Sheets shrouded the furniture on a dusty hardwood floor. Angie stood beside a floor lamp to the left of a sheet-covered couch. Her eyes glittered in the light as if she held back tears. Dan's gaze traveled her, then the room, coming to rest on muddy footprints crossing the floor.

"Someone's been here." He pointed to the footprints that led to the closed door behind Angie.

The duffle bag on his shoulder thudded to the floor, and he rummaged in it a moment before emerging with a flashlight that he clicked on and shone on the floor by his feet. More muddy tracks marked the hardwood. Dan followed them around the small space.

It appeared as if someone had entered and searched the living area before heading to the kitchen. The four kitchen cabinets were open and empty. The plug for the empty refrigerator was knotted through the door handle, keeping it open. Scuffed muddy tracks crisscrossed the kitchen floor as if whoever was here had searched each cupboard. Tracks led to both closed doors.

The room closest to the kitchen proved to be a small bathroom laundry combination. Tracks covered the floor in an impossible to sort out pattern. A plastic bin in the old, faded tub held towels, and a piece of petrified soap sat in a soap dish. The cabinet under the sink was empty.

Dan returned to the main room and gestured at the

door behind Angie. "The bedroom?"

"Yes. Someone went into the loft."

She pointed to a steep set of stairs, almost a ladder, to her left. Twelve-foot-high ceilings gave the main room an airy feel. Above the bedroom and bathroom, a railing framed a loft. "When I was a kid, I slept up there. That was my space. I thought it was great cause no adult could fit. Gram would come up once in a while to make sure I didn't have any critters stashed up there, but they pretty much let me decorate it however I wanted."

Angie bit her lip and looked worried.

"I'll check it out."

Dan climbed the stairs and played his flashlight over the scuffed hardwood floor. He had to hunch to fit under the five-foot ceiling. A mattress lay on the floor with a plastic bin beside it. Four more bins with the tops off stood right in front of the stairs. Someone had pulled off the sheets that had covered a small armchair, dresser, and a wooden table with two wooden chairs, and dropped the sheets on the floor beside the bare mattress. A large bank of windows, boarded now and framed with empty built-in bookcases, lined the back wall. An empty department store clothing rack stood in the corner.

Dan peered into the bins. Two were filled with books. One held board games, and one was filled with rocks, pieces of wood, small plastic containers of beads, dried up glue sticks, and other assorted craft supplies. Dan smiled, picturing a young Angelina in her sunny room making artwork to give to her grandmother. The smile became sad as he pictured her working on gifts for the parents too busy to come here with her.

"Everything looks okay," Dan called as he closed the lids before going back down the steep stairs. "I can see why you liked it. I wish I had a place like that when I was a kid."

"Where did you grow up?"

"Seattle. My mother died when I was twelve. I have no idea who my father is. Mom was great though. She tried really hard to be a good parent.

"You never knew your dad?"

"Nope. My birth certificate says Jack Tar, which is basically a generic term for sailor, so I'm guessing some sailor she met swept her off her feet. She never spoke of him, although she'd sometimes walk the shore and look sad as she stared out to sea. Frankly, it's why I was never into casual relationships. I didn't want to be like him and leave some poor girl having to fend for herself and my child. Not that my mother ever made me feel unwanted, but I'm sure her job caused her cancer, and she wouldn't have had to work there if my father hadn't bailed on her. When I have kids, I'll be a full-time dad."

Dan began removing the sheets on the furniture and folding them with Angie's help as he spoke. "When my mom knew she was dying, she got me a place at a boy's home, and I lived there until I was sixteen. I liked both the other boys and the Fathers who ran it. Saint Patrick's was a good place if you needed somewhere like that, and I would've stayed, but I got a job on a fishing boat and never looked back. I was born to be a sailor."

"So, you never finished high school?"

"Not officially. When I joined the Navy, I got my

GED, and I've taken classes to pass my advancement tests, but I don't have a degree or anything." Dan rubbed his hands together. His breath plumed in the cold air of the cabin. "Where's the woodpile?"

"Out back. A bilco door leading to the basement is back there too. Let's turn on the water and heat before Tiger freezes in the car."

SIX

———◆———

ONE OF THE BEST NIGHTS OF HIS LIFE

A COZY fire threw wavering shadows against the walls. In the kitchen, Angie chopped vegetables for soup. Dan took out a small radio from his duffle bag and fiddled with it until he got a local weather station.

"Ang, the storm is now officially a blizzard. We aren't getting out of here any time soon."

"Not a problem. I brought supplies for a week. There should be plenty to eat for at least four or five days."

Dan placed the radio on the green tile counter that separated the kitchen from the living area.

"Don't freak out, but if those were Candice's prints, the people who are searching for whatever she stole might come here too. You can't stay here, Angie; it isn't safe. What if they come while you're here? Once the storm breaks, we're heading back to Washington, and I'll rent you a room there."

She paused in her chopping to peer worriedly at him. "You think whoever wrecked my home will come here?"

"I'm sure of it if they know about this place."

Dan took out the small digital camera and flipped through the pictures. He stopped on the one showing the hole in her wall.

"See how they tore out outlets? That means whatever they're looking for is small. Small enough to fit into a soup can or a power receptacle. Every single outlet was torn out and searched. I'm guessing whatever Candice took was worth a fortune. Maybe a USB drive. Not money, because there couldn't be enough in that small of a space. Well, maybe money too, but that isn't what they're so desperate to find."

Angie handed him the bag of potatoes and turned back to her pile of carrots, peeling them as she spoke.

"Her husband was connected. I ran a quick search on my work computer. Joe Conti has ties to the Ricon crime family in New York. The Ricons are under investigation for tax fraud among other things. Maybe what Candice took can send someone important to jail. That would be serious enough for them to search for it."

"Whatever it is, we want no part of it." Dan took a kitchen knife from the drawer and began peeling potatoes. "I'm sorry, Ang, but I think you need to accept this place will be trashed too. Sooner or later they'll realize you own it and someone will come look. When we go, take anything you don't want to be destroyed."

"Nothing remains really besides the quilts. It makes me so mad that there's nothing I can do about any of this."

"This house is too far in the boonies for the police to even patrol it."

Dan began cutting up onions as he debated what to say next. Whoever had destroyed her house was serious about finding what Candice had stolen. He was worried they'd come after Angie if they didn't find what they were looking for soon. The police had informed them the room Dan had rented in Tijuana had been ransacked the day he left. The apartment Candice rented in Chicago had also been ransacked.

Whatever they were searching for, they weren't going to give up without at least confronting Angie and him. He decided they could talk about it later. The pallor of her skin and circles under eyes revealed her stress. A couple of days in the quiet here and he could talk to her about it on the way back to Washington.

Tiger leaped to the counter. Dan narrowed his eyes. "Off."

The cat jumped down and wound around his legs.

Angie laughed and gave the cat a piece of raw chicken.

"He never listens to me to that good," she said.

Dan quirked and eyebrow, a smug smile on his face. "The Navy spent a fortune teaching me the voice of command. Glad I can finally put it to use."

Angie giggled. "Do you serve on a ship?"

"Sometimes. What I do is specialized and confidential. I can be assigned anywhere at any time as needed. Right now, I'm officially on leave, but when I'm working, I carry a beeper and have to report to base within thirty minutes once it goes off."

"And you don't know where they'll send you or for how long?"

"Could be anywhere. Generally, it's a few weeks, most of which is spent traveling, but I've spent a few months on assignment in the past."

"That must be hard on the families."

"It can be. The Navy makes a real effort to support the spouses though. Ship assignments can run for months. With video chat and email, ship duty isn't so bad. You can talk almost daily. Not that talking can replace real contact, but it's better than nothing. When I get called out, I can't bring a cellphone, and I'm rarely sent anywhere there is phones or internet, and because of the, ah, secretive nature of my work we don't call in unless we're on a base."

"You don't go alone then?"

"No. I serve on a seven-man team. My teammate Juan died on the last mission, so we'll get a replacement."

"What you do is dangerous then?"

"No more so than any soldier faces. Hell, maybe even less so because we're so well trained." Dan wiped his eyes and sniffed. "Onions always make me cry."

"Cut them under water. Or let me cut them. Onions don't bother me too much." Angie gave him a quick hug. "I'm sorry you lost your friend."

"God, me too. Juan was a great guy and my best friend. The killer is, he died a hero and no one except the team will ever know it. We can't say anything, and he has no one to mourn or remember him."

"Not true. You remember. Love doesn't die. You can keep loving him and his memory will live with you."

"Awful wise for one so young."

Angie shrugged. "When my parents died I saw a counselor. Time helps. Everything the councilor said was true. The anger, loneliness, fear, all the stages of grief. But mostly I think of that when I'm sad and miss them. I remember they never stopped loving me and I don't have to stop loving them."

Dan nodded, and they continued making the soup in silence.

———————◦ ◆ ◦———————

The power went out at ten the next morning. Dan brought in the woodpile, stacking it around the room. "Keep the bedroom door closed. I'll move the mattress in here. There's already two feet of snow outside, and the storm has another day at least. This wood might need to last a week."

Angie's eyes widened.

"Nothing to worry about. If we run out of wood, we can walk to the neighbor's house. I promise we won't freeze, but I'd rather stay here so we'll only heat this room. I'm going to use that roll of plastic in the basement to seal off the loft. Get everything from the bedroom so we don't need to go in there. The kerosene heater can keep the bathroom warm enough the pipes won't freeze, but there won't be hot water just the toilet."

To Dan's surprise, a grin flitted across Angie's face. He rose an eyebrow, and she laughed.

"I was just thinking of the copper tub my granddad kept in the basement. When I was a kid, and we lost power, he'd place the tub on a quilt before the fire and Gram would heat the water in the kettle. See that hook? The pole there lets you tip the kettle into the tub. They would hustle me through my bath and put me in their bed. At the time, I thought it was to keep warmer, now I realize they wanted privacy to bathe before the fire. I used to think Granddad cut the power on purpose sometimes because he liked roasting things over the fire. Now I think he just liked watching Gram wash in the firelight."

"Mmm hmm," Dan made an indistinct sound.

Angie flushed and hurried into the bedroom. Dan laughed and went to the basement to get the roll of plastic. Try as he might he couldn't banish the image of Angie bathing by firelight.

Before he sealed the loft, he brought the five bins downstairs. Two kerosene lamps gave enough light to see, but not enough to read by. Angie had dug up a cauldron that hung from the hook beside the fire. Two long metal skewers, which held an assortment of chopped meat and vegetables, hung from small hooks hanging from a metal strip with a wooden handle built into the mantel.

"Granddad designed this," Angie said as she picked up a yellow mustard bottle from the mantle beside a thick oven mitt. The writing on the bottle was so worn it had disappeared. "Every ten minutes we squirt the top and let the sauce trickle down and turn it a quarter turn. This was my favorite meal."

The smell of roasting meat filled the room, making Dan's mouth water. Dan glanced around for Tiger, surprised the cat wasn't there begging.

"Have you seen the cat?"

Angie stood and called the cat. An apologetic grimace on her face, she opened the bedroom door and entered, still calling for Tiger.

Dan shrugged on his coat and went outside. No sign of cat prints marred the snow. Thick flakes covered the tracks he'd made to the back of the house. Tiger's tracks would've disappeared in moments.

Inside the house, Angie continued to call, her voice rising in distress. Dan hollered outside as he trudged through the three feet of snow to the basement.

Back inside the house, Angie was opening all the cupboards.

"Maybe he's stuck in the loft," Dan suggested.

A relieved smile on her face, she straightened and closed the cabinet door.

"Of course, the loft. He's been here, and we used to sleep there."

"Really?" Dan said in surprise. "How old is he?"

"Fourteen in May. Gram got him for me when Grandad died. We spent every summer here until I turned sixteen and Gram got sick. She died when I was in college. I hate to admit this because it sounds horrible, but I missed her more than my mother. Gram and Grandad practically raised me. Every day after school she greeted me with snacks and a hug. We lived in a two-family home, but I spent way more time in their half of the house. To this day, I don't know my father's favorite color, but indigo blue was Granddad's. Every recipe I have came from Gram. I can clearly hear her voice in my head but can't remember what my mother sounded like."

"Isn't that weird? I can remember what my mom and Father Calbert sounded like too." Dan exchanged a sad smile with Angie.

Angie headed up the stairs and eased the plastic

aside. Dan followed, carrying one of the kerosene lamps. No Tiger greeted them. Angie's eyes swam with tears.

"We'll find him. He couldn't have gone far." An arm around her shoulder, he sat back on his heels.

Angie paused as she turned back to the stairs. "That's weird. Did you move the dresser?"

"No."

"Maybe he's in the laundry chute." Excited now, Angie crawled over to the small dresser and pushed it aside. White paneling covered the walls. Two fingers pressed in what Dan thought were knot holes and the panels lifted and Tiger leaped out.

Angie sat with a soft cry and buried her face in the cat's fur.

Dan crawled over and stuck his head in the space revealed. A small ledge surrounded a two-foot square hole. Once the cat's weight was off the shelf, a board covered the hole. "Where's this go?"

"Bathroom. Gramps made it for me. He was afraid I'd fall carrying garbage and laundry down the stairs. I was afraid of spiders crawling from the hole, so it closes automatically. Tiger must have entered and stepped on the board that closes the door. Good thing he's still agile, or he might have fallen and hurt himself."

"I never noticed a hole in the ceiling," Dan said.

"Comes out of the wall like this one. Gram didn't want dirty clothes and stuff dirtying up the bathroom."

Dan ran his hand over the floor panel making it release and reset. "Your grandfather was a real craftsman. This work is excellent."

"He built the entire place. At one time, he planned

on adding on but as there was just us three, and I loved the loft, he never did."

Once they returned downstairs, and Dan had sealed the loft again, he went into the bathroom. Another paneled wall lifted beside the washing machine, and a plastic wrapped bundle tumbled out. Dan put it aside and laid on the floor to peer up the chute. Another plastic wrapped bundle was wedged inside. In a minute, he had two more on the floor beside him. He brought all three into the living room and handed them to Angie.

"Found them in the chute."

Eyes wide, Angie unwrapped the black plastic. Bundled stacks of money were tucked inside a paper bag. The second package held money and a ledger. The third held more money.

Dan took the ledger from Angie's trembling hand and flipped through it. "Candice. I recognize her writing. Jesus, there's almost a million dollars here. Three hundred sixty thousand from you. Sixty thousand from Claire Everwood. The rest from a Deborah Singer."

"Mine?" Angie sounded hopeful and confused.

"According to her notes, this is the cash she took from your accounts. Jeez, Ang, didn't you spend any of your pay?"

Angie snorted. "It isn't all my pay. Most is from the sale of my parent's house when it finally cleared probate. But I told you, I worked all the time and never went out. I'm going to spend it now though."

Dan snickered. "Well, before you spend it, you need to report it and get it back legal. And let's face it, that might not happen."

A frown on her face now, Angie fingered the stacks of hundreds before her. "Unless I don't report it."

"And then what? How do you explain this amount of money? If you don't report it and someone finds out, you can go to jail a long time for fraud."

"I guess."

She sounded so disappointed Dan laughed.

Her thumb fanned the money, making a dull whir. "You're not tempted at all?"

"Not really, no." Dan shrugged and put the money back into the plastic bags. "I can afford anything I want. To me, it isn't worth the risk of jail."

A deep sigh escaped her. Again, she fanned the money, then began stacking it back into the bag. "I'm going to be seriously pissed if I don't get my money back now."

Dan snickered again as he emptied the books from the plastic bin. Muttering under her breath, Angie helped him.

Once the money was in the bin, Dan carried it outside and buried it in the snow against the cabin wall.

"Got the money on ice," he said as he slapped his gloves together when he came in.

She snorted. A glint in her eyes, she pointed to the monopoly game she'd taken from the bin. Marinade bottle in her hand, she turned from him to douse the meat.

"Let's play. I warn you, I'm a cutthroat gamer and show no mercy."

Dan kicked off his snowy boots and stood before the fire, rubbing his hands. "Wouldn't have it any other way."

That night, as Dan laid on the couch and watched the firelight dance on Angie's hair as she slept, he wished he'd met and married her. Angie was easy to love. This had easily been one of the best nights of his life. He didn't know if that made him pathetic or not.

Served piping hot and eaten with their fingers, the sauce she'd used on the meat was delicious, but the company was what made the meal so good. The smell of slightly burnt buttery popcorn still filled the cabin. Tiger curled beside him, purring with his chin setting on Dan's arm.

The sound of her laughter when she was winning and her insults when she wasn't seemed to linger in the air too. He hoped the storm raged for a week.

He got his wish.

SEVEN

---◆---

HE'D NEVER FELT LIKE THIS ABOUT ANYONE

ANGIE peered out the door after Dan. The snow had stopped falling, leaving the woods surrounding the cabin swaddled in white. Cold air gusted snow into drifts around the car. Dan's shoulders were hunched, his hands deep in his coat pockets. Angie knew it wasn't from the cold.

"How come I keep forgetting he's in mourning?" she murmured.

A frown formed lines on her brow as she closed the door.

Why can't I find a man like him?

The frown deepened as she took out her cell phone and called Parker.

"Angelina, I expected to hear from you sooner," Parker said.

"It's Angie. My name is Angie."

"Your name is Angelina. Stop being petty."

Angie gritted her teeth but dropped it. "I'll be back in town in a day or two. Once the snow clears—"

"The insurance company will have your home repaired by then?" Parker interrupted, sounding amazed.

"No, but Dan thinks it's too dangerous to stay here and offered to rent me a place."

"That man is still with you? Jesus, Angelina. He could be a psychopath for all you know. And you're staying alone with him in an isolated cabin?"

"Not like I have a lot of choices," Angie said briskly, biting her lip against what she really wanted to say. A break up should be done kindly in person, and she wanted to set a date with him to do it.

"Don't start. You know my policy on lending money. Come stay with me and leave Tiger at the vet or let that man keep him."

"Don't start? What the hell is that supposed to mean? Did I ever ask you for money?"

"No, but obviously, this call is about that. You still haven't reimbursed me for my plane ticket to Mexico. I left the country to help you, missing a day of work. Time and money I'll never see again."

Anger made her teeth clench, and she took a deep breath. "No. This call was to tell you I was returning and wanted to see you. I have no intention of asking you for anything. Send me a bill for your expenses. Not that you helped me. You left me there."

"Now don't get all upset. I'm happy to help. Didn't I risk my job to locate that woman for you?"

Angie took a deep breath and forced her voice to calmness. "No— you didn't. You clicked a few keys and told me where my card was being used." Angie couldn't help the tight, bitter sound of her voice. She'd asked him to come with her to Tijuana, and he'd refused. "It isn't like that was breaking the law or could get you into trouble."

"Doing credit searches isn't my job."

"Oh, my God, really?" A snort of laughter that she tried to stifle burst free.

Parker made an annoyed sound that turned to stony silence as she continued to laugh.

"On second thought, I rescind my invitation of hospitality. It's obvious we're unsuited and your ungrateful. I can't overlook your improper behavior."

Angie giggled again. "What improper behavior? It's not like I wrecked my own place or stole my own money. And what should I be grateful for?"

"Are you sleeping with him?"

Angie gasped, angry again. "No, but I wish I was."

"Goodbye, Angelina." Cold and angry, Parker's voice dripped contempt as if her name were a swear word.

"Good riddance, Parker," Angie said to the dial tone. He'd already slammed the phone down.

Angie sat with a thump on the old plaid couch, put her feet on the scuffed coffee table, and laughed. Truth at last. She didn't want Parker, she wanted Dan. Someone so kind they'd go out of their way to help a stranger. Not Parker who only offered help on his terms if he thought something was in it for him.

"I need to stop pretending to myself," she said to Tiger as she scratched his ears. The cat obligingly began to purr. "The first night Parker and I had sex I should've ended it. Six minutes and that included undressing. What was I thinking? Our first encounter was cold and passionless. No wonder he's still single despite his looks." She petted the cat a minute. "Why is Dan still single? A good-looking guy like him should've been snapped up by now. There must be a major hidden flaw, but damned if I can see what it is."

The cat made no answer, circling and settling down in her lap. Angie closed her eyes and leaned her head back, visualizing Dan shaving that morning. Shirtless, crouched beside the fire in the dim room, firelight had played along his shoulders as he laid the steaming cloth against his face. She'd wanted to go to him and run her hands over the muscled planes of his back and breath in his scent.

A deep sigh escaped her as she sat and stretched. A pointless fantasy. Soon, he'd return to California, and she'd never see him again. *Well, maybe at the divorce.* Besides, he'd shown no interest and made it perfectly clear he was helping her to ease his guilt over his dead wife.

"Let's not kid ourselves, Tiger, this is for Candice, not me. I can't imagine how he feels losing her so violently and then finding out this horrible truth. And honestly, I know what his flaw is, and it's a doozy. Who wants to be married to a man who is gone so much and unexpectedly with no idea where he is or when he'll return?"

Tiger opened one eye and yawned, showing white, pointed teeth and a long pink tongue.

"Right, honesty. I'd wait for a man like that." She closed her eyes again and leaned her head back, one hand stroking the cat.

———◆———

Dan grasped the shovel and leaned on it panting, his breath misting in the air before him. The furious expenditure of energy hadn't helped. He didn't think anything would help. Falling in love with her was stupid. In days, he'd be gone, and she wouldn't even think of him except as an amusing story to tell her friends. Even if he asked her on a date, and she agreed, it would go nowhere. California to Washington was too far. An educated, beautiful woman like her wouldn't agree to date a man like him anyway. She had a good career and a life she loved here. What did he have to offer her? A life alone on a Navy base.

For her, I would quit and live in Washington. The thought shocked him.

He loved his job and had never considered resigning before. Any security firm anywhere would be glad to have him, but he'd signed a contract and had three more years before he could quit.

"She won't wait three years," he whispered into the cold wind.

He turned and faced the cabin. The driveway and car were now clear of snow. Tears froze in his eyelashes. Never in his life had he wanted anything this much. This would never be his home. His children wouldn't play here, making snowmen or crafts in the sunny loft. Some other man would come here with her to make memories and raise a family. He'd never see her skin by firelight.

Dan closed his eyes and lifted his face to the sky. What he could do was find her a safe place to live. Maybe even hire a guard until this Candice mess was cleared up.

For another hour, he cleared a path around the

building for no reason except to burn off energy.
Finally, chilled and tired, he returned to the warmth of
the cabin. Her warmth.

Angie greeted him with a smile and a bowl of hot
soup.

"Even though the snow stopped it can take a day or
two for them to clear the road this far out. Granddad
used to plow us out himself. When he passed, we
stopped coming in the winter. Gram didn't like to drive
the truck, but I think she missed his teasing by the
fire too much. Now, when I think back, I wonder how
my mom settled for the life she led with Dad. How
could she not want the kind of relationship her
parents had?"

Dan shrugged. "I think most people settle. Not that
they don't love their spouses, but not passionately.
Look at me and Candice. I was willing to settle. I see
that now, but I've learned my lesson and won't make
that mistake again. If I can't have what your
grandparents had, I want nothing."

Dan was surprised to see a tear trace a path across
her cheek.

She sniffed and wiped her eyes. "Me too. Granddad
would've liked you. He was a soldier in World-War-Two
and snuck Gram out of Germany after knowing her
one week. You remind me of him."

"Impulsive and reckless?" Dan grinned and tweaked
her ponytail.

"Kind and compassionate."

Angie gazed up at him, her lips parted and eyes
bright. Over the last few days, the dark circles had
disappeared and her skin now glowed with health.
Unconsciously, Dan took a step toward her. He wanted

to kiss her soft lips. The flush on her cheeks grew as he hesitated. He cleared his throat and turned away, placing his soup bowl in the sink.

"I'll get more water," he mumbled and hurried to the bathroom with the teakettle.

She would despise him if he kissed her. A kiss might make her think he was here to try to take advantage, that he was the kind of man who went with any willing woman. Candice had died a week and a half ago, and Angie would never believe he'd fallen in love with her so soon.

She'd think he was fickle, and maybe he was, but he'd never felt like this about anyone before. *Why the hell did she have to be so perfect? So exactly what I want. Two more days. I can keep my hands to myself for two days.* He splashed cold water on his face and waited to return until his eyes stopped stinging.

EIGHT

ONE MORE NIGHT

TWO days later, Dan stood in the driveway and watched the state plow go by. The driver lifted a hand. Dan waved back while inside he prayed for snow. An epic blizzard would be welcome.

The last week had been the best of his life. Despite the pipes that froze and soup for every meal, he'd never had a better time. Slowly, he trudged back to the cabin.

"Roads clear then?" She smiled but sounded disappointed.

"Yep."

"Can we stay one more night?" Angie asked and gazed at him with a hopeful expression.

Dan's heart leapt, and he grinned. "Sure."

"Great. Let's bring in the tub and clean up."

It had been a few days since his last shower. He

and Angie had washed their jeans and underwear in the cauldron and hung them on a line rigged by the fire after using the warm water to wash. Sponge baths and washing his hair in cool water held no appeal, but he wasn't sure his willpower was up to Angie in a tub.

Angie continued speaking. "We can hang a sheet on the line and have privacy. If someone does come and ruins this place, I want to bathe here one more time."

Dan regretted agreeing to stay. The idea of her naked before the fire had his pants uncomfortably tight. Luckily, she seemed oblivious to the effect she had.

"I'll, um, go get the tub." The cold would do him good.

"The tub is heavy. I'll help." Angie grabbed her coat from the hook beside the door and stamped her feet into boots. Twenty minutes later she was laughing as she filled every pot with snow and lined them up on the hearth.

"This could take a while," she said, grinning ruefully at him.

"We have all night." Dan's eyes darkened as her breath caught and a flush reddened her cheeks.

She lowered her head and spun away. Dan cleared his throat, for the first time all week uncomfortable with her.

"I'll pack up the car. Do you have everything you want to save?" he asked.

Angie licked her lips and nodded, her gaze glued to him. The pulse in her throat jumped, visible from where he stood. He wanted to press his lips against it. Instead, he grabbed the plastic bin by the door and hurried outside without bothering to put on his coat.

At the car, he placed the bin on the ground and leaned with both hands on the cold metal.

"Get a grip!" he whispered to himself. "Don't ruin your friendship by taking advantage!"

He took his time loading the car. The money in the bin he covered with quilts and placed in the back seat beside the bottled water they'd brought with them but hadn't used. Angie had sorted through the games and books. Most of them she'd wanted to save. Dan placed them in the trunk and tied it closed. He wrapped plastic from the basement around the trunk to keep out the snow the wind blew in swirls. Already a light dusting coated the road brought there by the wind.

The bin that had held the quilts now filled with snow, Dan headed inside. It took an hour to fill the tub enough to bathe.

Angie placed heated bricks in the water to keep it warm. The smell of roses filled the air from her bubble bath.

A small clear bottle with a picture of a rose on one side and the word Florian written in fancy script sat on the mantel.

"One of my favorite things. I'm so glad they didn't break it." Angie lifted the bottle and sniffed. "I don't know where to get this stuff anymore. Gram gave it to me. Nine years old and it still smells amazing."

It does." Dan winced at the deep, cracked sound of his voice. Desperate for a distraction, he moved a side table next to the tub and placed one of the lamps on it. Angie had hung a light sheet on the line. Dan replaced it with a quilt, not sure his self-control would be strong enough to resist her shadowy form.

She giggled as she watched him.

Tiger jumped into his lap as soon as he sat, and he obligingly began petting him. The cabin was shrouded in darkness and humid from steam. To Dan, the air practically crackled with sexual tension, and he wondered if she felt it too or if it was only his imagination.

A sense of expectancy hung over the cabin. He hadn't experienced anything like it since he was a small boy waiting for Santa Clause. The thought saddened him. He didn't want this to be a figment of his imagination, a fable he told himself.

Outside, dusk had arrived. Woods shaded the cabin on three sides, bringing night early. The boarded-up windows kept in the heat, leaving them in intimate warmth. Dan was glad the electricity was still off.

Conversations with Angie in the dark room were one of his favorite things. It seemed easier to talk honestly in the dark. He'd told her things he'd never spoken of with anyone. He'd shared his hopes, dreams, and fears. They had long conversations about everything from favorite books to politics. She adored nature stories and begged him for stories of his travels, eyes shining in the darkness, nestled in the quilt on the mattress on the floor. Hair tousled, and skin flushed from the fire, she gazed at him with fascinated interest.

He would miss those nights and the stories of her youth. The descriptions of her work and coworkers made him laugh and groan in sympathy. An office job would bore him to tears, but she made it seem interesting. He was brought back from his meanderings by her voice.

"When we get back to Washington, do you think my

apartment will be safe?"

"Yes. There'd be no reason to return and search again. I'm a bit worried they might think you have whatever it is on you, but by now they must realize they have the wrong Angelina."

The sound of splashing stilled.

"Am I in danger?"

"Maybe a little. I was thinking to hire you a guard. If I thought the chance was high, I wouldn't leave you."

"A guard? How could I afford one?"

"I can afford one. I make decent money. More than I need. My bills are small, and I have savings and retirement accounts." Dan tried to stop himself, but he wanted her to know he could afford to take care of her— forever."

"Three roommates. I remember," she said.

"Two now. Maybe the new guy will want Juan's room."

"Damn. I'm sorry, Dan."

"Don't be. You'd like Squirrel and Tom. Well, maybe not Tom, although when he tries, he can be a charming bastard. For you, he'd try, but don't get taken in. He flirts with everyone."

"You never did tell me why you call Enrique, Squirrel."

"Um, it's a long story involving crushed nuts and not the type you eat."

Angie giggled. "Do you have a nickname?"

"Yep— someday I'll tell you."

"That bad, huh?"

"Not really, but it requires explanation. Juan named me on our first mission, and the name took."

With a dull twang, the string holding up the quilt

snapped. The blanket fluttered to the floor as Angie shrieked, giggled and splashed.

Dan leapt to his feet and grabbed the quilt. Firelight shimmered on water droplets sprinkled over her arms that she'd crossed over her breasts. Bubbles floated in patches around her knees. The tub wasn't big enough to stretch out in. Hunkered as she was with her neck below water to hide her breasts exposed her legs. His heated gaze traveled her, and without meaning too, he took a step forward.

The smile fled her face as her eyes darkened. She straightened and reached a hand to him, exposing the tops of her breasts between strands of her long, wet hair.

Dan dropped the quilt beside the tub, kneeling on it as he took her hand. "Ang, I—"

The sound of a car interrupted him. He leapt to his feet and ran to the door. Frigid air hit him like a slap. The car slowed and turned into the driveway.

"Get dressed," he yelled as he slammed the door.

He jumped from the porch, landing in the path he'd cleared, grateful he had his boots on. To the right of the porch, a large snowdrift offered concealment. The drift reached almost to their rental car. Yesterday, he'd shoveled off the roof of the cabin, throwing the snow into piles around the house on top of the piles he'd made clearing the path. Bent over, he ran to the edge of the pile nearest his car.

Two men in a jeep parked behind his car and got out. Dan's gaze narrowed, he recognized one of them. The man who shot Carlos checked his gun and zipped his leather jacket. Black dress shoes on his feet revealed white socks. The other man removed his jacket and loosened a gun in a shoulder holster then leaned into the car and brought out a machete.

"If the girl is here, she'll talk." The man spoke with a thick Italian accent. Larger than the man who'd shot Carlos, his forearms rippled with muscle.

Dan's gaze flicked between them and settled on the Italian as his first target.

"Let's get this done and go home. I'm sick of this shit," the Italian said.

"Don't be in such a fucking hurry. You wanna end up like Carlos? The bitch is dangerous."

The Italian closed his door quietly. The man who shot Carlos shrugged and headed to the front steps.

Dan stifled a laugh that turned to a snarl. That man had blamed Angelina for Carlos's death. *No wonder they thought she was involved somehow.*

He waited until the men passed him, then jumped out and grabbed the bigger guy. One arm around his neck, he hit him in the solar plexus and grabbed his gun from the shoulder holster. The man stopped struggling as the gun reached his temple.

"Drop the fucking knife, or I pull this trigger. You have two seconds," Dan said.

To emphasize his point, he cocked the gun.

The knife thudded into the snow.

"Let me make this clear. We had nothing to do with Carlos's death. Your buddy there shot him. Angelina had nothing to do with Candice. Candice was never at her home. She did come here and hid money that we turned over to the police. There was a ledger, but it only listed her victims. She was here in November. I have no idea what she stole only that it was small enough to fit in a soup can or power outlet. We found nothing that small."

Dan tightened his grip on the man's neck and gestured with the gun to the other man. "You, whoever the hell you are."

"Benny," supplied the Italian.

"Right, Benny, then. Go home and tell your boss we aren't involved with this. We don't want a thing to do with any of this shit."

Benny's nervous gaze darted over Dan and his captive. "Like you'll just let us go."

"Yep. Drop the fucking gun. Get in your car and go. If I see you again, I won't hesitate to kill you."

"Drop the gun, Benny," the Italian said.

"Fuckers going to kill me if I do.

"I'm going to kill you if you don't! Don't be an ass. If he wanted to kill us, he could've. I believe him. The boss will too. We couldn't understand how she was involved. It was your bullshit story that convinced us. This search is pointless and a waste of time. It isn't here."

Benny licked his lips and backed away.

"Drop the fucking gun, Benny. I won't ask again," Dan said as he pointed the gun at Benny.

"Sorry, Tony, but I'm screwed if the boss finds out." Benny pulled the trigger as he turned and ran down the narrow path Dan had cleared around the house. Shots flew unaimed over Benny's shoulder as he ran. Dan returned fire as he staggered backward, holding up Tony's suddenly limp form. Inside the house, Angie screamed then called for Dan.

Dan let Tony fall to the ground, but it was too late, Benny had disappeared around the corner of the house. Snow soaked into his jeans as he knelt beside

Tony and felt for a pulse. Weak and thready, the pulse in Tony's neck slowed under his fingers.

"Fucker killed me." Blood bubbled from Tony's lips. "Tell Vin—"

A hacking cough interrupted him. Before Tony could finish his sentence, the light faded from his eyes.

"Lock the door, Ang!" Dan yelled and ran around the house the other way.

By the far-left corner of the house, footsteps marred the clean surface of the snow. Benny had run into the woods.

"Good riddance," Dan muttered and headed back to the front door.

Angie let him in. Tears sparkled in her lashes and trailed down her pale cheeks. Dressed in her flannel jeans with her wet hair in a ponytail making a wet spot on her blue sweater, she shivered. Dan hugged her, leaning down to breath in the scent of her neck.

"Call the police. I'll get Tiger. We're getting out of here," Dan said.

Angie had already thrown all their clothes into the bags. Dan grabbed Tiger and tucked him under his arm, swung his duffle over his shoulder, and let Tiger's bag dangle from the crook of his arm. Angie grabbed her bag and stared around the room with tear-filled eyes.

"Lock the door in case he comes back. Let's not make it easy for him. The dumb fuck will probably get lost and freeze to death in his leather jacket and dress pants. We have about ten minutes before he can circle through the trees in this snow in those shoes to get an angle on the front door."

Angie spoke to the police as Dan ushered her out

the door. At the sight of Tony laying in the red-tinged snow, she halted.

"Dan, is he dead?" High and shrill, her voice shook.

"Yes. Get in the car; we need to get out of here. For all we know Benny has back-up coming."

Angie took a deep sobbing breath and stepped forward, stumbling to her knees and struggling upright. Dan yanked her up and half dragged her to the car. The arm in his grasp trembled badly.

In the car, he handed her Tiger and threw their bags onto the backseat. "Stay down. Be right back." Dan grabbed the machete Tony had dropped and stabbed all four tires of Benny's car, leaving the knife sticking from the front driver side tire.

Back at his car, he grabbed the small digital camera from his bag and took close-ups of Tony and the car before he got in and locked the door. He dragged a blanket from the back and draped it over Angie who huddled on the floorboards with pupils so dilated her wide eyes were almost black.

Crouched on the floor clutching Tiger to her chest, she sounded panicked as she spoke on the phone.

NINE

Let's Stay Together Forever

DAN was already slowing the car as she dropped the phone and clapped a hand over her mouth. Dan reached over and grabbed Tiger as she fumbled with the door handle. The phone fell unheeded to the floor as she stumbled out and vomited in the snow.

Lips pressed tightly together, Dan put Tiger in the backseat, pushed the stolen gun further into his waistband, and followed. In the snow beside her, he knelt and rubbed her back as she shook and heaved.

"Take a breath. Everything's okay," he said

Her wet hair wrapped around his hand as she shook her head wildly. "No, it isn't. That man is dead, and he came to kill me." A shudder passed over her, and she retched again.

"That man came to talk to you." Dan took off his jacket and draped it over her head. Her skin felt icy cold under his hand, and her face was whiter than the snow.

"A machete, Dan? He was going to use a machete on me?" Now a thin pitiful wail, she trailed off into sobs as she fell into his arms, her entire body shaking.

"No, Ang," Dan lied. "He wanted to scare you is all. Nobody will hurt you. Get back in the car please before you freeze to death."

A scared, haunted expression on her face, she rose and grabbed a handful of fresh snow that she used to wipe her face. She grabbed another handful, put it in her mouth and spit it out.

Dan kept his arm around her waist, not trusting her legs to hold her up as she staggered to the car. In the car, she huddled on the seat.

Dan picked up the phone from which a man repeatedly said hello.

"One minute, please."

Without waiting for an answer, he put the phone on the dashboard and leaned into the backseat where he grabbed a quilt that he tucked around Angie. The heat set to high, Dan put the car in gear and picked up the phone again.

"Hello, this is Petty Officer First-Class Daniel Barstow. You were just speaking to my wife, Angelina."

From the corner of his eye, Dan glanced at Angie as he spoke on the phone. By the time they'd reached the main road, he'd told the story twice to the police and agreed to come to the local state police barracks. Two police cars with sirens blaring and lights flashing passed him, speeding toward Angie's cabin.

On the seat beside him, Angie shivered so hard he could hear her teeth chatter. Dan pulled over and got out of the car, leaving it running with the heat on high. He took a bottled water from the backseat, then slid her seat back and sat down, pulling her into his lap.

"Shh, take a breath and relax. That's right," he said encouragingly as she consciously slowed her breathing, taking deep breaths in time with his.

He rubbed her back with one hand, using the other to hold the quilt tight around her. In a few minutes, the shivering stopped and her breathing slowed.

Still pale and shaky, she thanked him.

"Your safe now and I'll make sure you stay safe. When you're ready, we'll go to the police station and get this cleared up." He handed her the water bottle. "Drink some. You'll feel better."

She obligingly took a sip and made a face. He cracked the door so she could rinse her mouth. After a few moments of sipping the water, she recapped it and dropped it on the floor.

"I'm sorry I freaked out..."–she rubbed her eyes with the heels of her hands– "This is too much, Dan. I'm not cut out for this— People dying and trying to kill me." A shudder traveled her body. "I never thought I was a coward—"

Dan tightened his grip on her, the self-disgusted tone of voice angering him.

Damn Benny to Hell!

"It's okay, Ang. Most people live their entire lives and never come face-to-face with violence. Don't feel bad that it upsets you. That doesn't make you a coward. Not wanting to be around violence doesn't make you weak or a bad person."

"How come it doesn't upset you?"

Dan's heart constricted. He was the kind of man

she was afraid of.

"Training. And it does upset me, but my training lets me function even when I'm afraid or angry. I didn't want that man to die." Dan took a deep breath, the scent of roses filling his nose. "Angie, I won't lie to you about who I am. If I could've, I would've killed Benny."

Another shiver passed over her, and she burrowed her face into his neck. For a minute, they sat together. Dan rested his fingers against her wrist, checking her pulse, which was nice and steady. A corner of the quilt made a makeshift towel that he rubbed over her icy hair.

His hands cupped her skull, fingers spread under her cold, wet hair, trying to warm her up.

She made a sound of contentment and turned her face to his. Without meaning to, he kissed her. The kiss deepened as fire consumed him. The touch of her lips on his heated his entire body, leaving him trembling and weak.

When the kiss ended, he was breathing hard and filled with fear. Never had he been this afraid or wanted something so much. With an act of will, he gathered his courage and spoke.

"Before we go turn ourselves in, I need to tell you some things. Please don't do or say anything you don't want too. Nothing has changed for me. I mean, I still want to help you." Dan heaved a sigh and groaned. "I'm not saying this right. What I mean is, I don't want to pressure or scare you. Before those men came, I was going to say I love you."

She tensed in his arms and ducked her head. Her wet hair fell forward, hiding her expression. Dan gulped hard and continued.

"Those men have changed my plans. Their boss thinks you're involved. You won't be safe in Washington. I have an idea to keep you safe, but I didn't want to offer it under false pretenses."

He took a deep breath and blurted, "Ang, you can come with me. In March, my team goes to Guantanamo for two months, and you could come as my wife. It's a restricted base and you'd be safe there. In no way do I want to pressure you." Dan groaned. "Look, I'm not good at this. I don't mean to imply you have to really be my wife. You could come there, and I swear I won't force myself on you or—"

A shiver racked her, and she kissed his cheek. Tears filled her eyes as she framed his face with her hands and kissed him. The touch of her warm lips on his filled him with hope. A low moan escaped him and he deepened the kiss, twining his fingers in her cold, wet hair. Hot and cold waves traveled him, leaving him lightheaded.

A catch in his voice, Dan said, "Whatever you want to do, I'll do. I can't quit my job for three years, but I swear I 'll come to you whenever I can. Stay with me."

Her breath caught in a sob and she kissed him again, leaning hard into his arms. She dropped her hands from his face to his waist and ran them under his shirt.

"Let's stay together forever. No matter what," she said.

"Yes." He wanted to say more, but the lump in his throat kept him from speaking.

Tears tracked his cheek as he kissed her, the heat of her touch inflaming him. He never wanted to let her go.

She said, "Don't worry about your job. We have three years to decide what to do. I can take leave from mine and maybe transfer. Accountants can find work anywhere, and I'm a really good one."

"I love you." Low and deep, his voice cracked with emotion.

"I love you too." She sounded breathy, shy, and full of hope.

"We'll work this out and stay together." He spoke in a whisper, resting his cheek against hers.

Euphoric now, he basked in her embrace, ruthlessly squashing the niggling voice of his conscious, not wanting to consider how he was taking advantage of her need for comfort. For ten minutes, they held each other, her hands wandering his back under his shirt. Tempted to touch her skin, but knowing he wouldn't be able to stop, he kept his hands on her jacket.

Sirens in the distance roused him. He felt drunk with desire, elated and scared she'd change her mind. He wished he'd rented a car with a bench seat so he could pull her close. Resigned, he moved back to the driver's seat and put the car into gear.

As close as the seatbelt allowed she leaned to him, resting her forehead on his shoulder with her arms around him.

A few minutes later, they passed a line of police cars. On the main road, which was clear of snow, he picked up speed. Traffic remained light until they reached the outskirts of town. Neither had spoken.

The smell of roses made his head swim, and he felt as if he couldn't catch his breath. Finally, he pulled over, removed his seatbelt and kissed her deeply. He lost track of time, caught up in her taste and touch.

"I could kiss you forever," she murmured as he drew back, breathing harder.

"I want to find somewhere we can be alone more than anything in the world, but we need to go to the police." Dan ran a hand over her damp hair as she stiffened. "There's no rush, Angel. We don't have to be alone until you want too."

"That I want. The police I don't, but you're right. Let's get it over with. I better call a lawyer too. The third murder in two weeks is bound to raise questions."

Dan drove them to the police station as she made calls and they went inside hand-in-hand.

An officer directed them to separate integration rooms. Dan was glad she'd called a lawyer. That is until the man showed up.

"Tell me this isn't your first case." Dan leaned back in his chair as his skeptical gaze traveled his lawyer. At twenty-four Rodney Basker appeared to be a teenager wearing his father suit.

A flush climbed the boy's cheeks.

"Never mind. It doesn't matter because we committed no crimes. Just get us out of here as soon as you can. Also, can you make sure our cat is somewhere warm?"

"Tiger is with Angelina. I saw her first. The police should be releasing her momentarily."

Dan sat up straighter. "And me?"

"That I don't know. I called your base and spoke to your commander. Someone from the judge advocates office should be in touch soon. I'm not really qualified to help service personnel."

Dan lifted an eyebrow. "Have I been charged with anything?"

"No. But I really think you need representation for the three murders you've been involved with."

"None of which I committed or in any way encouraged. For all three I was just an innocent bystander. A victim of mistaken identity in the wrong place at the wrong time."

"Yes, as to that, I could facilitate the annulment."

Dan scowled and leaned back in the chair. "Did Angie ask you too?"

"No, I just assumed..."

"We've decided to stay married."

"That might be wise. At least until this is all cleared up."

Dan said nothing, not wanting to explain that he loved her, and it had nothing to do with not testifying against a spouse. Besides, admitting they were in love might make them look guilty. He didn't care what this kid thought, he just wanted out of here.

"Make sure Angelina doesn't leave here alone. Benny is still out there and wants us dead. Do the police know who his boss is?"

"Not as far as I know. Sign your statement, and I'll see about getting you released.

"I want to return to my base with Angie as soon as I can. She'll be safer there."

"I'll see what I can do." Rodney rose and tapped the papers on the desk, neatening the edges.

━━━━━━━━ ◆ ━━━━━━━━

Four hours later, Dan left the room a free man. Angie dozed on the bench beside the door, the box containing Tiger by her feet. *Déjà vu* overcame him, the

86

way her blond hair shaded her face, the position on
the bench with her knees drawn to her chest. But this
time, the sight infused him with a protective love. The
bench creaked as he sat beside her, waking her. A
smile lit her eyes, although her expression remained
serious.

"Free to go?" she asked.

"Yep. Turning the money in went a long way toward
proving we aren't involved in this mess other than as
victims."

A glower on her face now, Angie turned and glared
toward the desk where the detectives sat quietly
talking. "My money."

Dan kissed her temple. "You don't need it.
Everything I have is yours."

"Pfft." she made a disgusted noise as she fished out
her cellphone from her front pocket. "Before you say
that, wait until you see the bill Parker sent me."

Dan let out a shout of laughter and hugged her.
"Oh, my God, I forgot all about him." The laughter died
as he pushed away to see her face. "He sent you a bill?
That goddamned bastard!"

"Yeah, I called him days ago to set up a meeting. I
didn't think it was right to break up with him on the
phone, but apparently he never received that lesson in
etiquette. The plane ticket, his lost wages and" – she
made a tu-dum sound – "pain and suffering. If anyone
should receive that, it's me."

Dan read the email Parker sent her. "What a
complete a-hole. Five-thousand dollars. Man, your
worth way more than that. I would've asked for five
million or so."

She snorted, then giggled. "He's just going to have

to wait. It'll take me three weeks of overtime to pay him back."

Dan forwarded the email to himself and handed her back her phone. "Don't worry about it. Let the bastard sue."

"No. I pay my debts."

"Our debts now. Can we go to California on the next available flight? I want us out of here and on base where you'll be safer. The police are tracking down who Carlos and Tony worked for. As soon as we know, I'll speak to their boss and explain Benny's lies."

"Can I answer tomorrow? I need to call my boss and landlord first."

"Angel, we'll do whatever you want. I'm hoping we can go to Gitmo early and get settled in there. The base is restricted so you would be safe there. Once this is over with, we can buy a place near base in California."

She smiled and kissed him, pulling him closer by his shirt. "We're going to raise a family, a real family that spends time together."

"A real family," he agreed huskily. "Thank God I met Candice in the bar that night!"

Angie laughed and punched his shoulder.

TEN

———◆———

I COULD DO THIS FOREVER

OUTSIDE the police station, sunrise turned the snow a rosy pink. Cold air nipped Dan's nose and caused his breath to plume before him.

"Brrr." Angie slapped her hands together and pulled the hood of her parka up.

In the car, Dan took Tiger from the cardboard box and placed him inside his jacket. "Another long night at a police station. This is getting to be a habit," he said.

Angie removed a glove and reached into his jacket to rub Tiger's ears. "What are we going to do now?"

"Stop at the first hotel we pass and get a room."

Angie grinned and leaned over to kiss his cheek. Dan turned into the kiss, weaving his fingers into her hair, cradling her warm skull.

"Mmm." He made a happy, aroused sound that

89

made Angie giggle.

He reluctantly pulled away and started the car. Angie took Tiger from his coat and put him in hers.

Dan turned the heater on high and then used his phone to find a hotel. "A Hampton Inn is five minutes away."

"Perfect," Angie said.

Dan reached over to rub Tiger's head, inadvertently brushing his knuckles against Angie's breast. She gasped and grabbed his hand.

"Ang, I want you more than I want air to breath, but I can wait. I'm sorry if you're feeling pressured or rushed—"

The cat leaped to the floor as Angie leaned over, pressing his hand to her chest. Blue eyes intent on his, she kissed his knuckles. "No, you aren't pressuring me. I want you just as much." She giggled. "Maybe more. I feel closer to you than anyone I've ever known. I can't believe we haven't even been together two weeks. It feels as if I've known you my entire life."

Dan used his free hand to smooth her staticky hair. "Hmm, let's see. If we'd dated normally, two four-hour dates a week, we've actually dated about five months if you subtract time spent in police stations and sleeping."

"Will you get tired of me? I mean, I love spending all my time with you, but you—"

"Never, Angel," Dan interrupted, resting his face against hers. "Every minute not spent with you will be torture for me. I'm really dreading returning to work."

"I'll be waiting when you come home whether you're gone eight hours, eight weeks, or eight months. We haven't known each other long enough to develop trust, but I assure you, I'm an honest, trustworthy person. Ask anyone."

Dan laughed and kissed her long and deep. "I do trust you, and you can trust me too. Wherever I am, whatever I'm doing, I'll be thinking of you, missing you and wanting to be with you. Nothing and no one will separate us. I can't wait to tell our grown children the story of how we met and fell in love, that God sent me an angel in my darkest hours."

Dan dropped his bag right inside the hotel room. He brought Tiger's green bag into the bathroom and emptied it, filling the food and water dishes and placing the litterbox on the floor after unwrapping it. He dropped a catnip mouse beside the bowl and sat on the toilet to remove his boots.

His sweatshirt followed the boots kicked into the corner. His hands were on his belt buckle when Angie entered. Her eyes locked with his as she pulled her shirt over her head and threw it on the floor by his. Still staring into his eyes, she loosened his belt buckle and dropped the belt on the pile of clothes.

He traced the lacy edge of Angie's pink bra as he leaned over to kiss her shoulder. His hands skimmed her sides, landing on the button of her jeans while she undid the button and zipper on his.

Heat followed the path of her hands as she slid his pants and underwear down. His breath caught sharply as she leaned over to push his pants to the floor, her hair brushing his erection. He ran his palms over the curve of her ass as he pushed her pants down, enjoying the feel of her soft skin and her small excited gasp.

Both her arms encircled his neck as she kicked her pants off and pressed against him to kiss him.

"God, you're so beautiful," he murmured between kisses as he unclasped her bra and ran his hands over her full breasts.

Pale-pink nipples tightened and elongated under his caress. Delicate and soft, his calloused palm rasped against her fair skin. Never in his life had he been this excited or wanted a woman as much.

He bent her backward and licked her nipple, making her shiver and moan. Skin smelling of roses tasted delicate, fresh, and slightly salty. She threw her legs around his waist and moaned when her breasts brushed his chest. One hand under her ass, the other splayed against her back, he kissed behind her ear, then the hollow of her throat.

"Bed?" Deep and husky, his murmured question seemed to echo in the tiled room.

"Here. Now." Low and throaty she answered as her hands wandered, lingering on his biceps.

"Mmm." He turned and pushed her against the wall, using both hands to lift her more until he slid inside her wetness. Both gasped.

"Oh god, Angel." He rested his forehead against hers, closed his eyes and held still, trying to calm the wild beating of his heart.

Tears trailed from Angie's closed eyes as she grasped his shoulders and sobbed his name.

He fumbled with the water controls with one hand. Still holding her pressed tightly against him, he grabbed the small bottles of shampoo and the wrapped soap, stepped into the shower, and lowered himself into the tub until he was sitting with her astride him.

"You have the most beautiful breasts I've ever seen."

Water trailed in rivulets around her breasts as he leaned her back and sucked a pink nipple into his mouth, caressing it with his tongue as he massaged her other breast, his thumb circling the nipple, making her squirm and gasp.

His hips jerked against her, and she cried out. She was going to make him come in seconds, and he wanted to stay inside her for hours– forever.

Braced on her hands, she leaned back even more and circled her hips on him, her breath coming in short pants.

"Oh god, I'm sorry," he said as he came.

For the first time in his life he'd made love, not just had sex, and the difference was indescribable.

"Stay inside me," she murmured as his hips jerked uncontrollably against her.

It occurred to Dan they'd used no birth control, and he didn't care. "Sorry, Angel. Next time will be better for you."

"This is good."

"I could've made you pregnant."

She groaned and pressed hard against him. "I have an implant, but I wish I didn't. I want your babies, Dan."

The soft sounds she made excited him, but her words excited him more. He rested his hands on her hips and kissed her, slipping from her body.

Her disappointed sigh made him wince.

Dan felt around for the soap he'd dropped. Wet wrapping stuck to his fingers, and she giggled when he tried to flick it off. The small bar lathered in his hands and he soaped her back and breasts. She took the soap from him. While she soaped his chest and back, he washed her hair, massaging her scalp with his fingers.

"Mmm, I could get used to this," she said as she tipped her head back, letting the warm water rinse the soap.

Dan's gaze heated at the sight of the bubbles trailing across her skin. For ten minutes, they washed each other. He learned her feet were incredibly ticklish and had her shrieking with laughter as he tried to wash her toes. Touching her neck and inner thighs made her close her eyes and gasp. Kissing them made her groan. The hungry sound she made caused his cock to throb.

They stood in the shower, her back to his chest as he explored her body, learning what she liked. Every sound she made he committed the cause to memory, wanting to please her.

"I love you," she said as she turned in his arms and pulled his face to hers.

He turned off the water and wrung out her hair as he kissed her, and she laughed when he picked her up and stepped from the shower to set her on the counter. The two small towels the hotel supplied barely covered her. The one he wrapped around her legs she removed and used to dry him, hopping off the counter to reach his back after rubbing his hair. Once he was dry enough for her satisfaction, she used the damp towel on her hair.

"Turn around." He handed her the built-in blow-dryer and combed her hair until it was only damp. His erection pressed against her towel covered ass. "Bed this time," he said when she dropped the towel and pressed against him, bracing her hands on the counter.

In the mirror, his eyes met hers as he kissed her neck and fondled her breasts until she panted and squirmed.

Again, he picked her up and carried her to the bed where he laid her down on the edge, then knelt before her.

"Lay back, he murmured as he kissed from her breast to her thigh, using his hands to spread her legs. She exhaled a shivery moan as his tongue caressed her.

Even her taste was delicate. He licked her until she begged him to make to love to her and yelled his name as he slid inside her. He meant to go slow, but before he knew it, they were rolling on the bed both groaning and calling out as they thrust against each other.

The warmth of her soft skin and the sounds she made excited him like never before in his life. When he used his hands to push her legs back, giving himself a deeper angle, she cried out and tensed.

Hands and legs urged him on when he hesitated. "Don't stop. Harder..."

Dan resumed his movement, thrusting hard, the slap of flesh on flesh filling the room as she began to keen. He fought his release wanting her to come, concentrating on her. She shuddered with her climax and sobbed his name, and he let himself go, spurting hard as her hips jerked against him.

"Let's do that a million more times. Next time come on my breasts. I want to watch," she said breathlessly.

Dan closed his eyes and kissed her as he contemplated the many positions he wanted to try with her. The kiss started soft until she groaned and deepened it, thrusting her tongue into his mouth and pressing his head to hers.

When he drew back, she was breathing hard and immediately reached for him again.

"Oh God, yes!" she yelled in a whisper as he slipped his fingers inside her and took her nipple into his mouth.

His gaze on his fingers sliding into her body, he moaned, "God, you're so beautiful. I could do this forever."

In moments, she was writhing against his hands, slippery with desire. Two fingers inside her and a thumb rubbing her clit, she came again. The inner muscles of her vagina clenched him in spasms as he slid inside her. Her legs were shaking as she yelled 'oh God' over and over until he pulled out and came on her breast, making her moan and buck. On an elbow, he leaned over her as she smeared his semen over her nipples. Half-lidded eyes stared down at her breasts.

"Mmm, that's so hot." A deep husky murmur, her voice sent a bolt of desire through him. One hand still on her breast she used the other to pull him down for another kiss.

"I love you," he said.

A brilliant smile answered him. He rose and headed to the bathroom. At the door, he glanced back. Her eyes were closed, and a small smile curved her lips. Her blond hair was spread in wild disarray against the pillow, one hand was still pressed to her breast, the shine of his drying semen between her spread fingers.

Never had he seen a more erotic sight.

A minute later he returned with a damp cloth and found her asleep. She murmured his name and snuggled closer as he wiped her off. In minutes, they were both asleep.

———————◆———————

Steam filled the shower, beading on the cracked linoleum. Angie knelt before him, taking him into her mouth, the water cascading over her bowed head onto his thighs. A hand on his balls, she sat back on her heels and glanced up at him, a trick of the light shading her features until she resembled Candice. Dan drew back.

"No, not here like this. Let's go to the bedroom," he said.

Angie rose and wrung out her hair, turning from him and using her hands to brush the water from her body, one foot pointed and giving her ass an extra wiggle. The pose, while erotic, seemed cold and dispassionate.

Dan frowned and grabbed a towel to wrap around his hips. A high, mocking laugh followed him from the bathroom.

He plumped the pillow behind his head as Angie moved to the other side of the bed.

Soft and sweet, she whispered, "I love you," as she paused at the foot of the bed. Water beaded on her skin, pink nipples peeking from her water darkened hair.

Dan patted the bed beside him. A shy smile on her lips, she turned and pulled the cord, opening the drapes.

"No!" Dan yelled as he leapt to his feet, knowing what would happen.

The air solidified, slowing his movement as he reached for her. Sunlight haloed her body as she turned to him and the glass behind her shattered. Her smile disappeared in a rush of blood and gore. With glacial slowness she fell, hitting the floor as he reached her.

"No!' he screamed and bolted upright.

Angie sat beside him and fumbled for the light switch. Unshed tears burning his eyes, he grabbed her and buried his hands in her warm, golden hair, hiding his face in her neck.

"Bad dream?" she asked as her soft hand rubbed his back.

"Don't go near the windows. Promise me, you won't go near them."

"I won't. I promise." She drew back and kissed his lips. "Are you okay?"

A continuous shiver rippled his muscles, the image of her face and memory of Candice's hot blood on his skin making him nauseous. A glance at the bedside clock showed they'd been asleep less than two hours.

"Go back to sleep, sweetheart. I'm okay, just a bad dream, but stay away from the windows."

She laid her head on his shoulder. "I will."

Hands still fisted in her hair, he laid back down, taking her with him. Her sleep-warmed skin against his was comforting. He released her hair to tuck the blanket around them, then rested his hand on her hip.

The sleepy, contented sound she made aroused him, but she needed rest. Warm lips grazed his neck as she rubbed her hand through his hair and over his chest. Fingertips traced his growing erection, and she began kissing his chest, flicking his nipples with her tongue and rubbing against him as her hand fondled him. In a minute, she was astride him, rocking slowly with her head thrown back. Her hair brushed his thighs her back was so arched.

Both hands on her hips he helped her move, lifting her to give himself room to thrust. It didn't take her long to climax and fall limp against his chest. A few hard thrusts later he came too. Relaxed and comforted, he drifted to sleep, her warm weight on his chest, her hair blanketing him.

ELEVEN

———— ◆ ————

This Needs to be Handled

AT TWO-TEN he opened his eyes again, spooned around Angie who still slept. Tiger stared into his eyes from inches away.

"Hungry, pal?" Dan whispered as he released Angie's breast to rub the cat's head. Tucked tightly against him, Angie fit as if made for him. "I sure am a lucky man." He kissed the top of Angie's head and eased out from under the covers.

In the bathroom, he fed the cat before brushing his teeth and using the toilet. Back in the main room, he grabbed the notebook on the small table beside the window and cracked the curtains enough to read a list of local restaurants, three of which delivered. He used the room phone to order hamburgers, fries and a salad. Free coffee sat beside the coffeepot on the table. He filled the pot but didn't turn it on, not wanting to wake her.

Back in the bathroom, he took a quick shower and dressed in his jeans, leaving his shirt off. While he waited for the food, he called his commander.

"Morty?" Commander Darmin sounded exasperated. "Dead bodies are piling up around you."

"I didn't kill any of them," Dan said.

Darmin snorted.

"My wife is in danger. Can you arrange for us to go to Gitmo early?"

"Your wife, huh?"

"Angie and I are staying married. Not just for her safety, but because I love her, and she says she loves me."

"I see," Darmin said in a thoughtful tone. "Is this going to be a problem?"

Dan snorted. "Yes, sir, it is. At least until I find out who Benny's boss is and we have a chat."

"Don't 'chat' with him without talking to me first. The boys can keep your wife safe."

"While we're here we can, but I need her safe while I'm called out. This needs to be handled."

"And you have no idea who Benny's boss is?"

"Joe Conti seems like a good place to start. But it seems unlikely he'd come after Angie or that he could be in charge of anyone." Dan ran a hand through his close-cropped blond hair. "Look, violence freaks my wife right out. I need to settle her somewhere she not only is safe but feels safe. A service wife was never in her plans, and she has no experience with what to expect, so I sort of need to ease her into it if I don't want to scare her away."

Darmin bit out a sharp bark of sarcastic laughter. "Jesus, Morty, that's a tall order. Doesn't she know what you do?"

"Not yet and tell the guys not to tell her. Let her think we're just regular sailors until she has some time to adjust. Seriously, sir, let her have time to get used to her new, um, situation without stress. Or any more stress than she already has."

"Oh, for the love of... Starting out a marriage with lies isn't a great idea."

"I'm not lying. If she asks, I'll tell her, but who does it hurt if she thinks I do a regular job?"

"Regular job?" Commander Darmin repeated questioningly as if he were turning the words over in his mind.

Angie entered the bathroom wrapped in a sheet. Dan mouthed, 'one minute, my boss,' kissed her brow and went to the bedroom.

"Guard duty, patrols, normal things," Dan said softly.

"Sure, normal things." Darmin made a sound of amused disgust. "Let me see what I can do about getting you sent early. I'll call you right back."

Dan started the coffee while Angie was still in the bathroom. She came out wearing his t-shirt, which barely brushed the top of her thighs. The kiss she greeted him with curled his toes. Before he could pursue it, someone knocked on the door. She giggled at his disappointed groan.

"Get that, and I'll call my boss." Her hands trailed down his arms as if she were reluctant to release him.

Dan checked the peephole, then opened the door a crack, giving the delivery man most of his remaining cash.

By the time he set the food on the table, Angie

spoke with her boss. Without touching her, he stood behind her. Heat radiated from her as if the heat she caused by her touch surrounded her. She took a step back until her body pressed against him. Dan loved how much she liked to touch him.

He slid his hands under her shirt, brushing her sides with his palms, then cupping her breasts and massaging. She turned a gasp into a fake cough before she covered the phone with her hand, giving him a lustful look over her shoulder.

Buttocks pressed against him, she held the phone to her ear with one hand and used the other to press his hands against her breasts.

"Yeah, Janet, I'm sure," she said. "Until this stolen identity stuff is cleared up it isn't safe for me to return." She gasped again and cleared her throat as one of his hands wandered lower. "No, put me on indefinite leave. I don't know if or when I can return."

Dan dropped his pants, letting them fall to the floor and kicking them off.

Her voice rose as he bent her slightly, taking her from behind. Her free hand pressed him to her as she arched her back, sliding onto him in slow, short thrusts, making him moan.

"Yes, I'll call when I know anything, and I'll text you my address. Thanks, Janet. She dropped the phone, braced her hands on the bureau and exhaled a deep gasp as he placed both hands on her hips, pulling her hard against him.

"Yes." Deep and low, she encouraged him, meeting his thrusts with her own.

The softness of her body felt perfect against his. Heat built in his chest and spread to his groin. He could make love to her forever and it wouldn't be enough. The feel of her skin against his, her soft sighs and moans, the warmth of her body– he craved it.

When her legs stiffened and she fell forward, he thrust harder, knowing she was close. With a deep groan, she came and collapsed, unable to support her own weight. He caught her and laid her face down on the carpet and let himself come in a few quick thrusts, staying inside of her as her inner muscles clenched him.

Tears on her cheeks, she turned in his arms, hugging him as tightly as she could.

"Every time we make love I feel closer to you, as if your connecting us, making us one. Dan, I've never made love before. I thought I had, but that was just sex, nothing like what we're doing."

Dan chuckled as he smoothed her hair, then kissed her temple. "Me too. I feel it, Angel. We're forging an unbreakable bond."

For a moment, he caressed her as her hands wandered his body as if memorizing him.

"Ang, we'll have problems and disagreements, but nothing can come between us unless we let it. If I do something you don't like –anything at all– tell me and I'll change. I'd do anything to make you happy."

Balanced on one hand, she leaned over him, her hair curtaining them in a golden cloud. "I'll be honest with you and tell you right away if something is wrong and you do the same. Be yourself. If you hate cats, I won't leave you, but I do need to know."

Dan let out a shout of laughter. "Tiger is awesome. I like dogs too, but my job doesn't allow for pets. Honestly, I'm a bit worried about my job upsetting you.

The adjustment will be hard on you. Tell me right away if your lonely or bored or anything at all and I'll do my best to help, but please don't let it build up until you leave. Three years, Ang. If you hate my job, I won't re-up."

One finger traced his cheek and smoothed his eyebrows as her blue-eyed gaze searched his face.

"Frankly, I don't know how I feel about your job, but three years is plenty of time to decide. I do know I won't leave you though. Not for anything. We belong together."

TWELVE

───◆───

You're Too Good to Be True

SUNRISE lit the room a soft gray. Thick drapes hung to either side of the large picture window, framing the view of a busy airport in Windsor Locks. Dan's teammate JT had paid for this room on his credit card, leaving Dan feeling safe enough to leave the curtains open. That and there were no other buildings with line-of-sight into this room. The nightmare he'd had of Angie being shot still made him shudder.

JT had deposited two grand in his ATM account and put this room on his credit card without complaint. He'd offered to look into Joe Conti for him too and agreed to ensure the team didn't mention anything upsetting to Angie. Dan had only told him they'd gotten married in Vegas, and Joe Conti was connected and might have hired men to search her apartment.

Dan was surprised by how happy JT sounded for him. He'd been so caught up in his own pain over Juan's death he hadn't really noticed his teammates were worried about him. In hindsight, they'd been trying to help, but he'd pushed them away, wallowing in his misery.

He made a mental note to apologize. They were hurting over Juan's death too, and he'd been a selfish asshole.

He was glad he'd left though, or he'd have never met Angie.

A blush heated Dan's cheeks. The good-natured teasing from his boss and friend was sure to continue when he saw him in a few weeks.

Dan tightened his grip on Angie. Asleep on her stomach, her warm limp body was snuggled into his side, one leg curved over his and both arms around his left one as if even in sleep she craved his touch.

In the past, Dan had always prioritized his job. Proud of what he did and how well he did it, he'd always thought he'd continue to do it until he died or age forced him to retire. Now, his plan had changed. Whatever she wanted, he'd do. And maybe he'd do some things she didn't want– like visit Joe Conti and end the threat he represented.

Murder wouldn't be his first choice, but he'd do anything to keep his nightmare from becoming a reality. If Joe had a hand in Candice's death, his days were numbered. Not for love of Candice— but love of Angie.

He stroked Angie's bright hair as he debated his options.

Angie's dislike and fear of violence was real and

107

deep. Real enough she'd tried to go home at the first sign of violence instead of confronting a woman who'd stolen everything she had. Dan realized his job would be a serious issue in their relationship.

Right now, they were running from crisis to crisis, clinging to each other, but he needed to know she'd stay committed once everything was settled. In every way he could, he'd ensure she was happy.

Money had never been important to him. Now he wished he'd hoarded it so he could buy her whatever she wanted. One hundred and seventy-four thousand dollars in the bank wasn't even half of what Candice had stolen from her.

A frown crossed his face. In the last month, he'd spent almost twenty thousand dollars, and he'd have to spend more, lots more, just replacing her possessions. She needed everything from clothing to a car. He sighed and ran his fingers through her hair. The bonus from their last mission could go toward that. Blood money for Juan's death. Juan would be happy to help to him though, and it eased him thinking of how much Juan would like Angie and how happy he'd be for Dan.

Besides, if he really needed money, he could break into his retirement fund or sell a few of his guns. He was doing a mental inventory of his rifles when Angie stirred.

Without fully waking, she reached for him, nuzzling his neck with soft kisses as her hands trailed him. The delicate touches aroused him and his body responded to her. He glanced at the bedside clock and snickered under his breath. They made love about every four hours. On one hand, he hoped he could keep up this pace, and on the other, he hoped soon they'd be sated longer. Thoughts of her distracted him badly and that would be dangerous for him at work.

All considerations fled his mind as she slid on top of him. The slow swaying of her body on his was the perfect way to wake up. His attention now on the soft sighs and moans she made, he held himself back until she came.

Tiger leaped onto the bed and meowed plaintively as they kissed. Angie laughed and rose, speaking over her shoulder as she headed to the bathroom.

"What's the plan for today?"

"This." Dan stole her pillow and plumped it before placing it beneath his head. "Until I hear back from my boss, we're staying here. I've asked to get sent to Gitmo early, and I was thinking we could go to Florida in a few days so you can shop. You'll need shorts and swimsuits, warm weather stuff, but we should shop here too and get cold weather stuff."

Angie exited the bathroom brushing her teeth and made a face at him.

"Was the face because you don't like shopping or over our money?" he asked.

The grimace on her face deepened, and she returned to the bathroom where water ran in the sink. He waited until the toilet flushed and shower came on before joining her. After using the toilet, he stepped behind the shower curtain and lathered his wife's hair.

"Mmm, you do that so good maybe you should become a hairdresser," she said.

Dan laughed and kissed her neck, then turned her to kiss her lips, running his fingers through her hair as the water rinsed it. "Move over so I can rinse off."

While he shampooed and rinsed, he spoke, "Let's go to Verizon and add you to my phone service and then to Best Buy."

"What do you need there?" She stepped from the shower and toweled off, sounding interested.

"You need a computer to replace yours. We can buy a desktop and have it shipped to Gitmo, or you can wait until we get to California and buy one there. Either way, we're getting you a laptop and a tablet to replace the ones from your apartment."

Water dripped to the floor unheeded as Dan turned the shower off and stepped out, taking the damp towel from her hand. "What's mine is yours and vice-versa. Forever, Ang. No barriers between us, not money, friends or distance. If you need or want something, buy it. Once we get to base, I'm putting you on all my accounts. I trust you to have sense when buying things."

Angie turned away and fussed with her wet hair.

Dan placed his hand on her shoulder and squeezed lightly. "Money can be a serious issue in any relationship. You make more than I do. Is it going to be a problem if I spend your money?"

Eyes wide, she turned back to him. "I hadn't considered that." A frown formed on her brow. "But I'm out of work now."

"True, but that could change. Anything can change except that I love you. So, let's decide now how we're going to handle money. I vote no mine or yours, but ours. We both spend what we want and talk over major purchases. In fact, I vote you're in charge of finances. Look over my records and tell me what I need to change."

She grinned and hugged him. "Sometimes I think you're too good to be true. I keep waiting for something I can't stand to pop up."

Dan winced, hiding his expression in the curve of her neck. "Nobody is perfect. My job is going to be hard on us, I know that, but I'll do everything I can to make it easier. Now I'm worried about disappointing you."

Angie drew back and framed his face with her hands. "I'm worried about your job too, but not too much. Three years isn't too long. I can stand anything for three years to be with you."

"And our money?"

Angie smiled, dropped her hands and grabbed the hairdryer. "Is ours. Let's go shopping."

———— ◆ ————

Before they went shopping, Angie spent three hours going over Dan's finances.

"You're going to ruin your eyes using that small screen," Dan said as he shined an apple against his t-shirt.

While she checked his banking records, he'd gone out for food. A half-eaten Italian sub sat on the table beside her.

"We can't shop until I know what we can afford. Mr. Basker hasn't heard yet if I'm getting my money back or not, so I need to plan as if this is all there is. Your pay is confusing as hell. What's all these large sums?"

Dan glanced over her shoulder. "The bigger ones are resigning bonuses." He hesitated. "The smaller ones are hazardous pay bonuses."

Angie grabbed the pen and stationary provided by the hotel and wrote a moment. "So, we can't count on those either. I assume the monthly deposits are your base pay?"

"Yep." Relieved she sounded so matter-of-fact about this, he relaxed and ate the apple.

She tapped the pen on the tabletop a few moments. When she stilled, an uneasy expression covered her face. "And you have no choice in these assignments?"

Apple forgotten on the nightstand, Dan crouched beside her and took her hand. "No. But, Ang, even the 'hazardous' ones aren't that dangerous because of our training."

"Juan died." Soft and low, her voice shook.

"Yes, and technically he was on a mission, but that isn't what killed him. Juan died saving a ten-year-old boy from a crazy man with a gun. The hell of it was, if he'd waited, we could've taken the man out, but Juan freaked and rushed in. Patience is key in our work. Most of the time we aren't even anywhere near the bad guys."

"Did he save the boy?"

"He did, and killed the man, but was fatally wounded himself. I wish to God he'd have waited for us." Dan stood and strode to the window where he stared out unseeing.

"Juan always hated abuse. Any kind of abuse got him really angry. He never spoke about his home life much, but it wasn't good." Dan cleared his throat. "Normally, Juan was the soul of patience. When we heard him enter, we ran to his position but were too far. That was the worst day of my life." Dan turned back to Angie. "Talking about him hurts. My point was if he'd waited and stuck to the plan, he'd have been fine. I'm careful, and my team is good. While I can't guarantee I won't be killed, I don't think my chances are any worse than firefighting or police work."

Angie rose and hugged him. "I don't think I'll ever not worry."

"Me either, about you. The problem when you love something so much is you know it's going to suck when you lose it."

For minutes, they held each other in the weak winter sunlight. Finally, Angie stepped back. "Let's both promise to be careful and take no unnecessary risks. When we have kids, we'll take out big life insurance policies so they'll be okay no matter what happens to us. I can say from experience it was a relief to receive the money to pay for my parent's funerals. At the time, I had no savings and big student loans. The fifty thousand dollars went a long way toward easing my anxiety about caring for myself.

"I already have a policy, but I'll up it. We'll do whatever you need to feel secure."

A sad smile on her face, Angie kissed his cheek." Without Juan, we would've never met. If he hadn't died, you wouldn't have gone to Vegas or married Candice. To go through my entire life searching for you... I wish I could thank him."

"We'll never forget him." Dan's voice cracked.

The smile on her face became wistful.

"Juan Barstow has a nice ring to it," she said.

Dan grinned and pulled her to her feet. "Let's practice making Juan Barstow. We need to get it just right."

Angie giggled.

"Leave a paper on the inside of every box with our address and your name and ID number on it. That way, if the box gets damaged in shipping, you'll still get your things," Dan said as he slapped a label on the box containing her old board games, then stood back to survey his work.

Everything she'd salvaged from her apartments was packed and labeled. Most of it was going to California. The box containing the board games was going to Gitmo. A trunk full of clothes sat by the door labeled for Gitmo beside her duffle bag and new laptop case. Two new bicycles leaned against the wall beside a bright yellow bag holding her new scuba gear.

"I can't wait to learn how to snorkel and scuba dive." A folder with computer printouts in her hand, Angie opened the bag and admired her gear again. "You sure the stuff we ordered online will be sent to us?"

"Yes. Remember, use my name and P.O. Box for everything until we go there and get our own place. The Navy always knows where I am and will forward my mail. If you buy something that can stay in California, use Charlene's address."

"You're sure she won't mind?"

"Absolutely. You're going to like her, and she's looking forward to meeting you."

Angie bit her lip.

Dan gave her a quick hug. "JT's wife is used to helping us. The entire team uses her to order stuff when we don't want it shipped on. It really is no bother.

Angie stuffed the papers into the yellow bag and flopped on the bed. "Three more days."

Dan leaned over her, bracing his hands on either side of her head. "It's just a job, sweetheart. I'll go to work and come back at night. Once in a while, I'll be out all night doing night training, but I'll tell you in advance. Ronny Mitland, the guy replacing Juan, and I need to practice working together. Darmin set this up so we could train here where you'll be safe. No one knows we're in Florida. I don't expect to be called out while we're training, but if it happens, I'll make sure we speak. I swear, I won't just disappear."

Angie pulled him down for a kiss. "I love you more every day. Are you sure about confronting Joe Conti? Is that a good idea?"

Dan sat back and ran a hand through his hair. "Yes. It needs to be done. The man has a right to be angry about Candice. One day apart, Ang. I'll go and speak with him, and we'll sort this out."

"Where is he?"

Dan hesitated. He wanted to claim it was confidential but that would be a lie. "Not too far away, actually. He's off the Florida Keys on a rented boat. I'll go and work things out with him and be back before you know it. "

"What if he *is* the guy who sent Benny?"

"Then I'll handle it. And before you ask, no, I don't know how. It depends on what he says, but I *will* handle it. If he means to harm you, I'll ensure he can't."

Angie shivered.

Dan ran a finger along the skin of her cheek and held back a heavy sigh. She was delicate and soft;

all the things he wasn't.

"I'll be careful."

She nodded as tears clouded her eyes. He closed his and kissed her.

THIRTEEN

— ◆ —

SETTLE THEIR DIFFERENCES PERSONALLY

B LACK water stirred, a slight wave forming around
Dan's emerging head. In moments, the ripple
dissipated. He reached up and pushed back the
black goggles covering his eyes, letting them dangle
behind his head, using one hand to tread water in
sync with the flippers on his feet.

A hard grin formed on Dan's face. Joe Conti had
picked the wrong vacation spot. *Or hell, maybe he was
working, and this yacht and party were a cover for a
drug pick up.* From what he knew of the man it was
entirely plausible.

The water barely rippled as Dan swam around the
ship, searching for the anchor chain. Within minutes
he'd found it and removed his flippers, attaching them
to the chain along with his goggles and a small
canister of air.

A grimace of effort replaced his grin as he pulled himself up the taut anchor chain. The hole from which the chain emerged was too small to permit entrance but big enough to allow purchase for standing.

Balanced precariously, Dan leapt, grabbed the bottom rail, and pulled himself aboard in one smooth move. Crouched over, he ran to the pilot-house wall where he climbed up to the top deck.

A guard leaned against the rail with a rifle resting beside him and stared out over the ocean. He sucked in a hit from a joint held between two fingers and coughed.

Dan waited until he inhaled again and darted to the rail to let himself down. Dim light cast wavy shadows around the pool. The lawn chairs and pool seemed deserted.

He sprinted to the opposite end of the boat and lowered himself to the middle deck. A large potted palm stood beside a tight grouping of emergency life rafts. He placed his back against the palm and took a moment to survey the deck. No partygoers were in sight. Loud music and raucous laughter came from around the corner inside the main salon.

Familiar with this model of ship from long hours of studying boat design, he headed aft, climbed over the rail, and dropped to a private balcony attached to the master suite. A moment's work with a lock pick opened the door.

Dan paused inside the bedroom door and rolled his eyes at the heart-shaped bed in the center of the room. A disco ball hung from the mirrored ceiling.

"Tasteful. No wonder Candice ran away."

A quick search of the chamber netted Dan a pistol

in such disrepair he was afraid to fire it. Black grease gummed up a rusty firing pin, the gun would more likely blow your hand off then injure an enemy. Holding it outstretched between gloved fingers he stepped onto the small balcony and dropped it into the sea below.

"I'm doing you a favor, man," he murmured as the gun sank beneath the dark water.

From where he stood on the secluded balcony party noise came to him in clear bursts intermingled with muffled conversation.

The windows must be open in the room above me, he thought as he gazed upward trying to see but the angle was too sharp.

Three decks of living space fit quite a few partygoers, and by the sounds of raucous laughter they'd just begun partying. Dan relaxed on the floor to wait for this overdue meeting. He and Joe needed to settle their differences personally. If Dan didn't like his answers, Joe was a dead man.

Reminded of the danger his wife was in, he tensed, and a rueful smile crossed his lips. Angie would be angry he'd be late returning. His plan had been to sneak aboard to speak with Joe and return before she had time to worry, but the flight here had been delayed and liberating a small fishing boat had taken longer than planned. The size of the ship and the crowd aboard was another unwelcome surprise. Joe probably wouldn't return to his cabin for hours yet.

Dan heaved a disgusted sigh and tipped his head against the wall, closing his eyes and letting the balmy sea air relax him. The snatches of conversation he caught were typical and banal of the flirtatious variety with no real content. Parties like this bored him to tears.

A familiar voice caused him to jolt upright. Above his head, Angie spoke again, to Dan's ear sounding angry and scared.

"No, thank you, sir. If you'll excuse me?"

The reply, if any, was muffled. Dan leapt to his feet, cursing under his breath. "I knew I shouldn't have told you where I was going. Goddamn it, you're going to get yourself killed," he muttered as he stripped off his wetsuit and rummaged through the closet, searching for something to wear.

An angry scowl on his face, he slammed the closet shut and headed to the dresser. Joe was a good six inches shorter and a good hundred pounds heavier than him. None of Joe's suits would fit.

A bright red and orange pair of Bermuda shorts bagged around his hips. He hoped some of the guests had dressed casually enough he wouldn't stand out too badly. The bar in the corner supplied a bottle of rum, which he splashed liberally over his cheeks and shoulders before filling a tumbler. He duct taped his k-bar to his leg under the shorts, opened the door and sauntered down the hall, adding a stumble for effect. The guard beside the staircase smirked but let him pass unchallenged.

Glass doors open to the sea breezes led into the reception hall. Dan leaned against the rail, pretending to sip his drink as he eyed the crowd. The men wore tuxedos and gathered around gaming tables, expensively gowned women hanging from their arms.

Wait staff, serving drinks and *hors d'oeuvres*, wandered among the guests. A buffet by the back wall held ice sculptures that dripped onto the floor. While Dan observed, a waitress mopped up the puddle, hiding her glower from a groping guest.

Angie stood to the left of the buffet. Long, blond hair in an intricate knot left her lightly sunburnt shoulders exposed. A gold, form-fitting dress hugged her curves, showcasing the tops of the full breasts that Dan knew were the real deal. A slit almost to her groin allowed her left leg to peek through, revealing glimpses of a silver high-heel. Compared to the other women in attendance she dressed modestly, but to Dan's eyes, she seemed shockingly exposed.

A drunk man grabbed her arm, and Dan's hands clenched in anger. Her delicate skin bruised easily; the drunk would leave a mark on her. If he were beside her, no one would dare lay their hands on her. His angry gaze scanned the guests again. Every single guest wore formal wear. Dressed as he was, he couldn't enter, not without causing a scene.

Angie drew her arm from the man's grasp and backed away, a fake smile on her face as she nodded her head. The man with her pointed, and she nodded again and headed away. Dan's gaze followed the pointing finger to Joe Conti.

A cold sweat sprang up all over his body. His wife stood fifty feet away from a man who might have sent men to kill her. A man like Joe wouldn't listen to her or any woman. All he would see was a beautiful woman, and if he realized she was Dan's, he'd want her all the more. He needed to get his wife out of there. Another man approached her as she crossed the room.

He needed to stop her before she spoke to Joe. At the rate guests were intercepting her as she crossed the room, he had about five minutes. Not enough time to run back and subdue a guard to steal his tux. Dan headed to one of the smaller doors and gestured to a guest.

"'Scuse me, friend, would ya get me a refill?" Dan waved his empty glass at the man by the doorway who turned in surprise at being hailed.

"Are you speaking to me?" The man sounded incredulous.

"Don't want to disturb the guests and got carried away with the party favors."

"Party favors?"

"Sure, Joe bought the good stuff off me. Thirty pounds of Midnight Madness."

"Midnight Madness?" The man approached, sounding intrigued now.

"Ecstasy, my man. My own special blend. Get me a drink, and I'll give you a preview."

Dan held out his empty glass and turned away as if reaching for a bag beyond the door. Bait accepted, the man exited the main room.

Dan let him take the glass as he stumbled further from the door. "The bag's in the can." Placing an arm around the man, Dan led him to a nearby restroom.

"Ahh, here it is." Body tense, he waited for the man to move behind him, then whipped around and hit him in the neck hard with the side of his hand. The man gagged and choked.

"Sorry, pal. I need your duds."

Dan tugged him into the small room, glancing around before he shut the door to ensure the altercation hadn't been seen. Inside the room, he knocked the man to the floor, wincing as the man cried out. He fisted a hand in the man's white shirt and ripped the knife from his leg, terror for his wife making him rougher than he intended. The man stilled and held out his empty hands.

"Sorry, I'm sure someone will be by shortly to release you. Think of this as a great story to tell your friends," Dan said as he peeled a piece of duct tape from his leg and slapped it over the man's mouth. Moving fast, he stripped him and then used the necktie and socks to tie the man to the pipe under the sink.

"Be a good sport and don't make me quiet you permanently," Dan said as the man thrashed and moaned behind the gag.

The man stilled. Dan grabbed the jacket and left the room, leaving his erstwhile benefactor slumped on the floor in his briefs. With any luck, it would be a few minutes before someone stumbled on him. He was just donning his 'borrowed' shirt when a couple emerged from the doorway. They stopped and stepped back, eyes wide.

"Nothing to worry about." Dan continued to dress as he spoke, gesturing to the closed bathroom door with his chin." My friend had a few too many, but he'll be right as rain in an hour or so. He's puking his guts out; I'll check him again in thirty minutes." Dan pushed past the gawking couple and hurried into the ballroom.

Inside the room, he made a beeline for Angie and grabbed her arm just as she stepped forward to gain Joe's attention. Joe faced away from them chatting with a group of older men. Plastic surgery enhanced women hung from their arms. The men gazed at each other's dates with cold eyes– sharks looking for their next tasty morsel.

Angie pulled away as she turned to Dan. "Excuse me—"

Her practice politeness evaporated as she recognized him. Light leapt into her eyes and her cheeks flushed. Beneath his hand, her skin heated. Parted lips, which she licked as she swayed toward him, infused him with a wild lust. Her reaction was unconscious and unpracticed, the strength of her desire obvious in every line of her body.

"Let's dance, shall we?" He held out his hand to her.

A dazed expression on her face, she nodded and allowed him to lead her to the dance floor. He lowered his head and kissed her neck, enjoying the shiver that elicited. A man dancing nearby leered, making Dan's hands clench and reminding him of why he was there.

"Ang, go home right now. Don't speak to him, just leave. I swear I'll handle this," Dan whispered as he nuzzled her neck.

"But—"

"Go. Trust me, Ang. I'll explain later. I love you."

She tugged him down as if she were going to kiss him as she whispered in his ear. "I can't go. The boat to take me to shore won't be here for an hour or more."

Dan growled and pulled her closer. They didn't have an hour. The man he'd stolen this suit from could be found any minute and he was sure to raise a cry over being assaulted. Dan needed to be out of sight before that happened.

While he debated his options, he kissed her, the kiss heating despite himself. Mind made up, he took her hand and led her from the room by the main doors.

"Play along," he murmured as he nuzzled her neck while leading her to the stairway.

She glanced over her shoulder, a frown on her face. With one finger Dan turned her face to him and kissed her until her body fitted itself against him. One hand so high on her waist he was almost cupping her breast, he led her down the stairs opposite the ones he'd come up.

"Joe said we can use the third cabin," he said to the guard before the man asked him where they were going.

The guard smirked and rose an eyebrow but moved aside as Angie blushed and giggled. At the door to the third cabin, Dan pushed her against the wall, letting his hands wander as he kissed her while watching the guard from the corner of his eye. The guard stared as Dan opened the door and leaned down to pull her shoes off while she giggled. The man turned back to the stair.

Dan eased the door closed and pulled Angie down the hall around the corner and into Joe's room.

"We don't have much time. Stay here. If I'm not back with Joe in five minutes, go back on deck and mingle with the crowd until the boat comes to take you back. Don't go near him, Ang. I know his type. If he sees you, he'll want you."

Angie glanced at her dress, a skeptical expression on her face.

"Not because you're beautiful. There's a hundred gorgeous women here, but because you're mine. Believe me, the combination will be irresistible to him.

A man like him will be crazy angry to prove himself after his wife not only left him but stole from him. In his world, it's an eye for an eye, and he thinks I killed his wife. Please, don't let him see you. The less he knows about you, the better."

Suddenly angry, Dan spun away from her. "I can't believe you came here without speaking to me. These men aren't playing around. Benny killed two people already. What did you think you were doing?"

Dan exhaled heavily and turned back as Angie started to speak. "Never mind, we can talk later. Stay here on the balcony." He kissed her lips softly, resting his forehead on hers. "Jesus, I hate leaving you defenseless like this. Ang, these aren't good people who'd help you if you scream. These are drug dealers and prostitutes willing to kill their own mothers to make a buck. Stay hidden here."

Angie swallowed hard and nodded. She gave him a quick kiss on the cheek and slipped through the balcony doorway. Dan took a deep breath, straightened his too large jacket, and strolled into the hallway.

FOURTEEN

---◆---

I Came to Set Things Straight

HE GUARD eyed him, a slight smirk on his lips, but said nothing as Dan strode by.

Dan hurried into the party and headed directly to Joe. "Mr. Conti, do you remember me?"

Joe turned to him, an annoyed expression on his face that changed to fury as recognition set in. The men he'd been speaking to fell silent, seeming to feel the tension.

"Can we speak in private?" Dan asked.

"How the hell did you get aboard?" Joe's angry question rang above the music and talking. Guests around them quieted and stared.

"Please? I'll explain how—"

Before Dan could finish his sentence, Joe waved to a nearby guard.

"Fuck, and this could've been so easy," Dan mumbled under his breath as he stepped forward and

127

grabbed Joe, placing an arm around his throat and kicking his knee, making Joe stumble and choke himself. "NO ONE FUCKING MOVES!" The advancing men stilled. "This is a domestic dispute Joe and I are going to go clear up. If everyone acts cool, no one gets hurt."

Dan reached into Joe's jacket and removed the gun from the holster there. Without waiting to see what anyone would do, he dragged Joe through the doorway and down the stairs.

The guard's eyes widen as they approached, and he reached for his gun.

"Don't even try it." Dan gestured with his head for the man to move aside. "Joe and I are going to have a little talk and clear the air. If I wanted him dead, he'd be dead already. Move aside, and we can all get up in the morning."

The guard hesitated.

Dan pulled Joe past him. A glance back showed guests and guards intermingled at the head of the stairs but hanging well back. No one wanted to get involved. Snickers and whispers reached Dan's ear, everyone commenting that Joe had messed with the wrong woman's husband.

A grin flitted across Dan's face. *Good, let them think that.*

Dan shoved his captive through the door and kicked it closed behind him. "Look," he said without preamble. "I came to set things straight with us. Candice lied to me. If I'd known she was married, I would've never gotten involved with her." Dan released Joe and stepped away.

Joe rubbed his neck and glared.

"Not only didn't I know who she was, but the woman whose identity she stole had nothing to do with her. Whatever your men are looking for, she doesn't have."

"What the fuck are you talking about?"

"Did you send men to search Angelina's home?" Dan asked.

"Fuck no. What the hell do I care about whoever the hell Candice pretended to be?" Joe turned and ran for the nightstand that had held the gun.

Dan let him.

"Fine, I believe you. I thought that was a long shot, but someone is searching for something your wife stole."

Joe rummaged in the desk, his shoulders slumping.

"It's not there." Dan paced to the balcony doors and leaned against the doorjamb. "Let's clear the air between us. I get your angry I slept with your wife, but you gotta cut me some slack there as I didn't realize she was married." Dan winced as he spoke the words, admitting to having sex with another woman so baldly in Angie's hearing was hard.

"You fucking killed her."

Red-faced, Joe clenched his fists at his side, his angry gaze darting to the door, then about the room.

"No, I didn't. I was with her when she died, but I didn't do it. A guy named Benny knows who did. Do you have any idea who Benny is?"

Joe didn't answer. The red in his face deepened until Dan was afraid he'd have a heart attack.

"Joe, think, man. Would I be here trying to straighten things out if I'd killed her or had anything to do with it? I came to apologize and pay my respects.

We don't have to be enemies."

Joe snorted, but the red faded from his face. One hand rubbing the back of his neck, he began to pace the room. "Right. You broke in to make friends."

"I broke in to make a fucking point. I'm hoping the point is clear enough that I never see you again. If I learn who Benny is or works for, I'll drop you a note. I'm real interested in meeting him up close and personal too, so if you know who—"

"Vincent fucking Palgrino. Man operates out of Chicago. If I had to guess, I'd say it's one of his stooges. Are you sure he did it?"

"No, but I'm sure he knows who did. The man shot his partner by mistake and blamed Angelina, so now the boss thinks she's involved with whatever Candice had going on."

His voice both admiring and annoyed, Joe slapped his fist into his open palm as he said, "That woman was twister than a hedge maze. A better liar you never met, but I don't have to tell you that. Even knowing it was all a fake I fucking miss her."

Dan nodded.

Joe sauntered to the bar and fixed himself a drink as he eyed Dan speculatively. "Fucking Palgrino is too hot for me unless I want to start a war and I got a boss who won't go for that."

"Well, maybe I can help. He isn't too hot for me."

"Think you're a real bad ass, then?" Joe lifted an eyebrow as he pursed his lips and examined Dan. "Or are you connected too? Who you working for?"

Dan choked back a laugh. "Myself right now. Don't worry about me or who I work for. This is personal. I want it crystal clear here, harm to Angelina, or threats, or any damn thing, is gonna be met by a repeat visit. One you won't enjoy nearly so much."

Tempted to murder like never before in his life, Dan fingered the gun in his hand. With this man's death, Angie would be safer.

Joe seemed oblivious to Dan contemplating murder. He glared and said, "What– you think it's that easy? Come on board my ship, threaten me, then walk away?"

"It fucking better be. Lucky for you, I'm not a murderer." Dan slid the gun into his waistband. "I get you're in a position here. Be smart about it. No one aboard knows why I'm here or who I am. If you let me go in peace, we won't have a war, and as I said earlier, if I find out who killed her, you'll have back-up."

"You loved her then?" Joe asked, sounding wistful and sad.

"No, but I owe her. We didn't know each other at all, not really."

Joe nodded slowly as he sipped his drink.

Dan reached down and grabbed the wetsuit he'd left on the balcony. "I'll be going now. Please don't let me see you again."

Joe said nothing. Dan stepped backward, keeping his eye on Joe as he closed the doors. He grabbed Angie's hand and jumped over the side.

She shrieked as they fell, a thin gasping cry that ended as the water closed over their heads. An arm around her waist, Dan surged to the surface as he kicked off the shoes he'd stolen. Angry voices on the balcony warned him, and he dove again, pulling her with him and hugging the side of the ship. He made the corner before the first gunshot rang out. A hand clapped over Angie's mouth, he eased them to the surface. Wide, frightened eyes met his as she nodded frantically.

"Quiet," he whispered as he released her mouth.

She clung to his neck as he ripped his tuxedo off and wiggled into the wetsuit. The zipper on her dress stuck, and he growled as he ripped the fabric, the sound shockingly loud to his ear. As soon as she was free of the dress, he dove again and pulled her with him. In less than a minute, he reached the anchor chain and had gathered his flippers and the small oxygen canister. On the deck above him, men yelled back and forth.

Dan took a moment to tighten the strap holding the breath mask in place on Angie's face before diving. This time he dove deep and stroked hard away from the ship. Angie clung to his back, kicking her feet ineffectually. Dan swam until his lungs ached with the need to draw air, then surfaced as quietly as he could. His dive watch contained a compass that let him know exactly where he was.

A quick deep breath and he dove again, heading toward the boat he'd left anchored a mile away.

A thousand yards from the boat he surfaced and floated on his back, holding Angie's hand as she drifted beside him.

"Sound travels over water," he whispered. "Move slow and try not to splash. Joe is putting on a show now, and as long as we play our lines, we'll be fine. The two shots into the water were for appearance. If he'd meant to kill me, he would've fired sooner and had his men keep firing on the water."

A trembling hand pushed the oxygen mask off her

face. "I can't swim to shore, it's too far," she gasped. She clutched his hand almost hyperventilating.

"My boat is close. And even if it wasn't, the shore isn't too far. We could make it twenty miles. Try not to panic. Relax and enjoy the night."

Dan grinned and kissed her, slow movements of his flippered feet enough to keep them afloat.

"Loon," she muttered when he broke away, but her trembling had ceased, and she sounded happier.

Dan towed her to the boat where he clambered aboard, then lifted her in as gently as he could. The gold, strapless bra and matching panties she wore, see through now, enticed him.

"And my teammates say I have no restraint."

"Huh?" she made an inquisitive sound but didn't take her eyes from the bag he handed her.

He laughed as he started the engine. "Nothing. At least put on my t-shirt, or you're going to freeze."

In his shirt, she snuggled against his bare back as he drove them to the dock. He stuffed his wetsuit and her wet underwear into the bag. He wore his jeans and boots and eyed her doubtfully. His shirt revealed more than it concealed. The damp fabric clung to her curves.

"You need clothes."

His gaze traveled the dimly lit wharf. Boats of all sizes and types lined the dock, most with lights off, swaying unattended in the water. Two slips from them, a light burned in a cabin of a forty-foot cruiser.

"Wait here." Dan tied off the boat he'd borrowed and stepped onto the dock. A glance over his shoulder showed Angie hugging herself and biting her lip. Dan eased onto the deck of the boat with the light on. A towel laid on a folding chair beside a discarded sweatshirt. Dan scooped them both up and leapt over the rail back to the dock.

"Here, wrap the towel around your waist." He traded Angie the sweatshirt for the t-shirt and fully dressed now, took her hand and fished out his cell phone.

"Where were you staying?"

"Nowhere. I arrived, bought a dress, changed in the dressing room, and went to the wharf. They let me board with no problem."

Dan snorted. "I'm sure. Did you have a return ticket at least?"

She shook her head and bit her lip.

"Ang, your plan sucked. Honestly, I can't believe you even came here. What were you thinking?"

To his shock, she began to cry. "I didn't want you to get hurt. I thought because he was a man he'd let me on board and listen to me. What was I supposed to do, Dan? Let you get killed because of me?" Clearly distraught and sobbing now, she wiped her eyes with a fist. The childlike gesture melted his anger. She buried her face in his neck when he hugged her.

"Okay, I see your point, but I want a promise from you. You'll never sneak off anywhere again for any reason." He shook her lightly as she continued to cry.

"Promise me, Ang. We need to trust each other. My work will take me away for unknown periods of time, and you won't know where I am, but I won't sneak off. I need to know you're safe at home, not pulling harebrained schemes that can get you killed. Jesus, Ang, what if I hadn't gone tonight? Joe could've made you disappear. No one knows where you are. Never do something like this again!"

"What am I supposed to do?" she wailed.

"Trust me. If I say I can handle it, I can."

"What if something happens to you? How am I supposed to live with that?"

"Nothing will happen to me." Dan sighed and rubbed her back.

The worry, while justified and in need of soothing, was too complicated to handle here and now. Dressed as she was, she couldn't board a plane. His return ticket for six-a.m. gave him little time to get her decently clothed.

"First things first, Ang, let's go home." He ran a finger along the square of duct tape on her thigh. "Your license and my ATM card, I presume?"

She nodded against his shoulder.

"Smart girl. Okay, Angel, let's go buy you some real clothes."

FIFTEEN

———— ◆ ————

ZERO TOLERANCE FOR LIARS

THE KEYCARD lit the lock with a soft green glow.
Dan gestured Angie to wait and entered first.
After making sure no one waited inside their
hotel room, he beckoned her to enter.

"I know I'm being paranoid; nobody knows we're
here."

"Better safe than sorry." Angie smiled ruefully at
him as she headed to the bathroom to check on Tiger.
The cat greeted her with a loud meow and enthusiastic
rubbing against her legs. "What will we do about
Vincent?"

"*We* will do nothing. I'm handling it. I've already
spoken to the police in Washington and Vermont.
Chicago is too far for me to fly there and make it back
before work tomorrow, so I'll have to speak with him
on the phone."

Angie nodded and wrung her hands together. "Will that work? Your word against Benny's?"

"It can't hurt to try. Don't worry, Angel, this is only the first option, not the only option." Dan hugged her, breathing in the scent of her skin, a faint smell of roses overlaid with ocean and sweat. "Promise me again you'll never run off on your own like that. If anything happened to you..." Dan kissed her neck as she nodded.

"Let's get this over with." Dan released her and grabbed her laptop. After a quick search he had a phone number. Fingers crossed, he dialed the phone. It took him forty-five minutes to reach Vincent. Passed from one flunky to the next, his call was transferred twice before Vincent spoke.

"I'm a very busy man—"

"Let's cut to the chase then. Your man Benny is a lying asshole. He shot Carlos and Tony. Not me. Angelina had nothing to do with anything."

"Excuse me?" Clipped and angry, Vincent spoke loudly. "You're very mistaken. I have no 'man' Benny nor any idea what you're babbling about, and frankly—"

"Right." Dan interrupted again. "Whatever the hell you're looking for, neither Angelina or I have it. Candice visited Angelina's cabin in Vermont in November and all she left were bags of money and a ledger. Both of which are in police custody."

"I see." Thoughtful now, Vincent spoke in a calmer tone. "I assure you, I have no personal acquaintance of any 'Benny.' My firm is very large though with numerous employees, it would be impossible to know them all. That being said, I'd certainly never employ a man so inept as to shoot his own partner— twice. Not that any person in my employee would do such of thing."

"Carlos was an accidental shooting. Tony wasn't. He killed him to keep him from reporting. The man's last words were 'tell Vin.'"

"And how did that lead you to me?"

"Candice led me to you. The police tracked her to Chicago. Pictures in the Tribune, of her on your arm, led me to you. When I met her, I had no idea who or what she was. Angelina and I don't want to be involved in this."

"This?"

"Candice's murder. Whatever she took. Whoever is chasing it. Nothing small enough to fit into an outlet was found with the money. Only the ledger, as I said. The ledger contained names of the women whose identities she stole and listed the money she took from each. There was no mention of men or items."

"While that's all very interesting, it has nothing to do with me. Candice was a thief and a liar, and I'm sorry I ever met her, but I had nothing to do with her death. Before she left me, she stole almost a million dollars in cash and jewelry. The Mexican police claim there was no sign of it."

Dan snorted. Angie bit her lip. Dan smiled at her, trying to project confidence.

"She had money," Dan said. "But I don't know how much. I never searched her bags. My ATM account was drained in the week we spent together, but her husband removed her body and effects before I could search them. Or maybe the Mexican police have them. Either way, only my clothes were in the hotel room when I returned from the police station." A blush climbed Dan's cheeks as he spoke of his time with Candice.

A sidelong glance at Angie revealed she looked troubled, but not angry. He'd be angry if she spoke of another man so intimately. Angry and jealous. He was luckier than he deserved to have found her. With effort, he wrenched his attention back to the conversation.

"As to jewelry; she wore numerous gold chains and had an assortment of gold and silver bracelets. Most had no stones or charms or anything, although she did have a diamond choker, which at the time I assumed was fake, but in hindsight was likely real. She had every gem under the sun in earrings, but again I thought they were good fakes. The two rings she wore I knew were real, but neither was a man's ring. The diamond appeared old, and the sapphire one had lots of small diamonds around it. But what happened to them, I couldn't say."

"That's the only jewelry you ever saw her with?"

"No, she had another ring," Dan said after a moment's thought.

Vincent inhaled sharply.

"She wore a toe ring. A narrow, gold band with a pink stone in it. But for all I know, she had twenty pounds of jewelry I never saw. I never looked in her bag."

"Joe Conti took her effects?"

"No idea, but the shakedown we got from the Mexican police makes me think they could've taken them."

"Guess I'll never see my father's cuff links again,"

Vincent muttered. "Insurance is covering my losses, but I'd like to get them back. Sentimental value, you understand."

"Sure, if I hear anything from the police there I'll let you know, but neither Angelina nor I have anything from Candice."

A quiet, hard laugh was Vincent's response. "As if you'd say you'd taken her money and jewels."

"Even if I wanted to, I didn't have time. The police arrived minutes after she was shot while I was being sick. They had me in custody for over thirty hours. The room was clean and her luggage gone when I returned. The police report will state everything I carried on me when I arrived at the station. I assure you, they were most thorough in their search."

"Hmm." Vincent sounded thoughtful again.

"Tony said Benny claimed Angelina shot Carlos. If you consider that objectively, how likely is it that an IRS agent got a gun through customs and was able to kill one armed man and run off another? And why would she do it? How would she know who they were or what they'd wanted? Benny's story would've made more sense if he'd claimed I'd done it, but I assure you, if I'd killed Carlos, Benny would be dead too. I don't leave live enemies."

"And yet, Benny is alive now," Vincent said dryly.

"Because I didn't intend to harm him. Tony and I were having a cozy chat. He was in front of me. Benny's first shot knocked him off his feet and into me, ruining my aim. Frankly, Benny shocked me by shooting. I never expected him to kill his own partner. I promise you, if I see Benny again, he's a dead man."

"Bold."

"True. Twice now he's tried to kill me and killed others instead. Any jury on Earth would acquit me with self-defense. Not that I'll get caught."

A soft snort of laughter met that. "This Benny character sounds like a real clown."

"And yet I'm not laughing," Dan said.

"No, nothing about this situation is funny," Vincent replied. "I'm sorry for your troubles, but they have nothing to do with me. Candice was a problem for everyone she met. Believe me; I now have zero tolerance for liars."

"Well, sorry to bother you then. I hope you find your cuff links. Angelina and I have a live and let live attitude. Benny and his ilk stay away, and we're willing to put Candice behind us."

"Yes, I too want to forget I ever met the woman." Vincent cleared his throat. "As I said, I'm a very busy man. If there's nothing else...."

Dan offered Angie a reassuring smile. "No, that covers what I wanted to say. Time constraints mandated this meeting happen on the phone and I hope we never meet in person."

"Our paths seem unlikely to cross." Vincent disconnected.

Dan set his cell down on the table. "I think he believed me. Keep an eye on Chicago obituaries for any mention of Benjamin or Benny."

Wide-eyed, Angie appeared dismayed. "You think he'll kill him?"

Dan grinned. "Hope so and good riddance. Benny is a cold-blooded murderer. Don't lose any sleep over him." Dan rose and gave her a hug. "No need to worry, Angel. In two weeks, we go to Gitmo. No unauthorized personnel can go there. If your cabin remains unsearched, or we see Benny's obituary, we can assume Vincent believed us. That doesn't mean we can skimp on safety precautions, but I'm feeling really optimistic here."

Soft and pliant against him, Angie breathed a sigh of relief on his neck. The small gesture filled him with heat. Everything about her excited him. In the month he'd know her, his entire life had changed. Everything he'd once believed important to him, no longer mattered. The woman in his arms had become his complete focus, her happiness and safety his life's goal. With the same dedication and focus he'd pursued becoming a Navy SEAL, he'd ensure they became a family. The word thrilled him.

SIXTEEN

---◆---

HESITANT AND HOPEFUL

SOFT island breezes ruffled Angie's hair as they exited the ferry carrying their bags. Dan carried the large plastic box containing Tiger. The green duffle bag holding Tiger's supplies and his black duffle banged against his shoulder.

Angie gave him a nervous glance and put her hand on the handle of the box. Dan moved out of the way of the departing passengers, set the case down, and gave her a hug.

"Are you okay?"

"Yeah, just a bit nervous. Tell me if I'm doing something wrong. Everyone else seems used to this and knows what to do. I'm afraid I'll make a mistake and get you into trouble or embarrass you." Angie crouched to peer into the cage by her feet.

143

Dan glanced at her worriedly. She wasn't checking Tiger; she was avoiding his eyes. He knelt in the wiry grass and took her hand, letting the duffle bags fall to the ground.

"Nothing you do will get me in trouble, so don't worry about that. As to making a mistake, they happen, but the Navy is really good to service personnel spouses and has systems in place to help them transition. We're both attending orientation tomorrow and if anything is unclear ask me, but don't worry— the Navy is also real fond of posting rules everywhere."

She giggled and kissed his cheek. Dan examined her, relieved to see the smile reached her eyes.

"We good?"

When she nodded, he gathered the duffle bags and Tiger's cage. The departing passengers had politely ignored them. Now that they were moving again an older woman stopped beside them.

"New here, honey?" Her kind gray eyes smiled at Angie.

Angie bit her bottom lip and glanced from Dan to the woman. "Yes."

"Don't worry, this is a nice place to live, and you'll make friends in no time. Come to the book club Tuesday at six. We meet at McDonald's." The woman held out her hand. "Gwen Anderson, my husband Pete has been stationed here for four years now, so I know all the secrets. The book club is a great way to make new friends even if you don't like to read."

"Thank you," Angie said, to Dan's ear sounding overwhelmed.

Gwen smiled, then rummaged in the large purse

she carried slung over her shoulder. She emerged with a bottle of lotion. "Take this; you'll need it on rainy days when the no-see-ums hatch. Regular bug spray doesn't seem to do a thing to stop them."

Angie took the bottle and thanked Gwen again. Gwen followed them to the bus stop chatting about local events, then waved and continued down the road on foot.

In three hours, Dan and Angie stood in the middle of their new apartment. Fully furnished, the small studio apartment lay on the first floor of a row of similar concrete structures. Dan watched Angie as she examined the room. The room reminded him of her cabin except there was no fireplace; instead, wide, double, glass doors led out to a small courtyard shaded by the upstairs neighbor's patio.

Right inside the front door, a kitchen was separated from the living space by a counter. The living room consisted of a blue sofa and matching chair. Before the couch sat a coffee table that had seen better days, a matching end table, and a built-in cabinet that held a television. An alcove to the side of the double doors held a queen size bed with nightstands on either side. Two long, thin windows above the nightstands filled the space with light. Adjustable reading lamps sat on the nightstands. Across from the bed, a doorway led into a small bathroom. The fixtures, while not modern, were clean and the color scheme a neutral beige and white. Another door led to a small walk-in closet.

"There's hooks here where we can hang a curtain to block off the, um, bedroom if you want." Dan pointed to the row of hooks across the front of the alcove. He loosened his collar as he turned and hurried to the glass doors. The bed tempted him, but she needed time to adjust. He tried to project confidence as she gazed at him anxiously.

"I don't think we need to bother, but if you want to, that's fine." Angie released Tiger from the box and cuddled him.

Dan glanced at his watch. "We have three hours before our things are delivered. Want to go get something to eat?" To his shock, tears sprang to her eyes. "Ang, if you hate it here, we can work something out."

"No, the place is fine. The tears trickled onto her cheek. She rubbed them away and headed to the bathroom, speaking over her shoulder. "I'm okay."

He followed. "You're not okay. What's wrong?"

"You feel distant as if you don't want to be here or... with me?" A sob caught in her throat and she leaned over and splashed water on her face. "On the ferry, when you moved away from me, I thought it was because we were in public and you were in uniform. But here in our home" — she took a deep breath— "Dan, if you've changed your mind about staying married or want time apart, tell me, okay? I can handle rejection. But—"

Dan laughed and grabbed her, sliding his hands under her t-shirt. "Sorry, I was trying to give you space to adjust." He leaned down and kissed her warm neck, breathing in her delicate scent. "I'm trying to be sensitive here, not sex-crazed. Figured you didn't need me throwing you on the bed and tearing your clothes off as soon as the door shut."

Both her hands fussed with the buttons of his uniform. "But you still want to, right?" She sounded hesitant and hopeful.

He laughed again. "Ang, trust me, I'll always want that. Today has sucked. First, having to rush to catch the ferry, then meeting with HSC to get our housing assignment when all I want to do is lay in bed with you, feeling you close to me. We got spoiled the last few days being able to stay in bed all day."

Dan pulled her closer until she couldn't miss how aroused he was. "Our life has been crazy these last few weeks, and we need to adjust to normalcy. That doesn't mean I don't want you desperately. It's hard for me to be near you and not kiss you and once I kiss you, it's almost impossible to keep my hands to myself. God, I'm sorry if you thought I was rejecting you."

"Can we hold hands in public?"

"Not when I'm in uniform." Dan's anxious gaze scanned her face, but she seemed calm.

"In our house when no one is here?"

"We can do whatever we want, but I'd rather take the uniform off."

She giggled and began undoing his buttons.

"We good, Ang?"

"As soon as I get you naked we will be," she murmured as her hands dropped to his belt.

Dan drew away and took her hands. "I need us to be okay everywhere, not just in bed. Are you unhappy here?"

A brilliant smile on her face, she pulled her hands away and hugged him, resting her cheek against his. "Yes, you're the best husband ever."

He loved how sensitive she was, but it did have a downside. Dan winced, glad she couldn't see his face.

"I love you. You're the only women I've ever loved." He placed a soft kiss on her lips that he hoped conveyed his love and sincerity.

SEVENTEEN

---◆---

OUR WIVES ARE MAKING FRIENDS

CHARLENE waved a manicured hand, and half stood. "Yoo-hoo, sweetie, over here."

Angie glanced up from the papers spread over the resteraunt table and smiled. JT slapped Dan on the back and gestured him on. Her attention back on the papers, Angie nibbled the end of a pen.

"Seems like our wives are making friends," JT said.

He was the same height as his wife, but she outweighed him by a good fifty pounds. Dan let his gaze linger on Charlene's curves a moment. *The word voluptuous had been invented just for her*, he thought as he sat beside his wife. "What's all this?"

Angie slapped his hand as he reached for a paper. "Don't touch," she said absently as she began stapling pages together. A minute later the table was clear, and three stacks of paper were placed before Charlene with an air of triumph. "Now, next year file separately and your refund will double. Tell JT Junior to take those classes and your child school credit can be used to bribe him."

Charlene giggled and flipped through the papers in front of her. "You're sure this is legal?"

"Absolutely. Normally, filing together would be best but in your situation filing separately will bring you a much bigger return because of the itemized deductions. In two years, the student credit is being rescinded, so JT Junior needs to take advantage of it now. Thirty-five hundred dollars is a big chunk."

"Bribable amounts." Charlene handed the file to JT. "Angie had a great idea to keep JT in school to finish his degree. If we drop him from our deductions and let him claim himself, he can get a big refund, but only if he stays in school."

"Sure, but then we lose money."

"Nope." Charlene grinned and handed him the files. "If I file separately, with itemized deductions, we'll get more back. And if I put the maximum into an IRA next year that's taken from my gross."

JT flipped through the papers. "These forms are so obtuse ten lawyers couldn't figure them out."

The plug from her portable printer dangling from her hand, Angie glanced up and smiled. "Well, I understand them, and I assure you, not only can your wife receive a bigger refund, but even with an IRA she'll have more at the end of the year."

"Why didn't our accountant tell her to do this?"

"Because all the different forms to fill in and file to separate your finances is complicated, but believe me, it's worth it. I filled everything in. Is all you three need to do is sign them. Most accountants wouldn't bother even if they know how because of the work involved."

Charlene frowned. "It didn't look that hard."

Angie laughed. "Because I know exactly how to do it. Usually, I'm on the other end of the pile, making sure those that try this do it right. My job was making sure no one got away with loopholes. I'm the guy who sends the auditors out."

Charlene made a face. "Eww."

"In my defense, I always called first to see if the paperwork was mistakenly filed before I siced the big dogs on them."

JT snorted. "I'm betting you weren't popular at parties."

"Actually, I didn't get out much, but in my experience, everyone loves to talk about their taxes."

Charlene nodded. "Gwen and Bet both stopped by with questions and Angie is going to look at their tax returns too. Not many of the spouses here have jobs, but back home she's going to be swamped."

A frown on his face, Dan took the case containing the printer from Angie. "Ang, you don't have too—"

"I don't mind." Angie turned to JT. "So, what were you guys up to today?"

Dan tensed, trying not to show it.

"Same old, same old. Perimeter checks," JT said as he leaned back in his seat. "The new guy is fitting in nicely. He isn't Juan, but he'll do."

Dan relaxed. They'd spent the day checking mines underwater. In a few weeks, they'd begin planting the new ones. Angie seemed to be settling in fine, but Dan thought she'd worry if she knew what he was doing. Charlene interrupted his train of thought.

"Invite him for dinner tonight." Charlene turned to Angie. "Don't forget, my house at six thirty. Bring a side dish, whatever you want."

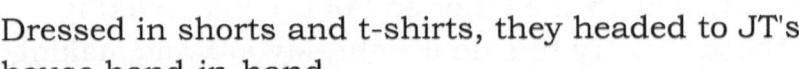

Dressed in shorts and t-shirts, they headed to JT's house hand-in-hand.

"Do you like the new guy?" Angie asked.

Dan pursed his lips and made a noncommittal sound. "I don't dislike him. I'm trying not to compare him to Juan, and that's hard. He's a lot younger than me and fresh out of training so a bit of a hotdog, but I remember wanting to prove myself too. Tom doesn't like him much, or maybe he's trying to slow the kid down. Sometimes it's hard to tell what Tom thinks."

"Will Ronny room with them?"

"Doubt it, he's married. Tom and Squirrel will be assigned new roommates."

"Are they mad you aren't coming back?"

"No. It's easy to get roommates. On base housing is always in demand." Dan took the towel wrapped dish from her, balancing it with one hand, he used the other to pull her closer. "Let's go swimming tonight," he murmured as he trailed kisses across her neck.

"Mmm."

The aroused sound of agreement filled him with heat, which the deep kiss she gave him fanned into an inferno. "Let's not stay long," he said as he pulled away.

"Long enough to be polite."

Dan released her and stepped away. She giggled when he used the dish of potatoes to hide his erection. "Don't, you're killing me," he said when she took his arm.

She laughed and released him.

"So, I heard back from my insurance company. The repairs should be complete by the end of the week. My landlord won't let me out of my lease, and by law, I can't sublease. Mr. Basker said he'll write the owner of the building for me, so maybe they'll break my lease, but as it stands now, I owe fifteen hundred in rent."

"Has Basker said anything about your credit card bills?"

"All of my cards are still frozen. No payments are due until the investigation is finished. Mr. Basker is hopeful though. He thinks there's a really good chance I'll receive my money back that we found in the cabin. So even if I have to pay the credit card companies off, I'll have the money to do it."

"Ang, we have enough money to do it even without that."

"Yeah, but I don't want to spend your money on that."

Dan stopped walking. "Our money. We share everything."

"Fine, our money, but I want to buy a house. One with enough bedrooms for an office for me and kids."

"And we will, but there's no hurry."

Angie resumed walking. "Well, I've been looking online, and houses by base are pricey. And I want one as close as we can get, so you have time to get there if you're called out."

"Okay, but there's no rush. I'm not going anywhere."

Her eyes lit as she smiled at him. "You're amazing. I'm so lucky to find you. Most men would be horrified by the amount of debt I'm bringing to the relationship."

"Honestly, it doesn't matter to me. If you get your money back great, if not, we'll pay off our debts and live in a smaller home, but we're still going to be a family either way. For richer or poorer in sickness and in health."

Angie bit her lip and stared at the ground. "Can we get married again?"

Before Dan could answer Ronny hailed him.

"Ronny, meet my wife, Angie," Dan said.

Angie offered her hand. "Nice to meet you."

"Likewise." Ronny's admiring gaze traveled Angie until Dan stepped between them.

"Is your wife coming?" Angie asked.

"Nope, she won't arrive for another two weeks. She could only get a week off." Ronny leaned forward and lowered his voice. "We aren't that serious. It's just a temporary arrangement while she's in school. She gets my bennies, and I get her when I'm in the area or like now if it's a spot she wants to visit."

Angie's eyes widened, and she grabbed Dan's arm. Dan kissed her forehead. "My wife and I are the real deal," Dan said warningly.

Ronny held up his hands. "Got it."

Charlene opened the door before they knocked. "Come on in and make yourself at home. Dan, can you watch the grill and make sure JT doesn't burn everything?" She took the potatoes from Dan and gestured with her chin for Angie to follow her.

In the kitchen, Charlene made drinks and introduced Angie to five other women.

In the backyard, the men gathered around the grill, beer in hand. Dan kept an eye on Angie all night. She seemed to be relaxed and having fun. After dinner, a game of poker began.

Dan gave his spot at the table to Angie. "My secret weapon. Prepare to meet your doom."

He kissed her what he intended to be a light kiss, but the touch of her lips on his distracted him.

"Okay, newlyweds, break it up," Charlene said as she handed Angie another glass of wine. "Cold beer in the cooler— help yourselves.

Angie blushed and straightened in her seat. Dan leaned over the back of her chair, enjoying the heat from her body. The glance she gave him was full of promise. A crowd gathered around the card table as the groans of dismay and the pile of chips in front of Angie grew.

"Damn, you brought in a ringer. She must have cleaned up in Vegas. Did you meet her at the tables?" Squirrel asked as Angie raked in another pot.

Dan laughed and tweaked Angie's ponytail. "For the life of me, I can't remember meeting Angelina. Vegas is a blur. I'm just glad I did."

Angie snorted.

JT rose and stretched. Charlene put an arm around his waist and every man there sighed enviously. Angie punched Dan lightly in the arm and grinned.

"Take me home; it's been a long day," she said.

The party broke up with much laughing and joking.

"I like your friends," Angie said as they walked home.

"We spend a lot of time together. One of the wives usually hosts a dinner party every week, even if we aren't around, but don't feel obligated to attend."

"That was fun. I wouldn't mind hosting one."

"Talk to Charlene; she'll know how to set one up.

"She's been real helpful already. Is that part of her job, or should I say JT's job? Is his spouse supposed to keep tabs on the other wives?"

"I don't think she considers it keeping tabs, more like being friendly. And no, she does it because we're all friends. Our squad is real close. JT doesn't have to socialize with us, he chooses to. Same for all of us. Those meetings aren't mandatory. If I wanted, I could only see them during working hours, but we like to hang out."

Angie glanced over at the road leading to their house. "Where are we going?"

"Swimming. All day I thought about you in the water, wearing that blue bikini and imagining taking it off."

I don't have a suit."

"Me neither, but I'm willing to forgo the details." Dan led her to a small cove bordered by a reef.

At the water's edge, Angie glanced around. "What if someone comes?"

"No one will. This beach is restricted."

"Won't we get in trouble for being here?"

"Only if they catch us." Dan grinned and threw his shirt onto the sand.

"Why is it restricted?"

"They do training here, but not at night."

A ring of practice mines blocked the entrance of the small cove thirty feet out from them. Before the teams were cleared to work on the real deal, they had to clear these without mishap.

Dan lifted her shirt off and paused to admire her. Moonlight illuminated her, making her white bra glow.

Tan now from spending days in the tropical sun, the white of her breasts was a startling contrast when he slid the straps of her bra down.

"God, you get more beautiful every day." Deep and low, his voice cracked with emotion as he traced the swell of her breasts. Her soft aroused sigh filled him with anticipation. Their clothes made a small pile on the damp sand. Naked, Dan led her into the warm water. All day he'd been waiting for this. The touch of her skin against his while floating together. Connected by his cock inside her, she floated on her back, her breasts shining in the moonlight, so beautiful his breath caught. The surge of his hips made her gasp and reach for him.

Her legs were tight around his waist, her hips rocking with his. Her nipples hardened, the sensitive tips poking through her wet hair. Every caress and kiss elicited a gasp or groan. He loved how sensitive her breasts were. The strength and ease of her orgasms made him hot.

Never in his life had anyone responded to him like this. Every time they made love, he learned something new she liked as if his body was formed to please her. Able to recognize the sounds she made, he knew when he was in the right spot thrusting in a rhythm to make her come.

If he made her come first and held still feeling her orgasm when he thrust again, it would make her wild and her second orgasm would be twice as powerful, making her cry out his name. Tonight was going to be one of those nights; she already strained against him, groaning, close to release.

"Come for me, Angel, I want to feel you wet and hot

for me."

"Dan..." low and hoarse she wailed his name as she came, jerking her hips against him, her body falling limp supported by his hands in the water.

"Mmm." Dan stopped moving, letting her inner muscles clench him. When the sensations slowed, he surged hard against her, his head thrown back, seeking release as she panted hoarsely.

"Oh God, Angel. The lust that filled him when they made love heated him from head to toe. His balls ached for release. When he came, she screamed and came with him, the wild thrusting of their hips out of their control. It was all he could do to keep them above water. He waded closer to shore on trembling legs until he could sit in the surf with her on his lap. Exhausted and sated, he held her until their breathing steadied.

A quiet, soft laugh brushed his chest. "I don't think I have enough energy to dress and walk home," she said.

Wet strands of hair clung to his hand as he smoothed it back from her forehead. "I'll get you home safe, never doubt it."

Angie relaxed against him, soft moonlight illuminating her curves and delicate skin. The tropical sun burned her if she didn't take care. Unlike him. He could spend a day in the sun with nothing more than a darker tan to show for it.

An hour later, he helped her dress and carried her to the road. He would've carried her home, but once they were in public, she wanted to walk. The walk to their home took place in comfortable silence broken only by the occasional cry of a bird and singing of insects.

At home, Dan undressed and washed her, then himself. In bed, before sleep took him, he said a prayer of thanks. God had given him an Angel. No one and nothing would take her from him. There was nothing he wouldn't do to keep her.

EIGHTEEN

---◆---

HOOCHY MAMA NEEDS A TALKING TOO

ANGIE halted on top of the path leading to the shore, lifting a hand to shade her eyes and staring in astonishment. Ronny's wife, Dawn, had both arms around Dan's neck. They were up to their waists in the water, and Dawn's shrieking laugh traveled to where Angie stood.

Ronny, JT, Squirrel, and Tom stood facing out to sea. The men wore black dive suits and carried air tanks.

Charlene made a noise of disapproval as Dawn put her legs around Dan's waist. "Little hoochy mama needs a talking too."

Charlene linked her arm with Angie's and tugged her down the path.

As Angie and Charlene approached, Dan waded through the water and handed Dawn to her husband.

JT turned and glowered. Tom laughed and held out a hand to Dawn. She shrieked and laughed as she took his hand. Squirrel gestured with his chin at Charlene and Angie. Dan turned, an annoyed expression on his face.

"Hey, wait there and I'll come set up your tanks," Dan called and turned back to Ronny and said something to soft for Angie to hear.

Charlene handed a tank to Angie and put one on her back. She was fussing with the belt when Dan arrived.

"What was that all about?" Charlene asked and nodded to Dawn.

Dan blushed, sighing hard. "Afraid of fish or something."

"Humph or something. Be careful with that one, Dan. She has home-wrecker written all over her."

Dan laughed and tightened the belt around Charlene's waist. "Dawn's a harmless flirt. Ang and I are tight."

"Uh huh. Dawn tries that shit with my man and there'll be hell to pay." Charlene glowered at Dawn a moment before turning her glower on JT.

Angie said nothing, busying herself with the air tanks. The men had been teaching them to dive, and she liked it. Ocean life was quiet and peaceful, filled with colors and fish she'd never seen before. Until this moment, she'd really enjoyed it. Now she was uneasy. Her glance flitted to Dawn who held Tom's hand and giggled. The white bikini Dawn wore was almost see through, doing nothing to provide modesty.

Angie glanced down at her wetsuit and sighed. The thick neoprene flattened her curves. She eyed

Charlene enviously. Charlene's curves were so generous nothing could flatten them. Where Angie was sunburnt and freckled, Charlene was a gorgeous shade of caramel latte ten shades lighter than her husband's dark-chocolate skin. Tom was darker yet. The blackest black man Angie had ever met. His teeth were a startling white as he smiled, which he did now with abandon at Dawn.

Angie's gaze flicked to Ronny, but he didn't appear to mind that his wife was flirting with Tom. Angie knelt in the hot sand to pick up the swim fins. She handed a pair to Charlene and took a pair for herself, trying not to let Dawn bother her.

Dan loves me, she reminded herself as she took his hand and waded into the water behind him. Charlene took his other hand, and they followed him until the water grew deep enough to put the flippers on. The shore here was stony. Unless you took slow, cautious steps, you were liable to stub a toe. It didn't bother Angie at all that Dan helped Charlene. She tried to figure out why it bothered her so much when he helped Dawn.

She bit back a snort. Charlene didn't throw herself into Dan's arms. *Let it go,* she told herself.

JT checked that they'd connected the tanks correctly and lowered his face mask. Squirrel checked everyone's gauges, and they dove, leaving Dawn, Tom, and Ronny, on shore.

For thirty-five minutes, they swam around, exploring the ocean floor. A wide, rock reef separated the cove from the ocean, making an ideal spot for beginners to learn. Small schools of brightly colored fish made the reef their home. At low tide, the top edges of the reef poked from the water.

Angie and Charlene floated thirty feet down before a hole in a rock in which a moray eel made its home. JT swam up and touched the eels head, causing it to draw back until just its beady black eye remained visible. He gestured for them to follow.

A school of clownfish darted between red sea anemones. The bubbles from the oxygen tank attracted them. In moments, all three divers were surrounded by the small, orange fish.

Angie glanced around for Dan and spied him ten feet back, facing the other way. Charlene grabbed her hand and tugged her after JT. Both women stopped and backpedaled from the small octopus JT led them too. He grinned and poked the octopus, causing it to squirt dark ink as it swam rapidly away.

Finally, they returned to the surface.

On shore, Ronny lounged in a beach chair under a small umbrella beside a cooler. Tom and Dawn were nowhere in sight.

Dan emerged from the water carrying a string bag full of oysters. "I'm willing to share, but any pearls go to my wife. Someday, we'll have enough for a necklace."

Ronny offered them beer from the cooler as Dan squatted and began prying oysters open.

"Needs tabasco," JT said after he slurped one down.

Charlene giggled and kissed him, then whispered in his ear. A grin on her face, she took the oyster Dan handed her and ate it.

Angie sniffed hers. "Are these safe to eat uncooked?"

"Yep, but an acquired taste. Try one." Dan handed a shucked oyster to Ronny, then ate one himself while

Angie debated eating hers. Face screwed into a grimace, she poured the oyster into her mouth.

"Um, chewy and fishy."

Dan laughed and handed her another. A light in his eyes, he ate one and licked his lips. "Delicious."

By the time Tom and Dawn returned, the oysters were eaten, the shells thrown back into the sea.

"Now I'm hungry," JT complained.

"Me too," Dan said as he stared at Angie.

Her eyes locked on his as she slowly pulled the zipper of her wet suit down. Underneath, she wore her blue bikini. Dan's gaze riveted to her exposed skin.

Charlene glanced at them and rolled her eyes. "Let's go out to eat. I'm hungry too." Charlene took JT's hand and pulled him down the beach. He laughed and scooped up their air tanks.

Dan stood and removed his wetsuit. "Need help getting it off?"

The front of her suit open, Angie had made no attempt to remove it. He slid his hands inside and splayed them on her back, pulling her closer for a kiss. "It'll be easier to remove in the water." Without waiting for her to answer, he walked backward still kissing her, bringing her with him one slow step at a time.

The suit did come off easier. Dan let it drop from his hand. "Don't worry about it; I'll dive for it later. It won't go far," he murmured as Angie grabbed at it. "Those oysters work fast." He pressed his hips against her. Long and hard, he throbbed against her leg. She put her arms around his neck and let him support them both in the water, which came to his chest. She lowered one hand as she put her legs around his waist, pushed his bathing suit down, and hers to the side.

"Mmm, he made an aroused sound as he slid inside her. "No fair, we can't really move with an audience."

Angie laughed then flushed. "I forgot he was there."

Her arms back around Dan's neck, she kissed him. "This is nice too. I love how you feel inside me.

Dan groaned and flexed his hips. "I want to kiss your breasts."

"Yes," Angie said and gasped as she pressed her breasts against his chest, wishing she were naked.

Dan jerked his hips again. "Oh god, you're going to make me come just like this."

"Yes," She said again as her inner muscles clenched him. "I hate when you're not touching me. When you're inside me like this, I feel complete. Tonight, when we go home, I want you to make love to me again, long and hard. Tomorrow, when I wake, I want to ache from you. So all day I remember what you feel like. And you can think about me at home remembering and wanting to do it again."

"Ahh," Dan jerked his hips again.

Angie pressed hard against him as he came. The urge to squirm and thrust was almost overwhelming, but she fought back the need. They weren't alone.

Dan kissed her a long time. When they finally broke for air, he released her and dove, looking for her wet suit. A minute later, he surfaced carrying it.

"Let's go eat and go home. I'll need my strength.

Angie giggled and followed.

NINETEEN

---◆---

CHOOSE ME ON PURPOSE

DAWN glowered as she entered the laundromat. The laundry basket thumped onto the counter and tipped over, clothes falling to the floor. With her back turned and shoulders tight, Dawn snatched them up and crammed them back into the basket.

"If you have a problem with me, take it up with me. Don't be a bitch and try to get Ronny in trouble with his boss." Hands on her hips, Dawn glared at Angie.

Angie let the clothes in her hand fall to the bench before her. "I have no idea what you're talking about."

"Right, you didn't tell JT to tell me to 'reign it in'?

"No, that sounds like Charlene, and believe me, you're a fool if you're messing with JT."

"As if! He's a married man. I see that. I'm no home wrecker."

Angie rolled her eyes. "Dan's married too— to me."

166

"Yeah, but not really. Ronny told me you two got married in Vegas same as us. The benefits are awesome, not even counting the sex."

"We got married because we're in love," Angie said.

"Sure, right." Dawn snickered as she shook her head. "You fell in love with him in two hours, and it had nothing to do with his money."

Shocked, Angie paled and took a step back. "What the hell are you talking about? You don't know us."

"True. But Ronny told me you two married in Vegas while Dan was drunk after knowing each other for two hours. Ronny and I have known each other for years, so don't get on your high horse with me. Ronny is cool with our arrangement."

A red flush climbed Angie's cheeks. "Dan and I are married. It isn't an arrangement. We plan on being married forever."

Dawn tilted her head to the side, raising her eyebrow and pursing her lips. "Sure, whatever you say. And I'm sorry if I blamed you for what Charlene said, but I thought you were mad over yesterday."

Angie nodded. "And you wouldn't be wrong, but I didn't say anything to anyone. I'd appreciate it if you'd keep your hands off my husband though."

"A no-fly zone, sure I get it, but if he makes a pass, I'm grabbing on tight. Fair warning and all. I don't mean to be a bitch, but you seem kind of over your head here. Like you think he really loves you, and I'm sorry, but that isn't how it is. Ronny tells me lots of guys marry to get higher pay. It costs them nothing to get the comforts of sex at home and more pay while we get benefits, medical, school, dental, all that crap. Even trips like this one, all-expenses paid on Uncle

Sam."

"I guess some do, but not us. We love each other."

Dawn sighed and folded her clean clothes a moment. "Now I feel sorry for you. How can you be this naïve at your age? Your what, twenty-four? Come on wise up. What are the chances he loves you after two hours?"

"Dan and I have a complicated relationship, and it's nobody's business but ours, but I assure you, we intend to stay married and are in love."

"Whatever helps you sleep at night. Rest assured he's on my hands-off list. Unless he makes a pass, of course. But I won't make the first move."

"Ronny doesn't mind you sleeping with his friends?" Angie asked as she sorted her clothing.

"No. Why should he? He sleeps with mine when they let him. I fuck him whenever he wants, and we both know this is temporary. Because of his job, I try to be discreet, but he isn't home much, so it generally isn't difficult."

A bark of laughter, Angie couldn't stop, escaped her. "Discreet?"

Dawn laughed and gave Angie a rueful grin. "I admit I was a bit, um, enthusiastic, but the men here are so damn hot, and it's been a dry spell for me. Ronny has spoiled me for boys. Give me a man with experience and stamina any day over a three-minute, excited boy."

Angie laughed. "Just between us, Dan is amazing in bed, and now I feel sorry for you because you'll never know."

Dawn laughed and lightly punched Angie's shoulder. "No fair, now I like you and will feel bad if I take that ride."

Angie snorted with laughter as she shook her head. "Don't try that with JT and keep in mind Ronny will be working with these guys a long time."

"You really are a nice person," Dawn said. "I believe you really do love your husband. For your sake, I hope he loves you too." Dawn heaved a heavy sigh and gathered her clothes. "I better go apologize to Charlene. Not that I tried anything with her man, but I don't want his commander mad at Ronny."

"Good luck with that," Angie said cheerfully.

Dawn winced and shuffled out.

<hr />

Dan greeted Angie with a hug. "What are you grinning about?"

"Dawn is on her way to apologize to Charlene, and I was wishing I was a fly on the wall."

"For what?"

Angie dropped the clothes on the couch and lifted both eyebrows as she tilted her head. "As if you don't know. No one can be that oblivious."

"I never saw her flirt with JT."

Both hands on her hips now, Angie glared. "But you did notice she flirted with you, right?"

"Well, sure, but I didn't flirt back."

"Your hands were on her ass." Angie rolled her eyes and picked the clothes up.

Dan grabbed her arm and spun her to face him. "True, but it was either hold her or fall over with her on top of me. I gave her to Ronny as soon as I could. What was I supposed to do?"

"Push her off. Think about it, Dan. If some guy

169

grabbed me like that, what am I supposed to do? Let them, or push them off?" Angie yanked her arm from his grasp and hurried to the closet.

Dan stared after her, a frown on his face. "It's not as simple as that. Sure, if she were a stranger I could push her away, but even then I'm not sure I would if a scared stranger grabbed me. Not that she was really scared. I'm not an idiot. I realize she was using the situation to flirt."

Dan sighed and ran a hand through his hair. "I get what you're saying, and I'm sorry if I hurt your feelings, but honestly, I was caught off guard. Ronny is new to the team and was standing right there. Yes, I knew she was flirting, but I also thought there was some truth in her fear of the bottom. Ang, this isn't about her, but about us. Do you trust me?"

Angie exited the closet, glowering furiously. "Don't turn this around. This isn't about me acting inappropriately, it's about you. Whether I trust you or not doesn't mean you can grope other women."

Dan approached with both hands outheld. "Don't blow this out of proportion. Do you really think I was groping her?"

"Did you want too?

"Where's this coming from, Ang?" He reached for her, and she stepped back and crossed her arms. Annoyed and worried, Dan crossed his arms on his chest too and they glared at each other.

"Tell me the truth, Dan. Did you want too? Or should I say, do you want too?"

Dan rose his right hand. "I swear to God, the thought never crossed my mind."

Angie smiled, then frowned and bit her lip. "Am I

fool for believing you? Dawn says lots of soldiers marry for the extra money and free sex while they're on base."

"Ahh, Dawn says, huh?"

Angie shrugged. "She's a wild one, but I don't think she's a liar. She told me she won't make a pass at you but wouldn't reject one either."

"I see. Well, you have nothing to worry about. I don't plan on making one."

"Good to know."

"So, you spoke with Dawn and now think I married you for the money?" Dan's voice rose as his eyes narrowed. "Oh, and the sex."

"I don't want to believe it, but she had a point. I really love you, Dan. It would break my heart if you discarded me. Nothing you ever did or said makes me think you will, but I've been known to fool myself in the past and see what I want to see in people.

Angie held up a hand as Dan started to speak. "I tell myself if I love you so desperately that it's possible for you to love me like that too. Then I see your hands on her, and I doubt. Maybe I wouldn't if you touched me in public, but you don't. And yes, I know why, but it still feels like rejection. When I reach for you and you pull away, it hurts. I'm trying to get used to us, and I realize it's hard for you too, but then someone says I'm being naïve and kidding myself and I have to wonder if they're right."

"What am I supposed to say here, Ang? Either you believe me, or you don't. I married you—"

"No." Angie shook her head as tears filled her eyes. "You married Candice. Those promises weren't to me. Our marriage is legal only."

"Oh, Angel." Dan's voice cracked as he reached for her. Relieved that she didn't pull away, he nestled her face against his chest. "You're right, but I swear I mean them to you. When I married her, I didn't mean it. Hell, I don't even remember doing it." Angie stiffened. "Oh God, please don't be angry with me about that. I can't change it no matter how much I wish I could. Don't let me screw us up. Please, Angel. Marrying Candice was a mistake except that it brought me to you. I'm an idiot. I told you that the first day we met."

Dan rubbed his eyes and fell to his knees, taking her hands. "Will you marry me? Please say yes and choose me on purpose. Let me be your husband. I want to love you and take care of you forever."

Angie sank to her knees and kissed his lips. "Yes. Legally we're married, but I want to make you my promise and have you make one to me. When you're touching me, I feel your sincerity. If we made a real promise to each other, the Dawns of the world couldn't come between us."

"No one can come between us unless we let them. Don't let them, Angel. You have my promise to be a faithful husband. Whatever ceremony you want, I'll do, but I swear to you, you're already my wife in sickness and health for richer and poorer until death do us part." Dan sat on the floor and pulled Angie into his lap. "Life as a soldier's wife won't be easy for you. It isn't easy for me to leave you or withhold affectionate touches from you either."

"I know, but it still hurts. And I hate that I doubt when I feel your sincerity, but you're honoring a promise made to her, not me."

"How can I help?"

Amused and sulky, Angie answered, "Don't touch other women either."

"I see that I hurt you, and I'm sorry, but I really don't know what I should've done differently. It's not like I wanted to hold her."

"My head knows that, and I hate how clingy and insecure I'm being, but that doesn't make it go away. Jumping right into marriage like this is harder than I thought it'd be." Angie squeezed his hands and took a deep breath. "Should I go? Would that be easier on us— if we take our time, I mean?"

"God, no." Dan hesitated, his throat dry and a nervous, sick feeling in his stomach. "Do you want to go?"

To his dismay, she began to cry. "No, but I think I should. I feel like I'm pressuring you."

Dan scowled. "No, you don't. You feel unsure. Everything you've said screams you doubt me and want time to know my love is real. You're afraid I'm going to break your heart, that I don't love you but the sex. That I was happy with Candice and I'm happy with you and I'd be just as happy with Dawn or whoever comes along. But that's not true. I liked Candice. She was fun, easy to get along with, but she was faking, and I never loved her. For all I know, she hated everything about me. I like to think once I sobered up I would've noticed ..." Dan sighed. "Okay, that's not true, I noticed, but I was taking advantage of her willingness and didn't want to drive her away by confronting her."

Angie stiffened, and Dan tightened his grip.

"Not because I loved her, but because I didn't want

to be alone. And before you say I'm doing the same thing with you, that isn't true. What I feel for you is real and strong, and I'll feel it forever even when we're apart. Money had nothing to do with us. We could've taken that million and run if money was driving either of us, but it isn't."

For a few minutes, they sat on the floor wrapped in each other's arms. Tiger joined them head-butting and purring, making Angie laugh.

Sad and wistful Dan spoke, "See we're already a family. Don't break up our family, Ang."

Angie nodded, and they made love, but she was sad and unhappy. Dan fell asleep holding her close, feeling as if he were losing her. The next day he asked for leave to go the mainland and was denied. A furious scowl on his face, he went to Charlene.

"I need a favor."

"Sure, Dan. What can I do for you?" Charlene motioned him into the house, a worried frown marring her brow. "Is Dawn causing problems? I warned JT that girl was going to cause trouble with his men. Ronny might seem cool with her sleeping with whoever she wants, but what man would be okay with that? Right in front of him like she does? Please tell me you didn't..."

"Of course not! What kind of man do you think I am? Jeez, Char, I haven't even been married three months yet." Dan ran a hand through his hair and rubbed the side of his face. "Look, Ang and I got married quick, but we're in love. Dawn did make her doubt me though, and I want to reassure her. We don't have wedding rings or anything, but I can't get leave to go pick them out. Can you go?"

"Well, I could, but I shouldn't. Dan, she won't want wedding rings picked by me."

"Please, Char, I need Angie to know in her soul this isn't a fling for me. There are reasons she thinks it is." Dan sighed and glanced away. "Not that I was ever unfaithful to her or anything like that, but it happened so quick."

Charlene pursed her lips as she nodded slowly. "Tell you what, I'll go buy her an engagement ring. If you want her to feel special, remarry her in a church before God and your friends. Take time to pick out wedding rings and plan the event as if it's important. Rushed in Vegas is romantic an all but doesn't have the weight of a planned marriage."

Dan grinned, his eyes lighting. "Char, you're a genius. Can you go today?"

Charlene laughed. "Yes. Tell me what you want and how much to spend."

"Um..."

Charlene rolled her eyes. "Fine, give me a limit, and I'll pick something nice. Gold or silver setting?"

TWENTY

---◆---

MARRY ME

DAN returned to work feeling hopeful. Angie would love the symbol of an engagement ring; he was sure of that. They could plan a wedding, and she would feel the permanence of his love. A frown etched his brow as he slipped his flippers on. Angie was right, and he was a fool. No woman would be happy honoring a promise made to another.

"Get your head out of your ass." JT snatched the air tank from Dan's hand and dropped it into the bottom of the boat. "Forget about your woman problems or whatever has you so distracted you're putting on an empty tank before you blow us all up."

Dan blushed as JT handed him a new tank. "Take Ronny and make sure he's paying attention. Get the left line inspected and start putting in the new sensors. Don't fucking leave him alone until you're sure he knows what he's doing." JT put his hands on his hips, his lips in a tight line. "Tell me there's no problem between you? I can't let him work with Tom and explosives, that's just asking for trouble. If you're screwing his wife too, I'm getting his ass transferred."

"I'm a happily married man. Dawn means nothing to me other than being the wife of a teammate."

"Good to hear. Whatever the hell is distracting you, handle it on your own time. You good to go?"

"Hooyah!" Dan saluted and slid into the water.

JT sighed hard as he sat to put his flippers on. "This is going to be a long fucking mission," he muttered as he checked an air tank before slinging it on his back and following Dan.

———◆———

Charlene returned from the mainland with a black velvet box and two, large shopping bags. Dan grinned when she handed him the box.

"Have you thought about how you're going to give it to her," Charlene asked.

The grin on Dan's face faded. "Romance is going to be hard to do here."

"Fear not." Charlene smiled and handed him one of the bags. "Everything you need for a romantic beach picnic, fine wine, soft towels, good food. The food is in this bag so I can refrigerate it." Charlene lifted the other bag and gave it a slight shake. "Come to my house tomorrow at ten to pick it up. Take her for a romantic picnic, have brunch, spend the day. I was thinking maybe you put the ring inside a fresh caught oyster? She loves to dive."

"Char, you're a genius, and I love you. Thanks for

everything; you're the best." Dan kissed her cheek and hurried home to his wife.

"What? Angie asked. A wide smile grew on her face when he came in.

"Nothing." Dan tried to smooth his excited expression with minimal success judging by Angie's inquisitive stare. " I have the day off tomorrow and thought we could spend it together diving?"

"Sounds great." Head cocked to the side, she eyed him a moment. "What's going on? What's in the bag?"

"Picnic supplies Charlene brought me." He dropped the bag on the couch and grabbed her. She shrieked as he swung her around. "You make me so happy. I'm the luckiest man on Earth."

Her gaze soft and full of love, she kissed him. Every time her lips touched his heat filled him. With no effort, she could arouse him. The half-lidded glance she gave him now made him so hot he couldn't contain the moan.

He walked her backward to the bed as she began removing his clothes.

Sheets twisted under her sweaty body, tangling on his legs and ended up on the floor as she answered his every advance with her own. He'd fallen asleep with her hand on his cock and woken with his skin sticking to hers. Exhausted from their lovemaking, she hadn't stirred when he pulled away.

The sound of the shower hadn't woken her. The light kiss he gave her got a sleepy, mumbled, "I love you." He barely made it to Charlene's on time. When he returned, Angie was awake, freshly showered, and wearing a swimsuit. He grabbed the bags containing their dive gear and threw them over his shoulder while she donned a sundress over her swimsuit.

He took her to the same restricted beach they'd visited before. Charlene had provided an assortment of food, which Dan happily attacked. He was starving.

"Oysters for lunch." He grinned as he handed her another water bottle. "Stay hydrated."

When they'd finished eating, they donned their dive gear. Hand-in-hand they waded into the water. Angie carried a small underwater camera.

"Will there be any jellyfish?" she asked.

"Not at this time of day. High tide maybe." Dan gestured to the reef showing above the water. "Stay away from there; that's a razor reef. Sharp edges can cut you badly. Stay with me, okay?"

Dan began gathering oysters. Angie followed a school of half-inch brightly colored minnows as they circled Dan, trying to get a good shot. The fish darted in random directions, making them hard to photograph. Dan laughed to himself as she settled to the bottom with the camera before her, ready to snap a picture as they passed.

He returned to hunting oysters. Clear and calm, the peace of the sea relaxed him. Dan tied a bag half-full of oysters to his waist and glanced around for Angie. She hadn't moved. Determined to get her shot, she held the camera out, glancing around occasionally to spot the small school of tiny fish. Dan left her to it. She'd gotten some great shots. He planned to get her a really good underwater camera for her birthday.

When next he looked, she'd moved. For a moment, his heart leaped, but he spotted her to his left. The mines circling this reef were practice mines but had enough oomph to injure if stepped on. She was nowhere near the edge though. She pointed and gestured, indicating she wanted to go closer to shore, and he nodded and gave her a thumbs-up, making sure to make the gesture broad enough to be clear.

In a minute, he was close enough to see what had captured her attention; A shiny silver disk with a small, blinking red light. Horrified, he put on speed— too far to stop her and to slow to reach her before she reached the mine, he swam as fast as he could.

Heart in his throat, he prayed as she hovered above it. Before she could decide to touch it, he arrived and yanked her away. The wake of his passage stirred the sand on the bottom. The camera dropped from her hand. Dan's gaze followed it down as he pulled her, putting his body between her and the mine. He was still dragging her away when the mine exploded.

A blast of water tumbled them. Sand and small debris obscured the water, making it impossible to tell direction. In his arms, Angie jerked, then stilled. His heart pounded hard as he clutched her tightly to his chest. It was possible the mine would set off a chain of explosions, and he didn't want to inadvertently trigger one. The sand would clear enough in a moment to see bubbles to tell which way was up. The moments ticked by with glacial slowness.

Angie hadn't moved, not a twitch since the water had rolled them over. Before he could become truly panicked, her grip on him tightened.

He loosened his hold. The cloudy water settled, leaving them drifting in an embrace. Dan followed the bubbles to the surface and headed to the beach, towing his wife. "You okay?"

She spat her regulator out and removed her

goggles. "Fine, stunned. What was that?'

"Training mine. Maybe it isn't such a great idea to use this beach," Dan said sheepishly.

Angie snorted. "We better get out of here before we're caught and arrested."

Floating on his back now, Dan grinned. "You really knock my socks off."

Angie rolled her eyes. "I blow you away, huh?"

He laughed. "I love you so much. Will you marry me?"

She stilled, treading water beside him. "You mean it? A church wedding and everything?"

"Yes. Any ceremony you want."

A grin lit her eyes. "Yes."

Dan kicked his flippers off and pulled her close. The water buoyed her in his arms as he carried her to shore, kissing her. He set her down on the blanket they'd spread out and knelt to retrieve the ring from his shorts pocket and slid it on her finger.

"Oh, Dan." Tears clouded her eyes as she stared at the square-cut diamond ring. Set in a silver setting, the diamond was surrounded by small diamond chips that glittered blue in the sun. "You really mean it."

"I really do. Believe this is permanent. Trust in my love for you," he said, willing her to believe him.

Angie threw her arms arm around his neck. She hugged him for a minute before drawing back and kissing his lips. "We better get out of here."

Dan laughed as they gathered their things and headed out.

Thrilled with the world, Dan didn't care he would have to report setting off that mine. Angie had said yes, and she was happy. Angie laughed and made a cooing noise, bringing him back to the moment.

"Look, Dan, a kitten, and it looks just like Tiger."

Dan glanced to where she pointed and winced. A small orange kitten meandered its way across the minefield separating the base from Cuban territory.

Angie squatted, balancing herself with fingers clenched in the chain-link, diamond ring glittering in the sunlight, and called the cat in a soft cajoling voice. A guard approached.

"Move along, please."

Angie scrambled to her feet and flushed. "Sorry, just calling the cat."

Dan took her arm and pulled her away.

"Well, don't," the guard said shortly. "Never call animals from beyond the fence. Not that many can fit through the links, but we don't want to encourage them to cross the mine field. Anyone or thing that crosses gets shot."

Angie paled and swayed. "The kitten is on a minefield? That's a minefield?" her voice rose shrilly. "Dan, it's going to get killed. Oh, my God, I could've killed it. Can we save it?" Tears filled her eyes as she turned to him. Dan pulled her into an embrace and glared over her head at the guard who snickered.

"The kitten will be fine. It's to light to set off the mines. See those bushes? The Cubans planted a pricker thicket to stop their people from coming here and asking for asylum. The Americans used to have a minefield, but we took it out when the cold war ended. The Cubans still have one, but the fences and prickers keep people off it. The kitten can fit through the links if it wanders over here." He didn't mention that the guards would kill it before it could spread disease to

182

the animals on base. Angie was freaked out enough.

"The Cubans kept their mines? How come?"

Dan led her away, headed home as he debated what to say. The fact that the Cubans hated Americans might scare her more. Before he could say anything, she pulled away and glanced at his face, her own looking scared and horrified. "Are we in danger here? Do they actively hate us?"

"Some danger, but no more than any other base. We're well protected, and the perimeter is alarmed. The Cubans know they can't win and while they don't love us, we have a live-and-let-live policy."

For a few moments, they walked in silence. A deep frown on her face, Angie peered over her shoulder. "The fences and guards, the security checkpoints— everything should've told me. I'm seeing what I want to see again. This place is violent under the surface. Not a home— a prison surrounded by enemies."

The hand in his clenched as she shivered.

Dan hesitated, not knowing what to say. She wasn't wrong.

"The violence under the surface is terrifying. All these men ready to fight and kill." Another stronger shiver racked her. "Thank God you're not like that." She jutted her chin at the guard who walked his beat carrying an M16.

"Ang, I carry a gun."

"Yeah, but you aren't like him, so cold and blithe about shooting people."

Dan's heart began to pound. In her eyes, he would be worse than the guard. He was pretty sure that guard hadn't ever shot at anyone never mind killed someone. With three confirmed kills at six hundred yards and more unconfirmed... his hands began to sweat.

Seemingly unaware of the effect her conversation had on him, she continued. "I'm glad you're a specialist safe on a ship somewhere fixing things."

"Ang—"

"Yo!" Ronny called as he and Dawn came up carrying ice-creams.

For the first-time Dan greeted them with sincere welcome. Angie was distracted, and he hadn't had to lie or tell the truth.

Dan grinned at Ronny and slapped his shoulder. "Let's take the girls for pizza."

TWENTY-ONE

---◆---

I'M GOING TO REACH OUT AND TOUCH YOU

WILL you be sad to leave here?" Dan asked as he stacked the last box beside the door.

"Some, but I'm excited to start our real life."

"This is our real life." He tweaked her ponytail and laughed when she batted his hand away.

"Yeah, but I want a permanent home, a place that's ours. This is more of a vacation spot. Temporary.

"That sounds amazing— a home with you. I'm almost looking forward to going away so I can come home to you.

She laughed as she sat on the couch. Tiger jumped into her lap, and Dan handed her the feather chaser.

"Not me. I'm dreading being away from you," she said.

"I'll always come back." He sat beside her and took

185

the cat toy, teasing Tiger absently as he ran a hand over her hair.

"I'll still miss you."

"And I, you. Don't worry about our separations, they'll all be temporary. Basker called this morning, and nobody has been near your cabin."

"Our cabin."

"Our cabin," Dan corrected with a smile. The smile deepened as she settled against his shoulder. Tiger ran back and forth across their laps after the feather. Dan let the cat capture it and laughed when Tiger rolled onto his back, paws kicking, trying to disembowel the feather. "Take precautions, but I think Candice is behind us."

Angie leaned her head back and rubbed her temples. "Not really. Don't get me wrong, I'm thrilled we'll never see Benny again, but I still owe a lot of money."

"Basker seems to think not. I admit it isn't official yet, but he seems sure the debt will fall on Candice's estate. And you'll be getting your money back. Basker also said Deborah Singer has written you a check for fifty thousand dollars. A finder's fee; she's real grateful you didn't just keep her money. He also said Deborah plans to sue Candice's estate for pain and suffering and he says we can too."

"No, I only want what she took. Besides, with a husband like Joe Conti, that's just asking for trouble."

"I agree. When we buy our new home, we can afford a nice one. One with plenty of rooms for kids."

Angie held up her hand, admiring the engagement ring. "A big family. Maybe we could even adopt a few kids."

"I love you more every second. That's a great idea. If your serious, I'd love to talk to the fathers at Saint Patrick. You'll make such an amazing mother; any boy would have a better life with you in it."

"We're really going to do this? Have a family— an amazing life together filled with children and love?"

"We really are."

———————◆———————

Angie lay beneath him, her flushed skin slightly damp with perspiration. Her bright blue eyes met his as he knelt between her legs and she made a soft disappointed sound.

A rueful smile curved his lips. He was disappointed to leave her body too. Physically satisfied, mentally he craved her, the feel of her skin, the sounds she made, the pure physical closeness of the act; he wanted to make love to her for hours— forever. He didn't think he'd ever be sated with her.

"I love you, Angel," he murmured as he leaned down and kissed her.

Tears filled her eyes. Arms and legs around him, she held him to her, kissing him with her soul. When the kiss ended, he was breathing harder. Too soon for his body to respond to her, he knelt between her knees again. "I read this article once."

Her half-closed eyes opened wider, then narrowed as her lips pursed and head tilted questioningly.

"On how to give a woman a squirting orgasm. Supposedly, if you can do that, the woman will be your love slave."

Balanced on an elbow, she giggled and reached for him. "I'm already your love slave."

He took her hands and placed them on her legs. "Hold your knees back so I can see what I'm doing. I don't want to mess this up." He wanted this woman wild for him, for her to want him as much as he wanted her.

Her breath caught as a flush climbed her body. The flush deepened when he slid a pillow under her ass, tilting her upwards. Caught between excitement and embarrassment she stared into his eyes, exposing more than her body to him. One hand spread her wide as he used two fingers of the other inside her.

A gasping moan from her made his glance flick to her face. Her eyes were closed and her head back as she began to thrust against his fingers.

"I'm going to make you scream my name. God, you feel incredible." The wetness around his fingers increased, and he smiled as he kept talking, telling her what he wanted to do to her and how good she felt. He wanted to lick her and taste her excitement but didn't want to ruin his rhythm.

She was panting now as she surged against his fingers.

"When you come for me, I'm going to make love to you again. Warm wetness coated his fingers. She was so wet now he heard his fingers sliding into her body. The sound made his stomach muscles clench and his cock throb. "That's right, Angel, come for me. All night we're going to make love."

The noise she made now was between a hiss and a groan as she squirmed against him, her body tense and straining. His cock stood out hard, eager for her. The heat of her body transmitting to him, heating him from head to toe. She shrieked his name and came in a wet rush. Tight warmth welcomed him, and she cried out again. Her hips bucked against him as she shouted wordlessly, arching hard against him. She wrapped her legs around his waist, surging with him.

"Oh God, Angel." Not able to articulate how amazing she felt, he kept repeating, 'Oh God' and calling her name. It only took him two minutes to climax, and she screamed his name again as his hips bucked uncontrollably.

"Kiss me," she breathed and pulled him down to her sweaty body.

The scent of her glowing skin surrounding him. The rose lotion she wore was his favorite smell. Her fingers curled in his hair, holding him to her, she kissed him as if he were air and she was drowning.

The beeper on his nightstand trilled. A harsh metallic intrusion. He was so caught up in her kiss, for a moment he didn't recognize what it was.

"I could kiss you forever," she murmured as he pulled away to check the number.

Dan slammed his beeper down on the nightstand and snatched up his phone.

"This better be for real."

Angie cuddled against him, clinging to him as he stretched across the bed to reach it. He pressed her against his chest as he held the phone to his ear.

"Get to base. We go in thirty." JT sounded sorry and aggravated.

"God damn hell!"

Angie half groaned half giggled. "Go. Come back to me safe."

Dan made an inarticulate noise, almost a cry, as he pushed her down on the bed and kissed her again. He growled as he pulled away from her warmth. Her gaze followed his every move as he dressed.

The intensity of her stare flushed his skin. It took him two tries to button his shirt. He couldn't tear his eyes away from her. Naked, she leaned against his back as he stamped his feet into his combat boots. The arms around his waist tightened as she kissed his neck.

"Come back to me," she repeated.

With one last long look at Angie curled in the blankets, her mussed hair and rosy lips beyond beguiling, he grabbed the duffle bag from the floor of the closet and closed the door quietly behind himself.

———◦◆◦———

Angie hadn't answered any of his phone calls. When he'd reached the base in Guam yesterday, he'd tried all day, and both the house and her cell had gone straight to voice mail. His email held three letters from her all posted in the first two days after he'd left. The notes made him smile, her personality and love came through loud and clear.

He'd checked the messages and found a voice mail from Angie and didn't know what to make of it. She'd sounded upset but had said nothing other than to call her and left a number he didn't recognize. He hadn't bothered leaving a message, deciding to surprise her instead.

The flight home tested his patience almost beyond endurance. The voice message had gnawed at him all night. *Surely, she wouldn't leave him after their first separation.* Phone breakup wasn't her style at all. Even Parker, who she'd despised, had received a more personal break up.

His thoughts comforted him, but the mystery niggled. For the hundredth time, he reread all his messages from her. The first two were about her job options and a house she wanted him to look at. The last email just said she missed him like crazy. Then the voice mail where she sounded upset. *God, what if she'd decided she couldn't stand to be alone?*

"Relax, Muerte Segura." JT slapped Dan's jittering knee. "Get any more strung out, and we'll have to sedate you."

Dan winced at the reminder of Juan. Juan had been Dan's spotter on their very first mission and called him Muerte Segura until he died. The rest of the team usually called him Morty, but since Juan's death, they called him Muerte Segura occasionally as if to keep Juan's memory alive. The reminder of Juan was both a comfort and a hurt.

Tom chuckled and opened one eye, still leaning his head on the seat back. "He's in a hurry to get his dick wet. Dude lived like a monk for years and suddenly discovered girls—"

A choking gasp cut him off as Dan grabbed him by his shirt and twisted.

JT yanked him off. "Tom, knock the shit off, that's his fucking wife." JT forced himself between the two men, using both hands to push Dan back into his seat.

Tom held up his empty hands. "Sorry, man. My bad. Angie's one fine piece of ass, but I still can't believe you got married."

"Asshole," Dan snapped as he sat back in his seat and turned away.

JT snorted a laugh.

Tom sighed and apologized again.

--------•◆•--------

The duffle bag over Dan's shoulder slid down and caught in the crook of his elbow as he fumbled with his house keys, making the flowers in his hand hit the doorframe. The smell of roses surrounded him, and he smiled. The delicate fragrance reminded him of the scent of his Angel's skin.

The odor when he opened the door slapped him in the face. Blood rushed from his head so hard the room spun.

Something dead was in his apartment.

As he thought that his shocked gaze traveled the disheveled room before him. Prayers flew through his thoughts with lightning speed. *Please, dear Lord, don't let me find her in here. Don't let her have suffered.* A vision of Candice's head and the memory of her hot blood splattering his chest caused his knees to tremble. *Not my Angel, dear God, please not my Angel.* Unheeded, the duffle bag and flowers fell from his hand as he stepped into the room.

The room had been ransacked. Holes gaped in the walls and the furniture had been ripped to shreds. Bright shards of shattered glass glinted amongst the debris on the floor. The scent of decay was pervasive.

Food and broken bottles littered the tiles before the refrigerator, which had been dragged into the center of the small kitchenette and lay on its side with the door open. A cloud of flies rose as he passed but resettled to their feast in moments.

In the hallway before his bedroom door, Tiger's maggot covered, partially desiccated corpse lay in a rotting heap.

A soft cry escaped him, and he prayed again that she'd passed quickly and hadn't suffered, lying in pain and fear, calling for help. A memory of her calling his name as she orgasmed beneath him was so vivid that he could almost hear her, made him shudder. His breath hitched as he pushed the door of his bedroom open.

Deep rents marred the mattress, revealing the stuffing and springs. More maggots crawled over a dried blood stain in the center of his bed. Hot and cold waves traveled him. A fatal amount of blood had soaked his mattress.

His horrified gaze swung to the pile of blood-soaked bedding crumpled in the corner and his breath caught on a sob. Gasping now, he swayed as the room spun again. He stumbled on trembling legs to the corner and lifted a blanket from the pile on the floor. One-by-one, he dropped the blankets on his bed and caught his breath sharply when she wasn't under them. Hope and fear warred with horror as he searched his bedroom.

The nightstand on her side lay in smashed pieces. The contents were strewn across the floor. On his side, the drawers were dumped, but on top, dead center, his cell phone lay connected to a charger, 'call me' written in blood above it.

"Fuck that! I'm going to reach out and touch you."

The low, breathless ferocity of his voice shocked him. He stood still a moment, trying to catch his breath.

The light was on in the bathroom. Flies crawled under the door, their dark bodies casting shadows in

the slice of brightness outlining the doorframe. Breath
held, and tears in his eyes, he opened the door,
knowing a dead body would be on the other side. He
wasn't wrong. His breath escaped in a loud sob, and
he inhaled reflexively, then gagged on the stench.

Not his Angel, was his first thought. Relief made his
head throb as the blood rushed to his head again.
She'd taken one of the bastards with her. His knife lay
on the floor by the man's feet. A knife he'd gotten from
Juan and kept in his nightstand drawer. He wished
he'd left a goddamn Uzi in the drawer.

On closer examination, he recognized the man from
the alleyway in Tijuana. Benny. This man had chased
Candice and shot Carlos and Tony. Horror made his
breath catch as he took in the rotting, split tongue
protruding from the blue lips.

Back in the hallway, he crouched beside Tiger and
examined him. No wounds marred the cat's body, but
the rotted, desiccated state made it hard to determine
the cause of death. Dan's eyes scanned the room. Food
and water were readily available, so the cat hadn't
starved. Someone must have kicked him hard or
wrung his neck. And by the state of decay likely a day
or two after he'd left them. *That mother fucker had his
wife for almost a month.* Now trembling with rage, Dan
stood.

Two minutes later, he was on his way to the airport.
Vincent had her, he was sure of that.

———————•◆•———————

The cell phone in his pocket trilled, not the tone he'd
programmed for Angie. He glanced at the caller ID and
frowned. Tom. An hour and fifty-six minutes remained

before his plane landed. For a moment he debated whether or not to answer.

On the sixth ring, he answered. "What the hell do you want?"

"What the fuck is going on. I stopped by your place. Jesus, man," Tom said.

"Did you go in?" Dan glanced at the man sleeping beside him and lowered his voice.

"Where the fuck are you?" Tom asked.

"Fuck you, asshole, did you go in?"

"Yes, I fucking went in. I thought you fucking killed your wife. You didn't, did you?"

"No." Dan rubbed his forehead, then his eyes with the heel of his hand. "Did you call the police?"

"No, I called you. What the hell is going on?"

"Someone took Angie. Look, it's a long story, and I'm really not in the mood to tell it."

"By someone... you don't know who?"

"Oh, I fucking know, and the asshole is going to pay with his fucking life."

"Is she—"

Fear made Dan's voice harsher than he intended when he said, "Don't know, but he better pray to God she isn't."

"Do you need help?"

A hard laugh escaped Dan before he could stop it.

Tom sighed. "Sorry about earlier. I swear to god I'll never comment about your wife again."

Dan rubbed his eyes again, then stretched and rotated his shoulders, trying to ease the soreness. "I'm on my way to get her back. The man who took her is connected, a real badass. I can't ask—"

Tom sounded angry when he interrupted. "I fucking

offered. Don't be such a dickhead. Tell me what's going on."

"Angie isn't the woman I married. Well, she is, but not the one who married me."

"What the hell are you talking about?"

"Stop interrupting, and I'll explain." Dan told Tom how he'd met Angelina and then found out she was Candice.

"For real? is that true or are you bullshitting me?" Tom said incredulously. "How did you not tell us this? We just spent two weeks sleeping rough talking about fuck-all, and you're keeping this massive fucking secret from us." Tom sighed hard. "Never the fucking mind. What are we going to do now?"

"Vincent has her. He must think Candice told her or gave her whatever the hell Candice stole from him."

"And you don't know what that is?"

"No fucking clue. I'm just assuming she stole something because that's what she did. The woman was a thief in her soul. My Angie is nothing like her." Unshed tears burned Dan's eyes. His Angel would be terrified— if she were even still alive.

"So, what's with the 'call me' bullshit?"

Dan rubbed his eyes hard as he said, "How the fuck do I know? Maybe Vincent thinks I have whatever it is now."

"No, I mean, why didn't he call you? Angie could've called the base and had you tracked down and returned home. Why wait so long with no attempt to contact you?"

"Angie wouldn't know how to reach me or anything. She doesn't even know what I do. I mean, she knows I'm in the service and can be called out anytime, but we never talked about my job. If Vincent told her to call, the only number she had would be the main number for the base to ask for me. They would say, 'sorry he's out of reach of our communications' and asked if it were an emergency. Would Vincent want her to claim it was?

Tom cleared his throat and spoke hesitantly. "Would he keep her alive... I mean, it's been weeks."

Dan was silent a moment. The thought of her dead formed a hard lump in his throat, and he had to clear his throat to speak past it. "Jesus, I hope so. Why take her and then kill her without speaking to me? How urgent could whatever he thinks we have be? It's been months since Candice died."

"And you have no idea what it is?" Tom asked.

Dan squeezed the bridge of his nose with two fingers. "I wish I did. I'd give him anything to get my Angel back." A sob caught in his throat and a flush climbed his cheeks.

Tom was silent a moment. "This is going to be a disaster." Low and thoughtful Tom spoke as if he were considering his options. "Okay, so Vincent can't know you're back yet, but any day now someone is bound to notice this smell and call the police. If that happens, your beeper is going off, and you have to report or be considered AWOL."

"Guess I'm going AWOL, cause I'm not coming back without my wife."

"Yeah, I get that. Fuck," Tom exclaimed and then softer, "fuck," he repeated worriedly. "I'm heading back to your place and trying to hide the smell a few more days, but whatever you're going to do, do it quick. How long until someone notices Angie isn't around?"

"Not sure really. She took a leave of absence from her job and applied to a few by the base, so work won't miss her, but honestly, I don't know if she has friends that will or what they'll do about it." Dan's thoughts flicked to Parker, and he dismissed that as a worry. Parker wouldn't cross the street to help her.

"Where are you headed now?"

Dan hesitated. Tom could call the authorities and have him stopped, but Tom was a teammate who he trusted with his life. "Chicago," he finally said.

"Right. I'll call you back once I get a handle on this here. Check in with me before you do anything rash. Give me time to catch up with you."

"You don't need—"

Fuck that! We're a team. All in, all the time. We'll get her back, man."

Dan placed his phone in his front pocket and leaned his head back on the seat. First, he needed a gun. He closed his eyes and clenched his hands on the seat rest until his knuckles turned white— planning.

The plane landed right on time. Chicago's O'Hare International airport bustled with activity despite the late hour. A brisk wind brought the smell of the city to him as he exited. Streetlights illuminated the outside of the airport to daytime brightness.

Dan hailed a cab and leaned forward over the front seat. "The airline lost my luggage, and the kid next to me puked on me. Is there somewhere close I can buy some cheap clothes tonight?"

"How about a Walmart, Mac?"

Fifteen minutes later, Dan owned a pair of black jeans and a black hoodie. A dark blue ball cap pulled low over his eyes covered his blond hair. A thin nylon jacket, dark red on one side and black on the other, was stuffed into a bag with sunglasses and a switchblade. The cashier had risen her eyebrows but said nothing as she rang up his purchases.

He changed quickly behind the building and went back in to buy zip ties in varying sizes and a roll of duct tape, a stolen camo face mask crammed into his pocket.

Ready to put his plan into action, he headed to Thorndale Avenue Station in Edgewater.

TWENTY-TWO

———◆———

THIS HERE MAKES ME THE KING

IT TOOK Dan five minutes to find his mark at the train station. A young black man, sporting a crewcut with a red bandana tied around his head and a row of black slashes tattooed on his neck, leaned against the wall right outside the station. Diamond earrings caught and reflected the low light. A matching glint came from his right hand. The left was stuffed deep into a pocket of his baggy jeans.

Dan took out a money clip he'd made on the plane. A simple trick he'd learned in training, the money was folded in such a way to appear more of it was present than actually was. At the corner of the building, Dan paused and caught the kids eye, took out the clip and ran a thumb over the edge, fanning the money for a moment before replacing it in his back pocket and sauntering around the corner. A minute later, his quarry appeared, drawn irresistibly to the sight of cash.

"Watcha doin' in my neighborhood, man?"

Dan cocked his head to the side and pursed his lips. "Looking for a deal, but I don't think you got the chops."

"Fucker, I the king here and got me anything if you got the green."

"How about the heat? Can you turn it up? Like real high. I'm talking fifty-cal' with a full delivery."

The kid's eyes narrowed and he took a step closer.

"What's a loser like you need that shit for?" He pulled a pistol from under his waistband and held it pointed sidewise at Dan. "This packs enough punch for any shit you want. Go around asking for specials, and you might be taken for a five-oh."

"Fuck you. You can't do it, say the word, and I'll find me a real man."

The kid grinned at him, revealing a gold front tooth. "Fine, pay the toll and blow."

A hard grin tilted Dan's lips. "You man enough to take it from me?"

"Fucker" —the gun in the kid's hand jabbed at Dan's face— "This here makes me the king and—"

Dan grabbed the gun in the kid's hand and twisted hard as he stepped forward and to the side. A bone broke with an audible crack, and the kid let out a piercing shriek.

Dan hit him in the solar plexus. The kid sucked in a lungful of air and seemed to choke on it, making a gasping wheeze as he tried to exhale. Dan twisted the gun more as he drew the kid's arm down. The gun fell into Dan's palm. He stuck it into his waistband and hit the kid again as he kicked his feet from under him.

The kid fell to his side on the ground, still trying to draw in a breath.

"I was willing to pay, but this will do. Keep quiet, and we can part peaceful like," Dan said as he patted the kid down and removed a knife, which he pocketed.

The cell phone he dropped on the ground and stomped on, turning it into expensive garbage. An extra clip got a grin. The kid's glare ratcheted up a notch as Dan pulled a wad of cash, held by elastic bands, from the kid's front pocket. Dan weighed the money in his hand, then dropped it at the kid's feet, kicked him once, and ran down the alley.

On the main road, he entered the train station, retrieved his bag from a locker, took off the black hoody and ball cap, put on the red jacket and hopped a train to South Haven.

Fifteen minutes later, he hailed a cab outside the South Haven station and had the cabby drop him half a mile from the Palgrino house.

Homes in this neighborhood could more properly be called mansions, each set back from the road surrounded by fences or shrubs and electric gates. Cameras on top of the fences and hidden in the shrubs swiveled as he walked down the street.

Dan needed to get off the street before someone's security stopped him. He tried to project an air of innocence and carry the brown paper bag holding his supplies as if they were groceries.

A half a block past his target home, he found what he was looking for, a house with the lights off. This home was under construction. Scaffolding lined the front of the four-story brick house. Piles of dirt and stacks of pipes half-covered the large circular drive. Two large generators sat by the double doors leading into the house. The gate was open.

A security guard sat on a folding chair under a light hanging from a pole right inside the fence beside the driveway. The hum of the generator powering the light was loud in the quiet night. Feet resting on a milk crate, and magazine open on his lap, the guard paid no attention to Dan.

Dan kept walking. At the first break in traffic, he tossed his bag over the eight-foot wall and followed, landing lightly and crouching against the fence.

A copse of trees to his left offered concealment. He ran to it and crouched in their midst. The ball cap back on his head, he examined the gun he'd stolen.

Dan chuckled to himself. The king had good taste. He'd stolen a brand-new Glock Seventeen, which appeared as if it had never been fired. Two full clips gave him thirty-four shots.

The glare of a flashlight beam made him jerk back. The guard by the gate had risen and was approaching the house. Clearly not expecting trouble, the man held the magazine in one hand, using his flashlight to read it as he walked.

Dan put the black hoody over his jacket, stuffed a handful of zip ties into his pocket, pulled on the camo face mask and trailed the guard as he circled the house and examined every window and door.

At the back door, the guard turned the knob and shook it. Satisfied the door wasn't unlocked, he continued his patrol.

Back at the front of the house, the guard entered the garage and shook the door handle there before heading back to his chair beside the generator and jury-rigged light.

Dan got an idea. This would be a great place to take his captive. The house obviously had no power. He could bypass a battery powered security system easily if it even had one. Now he just needed someone Vincent cared about to trade for Angie.

The guard was paying no attention to anything except his magazine. Dan took the opportunity to scope out the yard. Cameras on the fence faced the street, but none pointed in at the yard. Security lights from the house next door cast shadows over the deep weeds in this yard. Cameras on the house covered the neglected lawn in the backyard, but they were all off.

Dan hopped the wall to the neighbors and a dog barked from inside the house. He grinned and dropped to the ground. A dog meant they either didn't have motion sensors or they would be set at dog height. On his stomach, he crawled along the fence until he reached the wall separating this yard from Vincent's.

This wall had a strand of razor wire on top. Thanks to Google Earth, Dan knew the eight-foot wall surrounded all twelve acres. A glance around disclosed a group of fir trees near the house. He debated another minute and headed to them, crawling on his stomach. Once in the trees, he picked the one closest to the wall and climbed, moving slow. The security lights hindered more than helped see. Background glare ruined his night vision.

Vincent's yard was mostly dark. Small solar lights picked out the covered pool and glimmered by the house. A single bulb hung above the door of the shed behind the pool house, leaving the pool house in a soft circle of light. Beyond the pool house, dark shapes blended into the distance. Dan assumed it was a garden with manicured shrubs or maybe a mini golf course. Beyond that, tall pines formed a barrier between the lawn and neighbor behind and to the left. He needed somewhere to hide where he could watch the house.

A sniper needed patience. In the past, he'd taken days to get into an advantageous position for a shot. Angel had stolen his patience. The urge to bust in and demand answers almost overwhelmed him.

But, to retrieve her, he needed leverage. And leverage would only come if he had something Vincent wanted.

TWENTY-THREE

---◆---

A NAIL IN HER COFFIN

ANGIE woke and kept her eyes closed, not wanting to face another day as a captive. The warm cocoon of her bedding enticed her to close her eyes and return to sleep. Instead, she jumped from the king-size bed, her feet sinking into the plush carpeting, and rushed to the bathroom.

The bathroom was larger than her bedroom at home. Marble and copper finishes shone in the light she flicked on, and she curled her lip at the walk-in shower that doubled as a steam room and a claw foot tub big enough for two...

She forced her thoughts away from the tub and choked back a sob. For the millionth time, she prayed for her husband's safety. He'd come for her, she was sure of that.

Vincent seemed sure of it too. A shudder traveled

her. That man scared her to death. On the surface, he oozed charm and cordiality, but his black eyes revealed his soulless state.

His father was even scarier, making no effort to hide his depravity and evil. Twice now Vincent's father had come to her bedroom in the morning and ordered her to strip. Naked and shaking, she'd stood before him, averting her eyes as he stared and commented to Gino. Unable to perform, he enjoyed looking. So far, he'd kept his touches to her hands when she was clothed at breakfast, but she knew it was just a matter of time until he did something worse.

Another shiver traveled her, and she turned the water temperature up. Hot water caused condensation to drip down the glass shower enclosure. Angie adjusted the temperature, waiting until it was just right before disrobing quickly and showering as fast as she could.

Gino would arrive promptly at eight to lead her to breakfast. A simple man, he followed instructions exactly and would drag her out in any condition he found her, no matter what she said.

The third day she was here, he'd come into the shower and dragged her downstairs naked and dripping wet to the amusement of the guards and her humiliation. She hadn't showered for days after until Vincent had said over breakfast she would shower daily, or Gino would wash her.

The tone of his voice, so calm and even kind, as if he were doing her a great favor, had made nausea roil in her stomach.

So, now, she slept fully dressed and rose at first light to shower. Not allowed a watch or any electronic device, she had to guess at the time. Afraid to guess wrong, she showered and dressed as fast as she could.

Once dressed for the day in Candice's castoffs, she sat by the window and gazed out over the front lawn through the decorative bars. As always, when Gino arrived, he leered at her, waiting for the opportunity to touch her. She was grateful the old man wasn't with him. Gino's emotionless gaze followed when she left the bedroom that was her prison. He never touched her though unless she broke a rule that allowed him to. Angie was very careful not to break the rules.

She never spoke unless spoken to and worked quietly four hours every morning then walked the grounds or sat outside trailed by Gino for two hours every day followed by four more hours of office work than dinner in her room. After dinner, she read files until she fell asleep and woke to repeat the actions the next day.

Gino removed her dinner, counted the utensils, and then locked her in until eight the next morning. At eight, he brought her to breakfast. Sometimes Vincent or his father attended, sometimes she dined alone. She much preferred to dine alone. Breakfast talk when they were there scared her to death. The two men made no effort to hide their criminal activity from her. Every word they spoke in her presence was a nail in her coffin.

No matter what Dan did to appease them, whether he gave Vincent the ring or not, Vincent would kill them. At least she hoped he'd kill both and not keep her. Angie knew too much. Maybe even more than they thought she knew. The financial aspects of the Palgrino family were complex. Multiple businesses, some legal, most not, but all intertwined produced a convoluted finical situation easily manipulated.

Vincent had her reorganizing and examining all aspects of his business empire. So far, she'd found twelve instances of fraud and six of mismanagement and she'd barely gotten started. The mismanagement was easily fixed. The thieves in his midst had already stolen millions from him, double billing, fictitious employees, and theft were major issues in Vincent's companies.

Angie prayed her access to the IRS mainframe would be rescinded, and at the same time, she hoped it wouldn't be. Without the access, she wouldn't have to endure Gino leaning over her, breathing on her neck, but they might decide they didn't need her, although she didn't use the computer for a lot of her work.

The stack of files and ledgers to still go through was daunting. While she worked on the computer in Vincent's office, Gino ogled her, occasionally rubbing his groin.

The day after she'd arrived, Vincent had her brought into the dining room. Still wearing Dan's t-shirt she'd fallen asleep in the night before, now blood splattered and vomit stained, Gino had pushed her to her knees at Vincent's feet.

Her gaze on the Italian loafer on the floor in front of her she'd trembled, afraid every breath would be her last.

Vincent had finished reading his paper as if she didn't exist. The crisp pages turning as he shifted in his seat were the only sound beside her panting, terrified breaths. One leg crossed over the other, he'd

laid the paper aside and snapped his fingers. Like a
trained dog, Gino pulled her upright by her collar,
revealing the skimpy pink panties she wore.

Cold, black eyes examined her. He snapped his
fingers again. Gino grunted and ran his free hand
under her shirt, cupping her breast and squeezing.

Certain she'd be raped any second, she'd struggled
in Gino's grasp, trying to speak.

"Please..."

Her begging was cut off by Gino's grip tightening on
her neck until the room darkened. Vincent snapped
again, and Gino released her. She'd fallen in a heap at
his feet, crying.

"Do one thing I don't like and Gino gets you,"
Vincent had said in a kind voice. "And you're exactly
his type. Stay useful, and you stay alive. Follow the
rules and don't cause me any problems and he won't
touch you."

Vincent had snapped the paper, straightening it as
he'd gestured with one be-ringed hand for Gino to take
her from the room. "Clean up and make yourself
useful." The last words had been spoken as if he
already thought she was useless.

Gino had placed her hand against the bulge in his
pants until Vincent cleared his throat. "She's a guest
until she breaks a rule. "

Gino had nodded meekly and had dropped her
hand, straightened, and gesturing her to proceed him
from the room.

"Be quiet. The boss doesn't like noise," he'd said as
he yanked her upstairs.

Every step they took filled her with dread. At the
doorway of the bedroom, he'd released her and

gestured her to enter.

"I'll be back in four hours. The rules are simple. Don't speak unless spoken too. Stay quiet and do what you're told." He'd hesitated in the door as she backed away on legs that trembled so badly she'd thought she'd fall. "I really want to hear you scream again," he'd said as if he were a child asking for an ice-cream.

Terrified by his childish, enthusiastic tone she'd peed herself as she sank to the floor with her arms over her head.

The vision of him wringing Tiger's neck and laughing as she screamed haunted her. The night he'd taken her, she'd dropped the knife and cowered as he wanted. For a moment, she wished he'd killed her then. The fear she lived with now was making her crazy.

Every moment of every day she expected him to come to her room and make her scream as he raped her before killing her. The smallest sounds made her jump. Food made her sick. A hazy of fear and worry clouded her mind, making her thoughts jumble and race.

One minute she wished for Dan and the next hoped he never came. Seeing Gino kill him would destroy her. Every day she was tempted to run when she was let outside. Not to get away, but because Gino would shoot her and this torture would end. The fear that he'd only wound her kept her from running. Wounded, she'd be his to do what he liked with. The screams from next door when he entertained left her no illusions about how he liked his sex.

Eyes closed, forcing herself to take deep even breaths, she tried to put everything except the work before her out of her mind. Gino stood over her shoulder and stared at her screen, reading every word she typed. He'd almost broken her hand three days ago when she typed the word Helpme. Before she could finish and type the T at the end of the man's name, he'd grabbed her and pulled her away.

Vincent had arrived an hour later. An hour spent in Gino's embrace with his excited breathing warming her neck and his hard cock pressing against her as his hands wandered her back, cupping her ass through her pants. She'd been afraid to try to fight him off. Instead, she'd stood stiffly in his arms, not willing to give him an excuse to run his hands over her.

Vincent had laughed and slapped his shoulder.

"Release her. No rules have been broken. A reward is in order though. I'll see to it tonight. Good job, Gino." Vincent had turned to her with a gracious smile that contrasted with his cold eyes. "Continue with your work, Mrs. Barstow. In the future, when typing anything that could be misconstrued point out the entire word to Gino first to avoid these instances. If you're under the mistaken impression that rescue is coming disabuse yourself of that notion. I've already met with and dealt with your husband."

The tears that had sprang to her eyes and trailed down her cheeks had made him smile. Angie had nodded, trying to hide her fear and sorrow with downcast eyes.

That night, huddled in her bed, Angie had cried and decided she would run the next day, forcing Gino to shoot her. By morning she wondered if Vincent had lied. By the time Gino had arrived, she'd convinced herself it was possible. It seemed more likely to her that if Vincent had Dan, he'd hurt her in front of her husband to make him talk.

The day after that, Vincent made sure Angie saw Gino's treat being escorted from the house. The young woman had limped. Long blond hair tied back revealed her swollen, bruised face and bite marks on her neck, obvious signs of abuse. Gino left Angie's side and kissed the woman, a blissful expression on his face. The young woman kissed him back. Vincent handed her an envelope, and the girl left without a backward glance.

Angie shuddered and pushed the memory away. At one, she followed Gino docilely. Vincent didn't attend lunch that afternoon. An elderly maid, who never spoke to Angie, served lunch in a beautifully appointed dining room. Solid silver serving dishes graced the antique sideboard. A crystal goblet held her juice, and perfectly prepared salmon and rice was served on china so thin light passed through it.

The food sat uneasily in her stomach but refusing to eat wasn't an option. The most she managed was requesting small portions. At one-thirty, she headed back to her room with relief. In her bathroom, she vomited, unable to keep the food down, trying to do so quietly.

Vincent had examined her with displeasure at their last shared meal, his gaze lingering on her thin wrists. She'd eaten everything put before her and managed to make it to her room before being ill.

No matter how hard she tried, she couldn't keep the food down. Sometimes supper was manageable if she ate small enough bites and took her time alone in her room but usually fear made her nauseous.

With grim determination, she focused on her work. For two hours, she organized her files mentally before asking to use the computer and inputting the information.

If she could get ten minutes alone on this computer, she could bring Vincent's operations down. A horde of agents would descend on this house. A bitter smile quirked her lips. Three minutes is all it would take to send messages for help to everyone she knew. But Gino never left her alone— not for a second. The perfect guard, he never talked to her or slacked in his observation. She'd hoped he'd get bored and tried typing for four hours straight, but he hadn't.

The day she arrived, Vincent had brought her outside and had Gino give a shooting exhibition. The man could shoot a quarter out of the air. Matter-of-factly Vincent had told her Gino had orders to shoot her if he even thought she might run. Angie made sure to walk slowly whenever she was outside.

At two, the silent maid handed her a light-blue jacket and offered her a matching wool hat. Angie accepted both, jammed the hat on her head and pulled the collar of the jacket to her chin, hiding her hair completely. If she were allowed, she'd cover her hair every day, or hack it off. The way Gino stared at it freaked her out.

Armed with a forty-five now, he escorted her outside, ten steps behind her. Whenever she left the house, he carried a gun. Not for her protection, but to stop her if she tried to run.

Angie headed to the open space surrounded by eight-foot walls and razor wire. Gino would let her walk alone here, standing back by the pool and staring. The sixty-foot separation was enough to let her lower her shoulders.

Huddled in the jacket, the collar pulled up to her cheeks, she paced the length of the wall, gazing at her feet.

TWENTY-FOUR

---◆---

THE SOBBING STUTTER NEARLY BROKE HIS HEART

DAN lay on his stomach under thick shrubs beneath an artful planting of trees beside the front gate to Vincent's home. It had taken him three hours to reach this position, and he knew he was rushing dangerously, but every moment he took to find her was another she spent in danger and afraid. He couldn't bear to think about how she was being treated.

So far, he'd counted nine armed men. At nine this morning, Vincent had left in a black town car with four other armed men. An older woman, dressed as a maid, had come outside thirty minutes ago and spoken to the armed man by the side door.

Another armed man sat by the driveway gate in a small gate house. The book in the man's hand didn't stop him from scanning the yard every time he turned a page.

Dan eased backward into the bushes. The back of the house offered a better opportunity for entry.

The watch on Dan's wrist mocked him. Three hours to get into the new position was two hours and fifty minutes too long. Dan bit his lip. Vincent might have no one he cared about. With no leverage, he had no way to force him to give Angie back. *I'll have to kidnap Vincent himself,* he decided.

He began inching his way to the back of the house. Each minute it took grated on his nerves until he wanted to scream in frustration. By mid-afternoon, he crouched behind a row of boxwoods beside the pool house and contemplated how to get into the house.

As he observed the bottom floor windows, the back door opened and a man exited with a gun drawn but held at his side. A moment later a woman left the house, and Dan's heart leapt.

His hostage.

The maid followed the woman and offered her gloves. Dressed in a heavy blue jacket with a matching hat pulled low, Dan was surprised when the woman shook her head and turned away. The maid retreated into the house.

Faced away from Dan, he couldn't see her face, but her gait was hesitant. Dan thought she was sick. The suspicion of illness was confirmed when she sank to her knees and leaned her forehead against a birch tree. The guard began to go to her until she pulled herself up and continued walking.

"Fuck," Dan whispered as his troubled gaze followed the woman until she left his sight around the corner of the house.

The guard shifted his position, never taking his

eyes off her. Obviously, she was a valued member of the household, but it would be beyond cruel to take a sick woman.

Lips tight, Dan turned back toward the house. *Vincent would have to do.* He'd take the fucker and force him to tell him by whatever means necessary.

Exactly one hour later the man retrieved the woman and they entered the house. Dan followed, boldly leaving the concealing shrubs and striding to the door they'd used. Finding the door unlocked, he entered and ran up the stairs. The first few rooms he poked his head into were empty.

His plan now was to find a good spot to wait in hiding, grab Vincent, and go, killing whoever stood in his way. The lesson learned from Juan's death troubled him. He realized he was rushing dangerously but couldn't force himself to slow down.

The first occupied room he examined appeared to be a man's room. One of the live-in help by the quality of the clothing in the small closet. A bigger bedroom across from the man's room held woman's clothing in a walk-in-closet. Dan's heart leaped, maybe another woman lived here. But his hopes were dashed when a search revealed the cold, impersonal nature of the space. A quick check of the adjoining bathroom revealed no makeup or other items usually found around women, but half used shampoo and conditioner bottles sat in the shower. Another employee room, he assumed. Disgusted, he decided to try the third floor.

He was still in the bathroom when the maid entered and placed a meal on a small table beside a window. As soon as the woman left the room, Dan headed to the door but changed his mind at the sound of approaching footsteps. Clothes brushed his face as he ducked into the closet, leaving the door open a crack.

His breath caught in a sharp hiss as Angie entered the room. The armed man followed and glanced around the room. Bright blue eyes examined Angie a moment. Neither spoke. Arms hugging herself tightly, Angie closed her eyes and turned, putting her back to the man in the doorway. The man reached out as if would touch her hair. Pale and drawn, with her lips pressed tightly together, she stood statue still beside the bed.

"Angelina?" the man spoke her name in a soft, childlike voice.

Angie began to tremble and sank to her knees, her arms wrapped tightly around her body. A curtain of hair swung forward obscuring her face. The man gazing at her smiled and stepped forward with a hand outstretched.

In the closet, Dan tensed. Whatever was happening terrified her. Every line of her body showed terror. Every move Angie made thrilled the man in the doorway. The bulge in the man's pants was clear evidence of his excited arousal. One thick-fingered hand dropped to his belt as he groaned.

Angie whimpered as she hugged herself tighter.

"The rules," she said in a quavering voice choked with tears.

The man halted and turned for the door, speaking over his shoulder. "It's going to be so good."

A piteous whine quickly stifled was his answer. The gun clutched in Dan's sweaty palm tracked the man to the doorway. If he'd taken one step closer to his terrified wife, Dan would've shot him. Only the memory of what rash action had cost Juan stopped him from the shooting the man as he left the room.

Angie reached to the bedside and pulled herself up. As the door closed, she raced to the bathroom and vomited.

Dan tensed, prepared to spring, but the man left, locking the door behind him. His heart pounding and tears in his eyes, Dan eased the door open. Angie ran water in the sink, rinsing her face and mouth.

"Ang?" Choked with emotion, his whisper was barely audible.

The trembling hands over her face dropped, and she swayed before spinning and falling, landing on her hands and knees. A terrified expression on her face, she glanced at the door as she stood again.

Dan grabbed her forearms, shocked by how thin she'd gotten. The pale, drawn look of her cheeks and the skeletal thinness of her once graceful fingers filled him with furious anger.

A low moaning noise came from her as she fell into his arms, then pushed him toward her closet.

"Get out of sight," she whispered in a voice that cracked with disuse.

Inside the closet again with Angie held to his chest, his face buried in her hair, he took deep breaths. The familiar scent of her was both calming and exciting, the dichotomy dizzying.

"Oh, thank God," he murmured and kissed her temple.

She pulled his face to hers and kissed him, a wild, desperate kiss. A soft sob escaped her when he pulled back. Both her hands fisted in his hair, and she pulled him back for another kiss. Warm breath fanning his cheek, she drew back and rested her lips lightly on his, taking deep breaths.

For a minute they stayed that way, unspeaking, breathing each other's air. The curve of her skull under his palm felt warm and alive, the soft weight of her hair in his grasp comforting.

No longer soft, her new angular hardness disturbed him. The muscles under his hands felt tense and fragile.

"Let's get out of here," he finally said as her breath calmed.

"You're okay. You're okay. God, I thought they'd killed you." Again, her breath caught in a sob, and she burrowed her face into his chest, ran her hands under his shirt, and began to cry choked, gasping sobs that shook her entire body.

"Angel, we need to go." Dan tried to take a step toward the door. She gripped his waist with both hands, trying to speak as she held him in place.

The words she forced out between sobs stuttered. "N—N— no, h— h— he won't come i— in. Pleeease, I— I—"

She gave up trying to speak and let herself cry, collapsing into his chest, sliding down his body until she huddled on the floor at his feet, grasping his legs.

Dan's gaze darted to the door. Every moment they spent in here was dangerous, but he couldn't drag her away in hysterics either. He squatted beside her, and she tried to get closer, throwing her arms around his neck now, her tears trickling down his cheek.

"Okay, Angel, take a second and catch your breath. We're okay, and you're safe now." Dan kept his gaze on the door as he whispered endearments in her ear. He stroked her back with one hand while supporting her weight with the other.

The crying slowed, and she sat back. His shirt in a vice-like grip in one fist, she rubbed her face with the hem of her shirt. "Gi—Gino won't come in t—till eight tomorrow. Not f—for crying anyway. A— as long as we're quiet, we h— have time to plan."

Lips compressed, Dan nodded, sat on the floor, and pulled her into his lap. His heart beat hard, adrenaline making his hands shake. The ragged breathing caressing his neck infuriating him. Questions caught in his throat. Now wasn't a good time to ask or learn the answers. Not while he was so on edge and she needed him calm and professional. Later, when she was safely away, he'd ask about her time here. Maybe. He didn't know if he could bear the answers.

It took ten minutes for her breathing to calm. Ten minutes of building anger and worry over her condition. Her voice was thick with tears and blurry when she spoke.

"Thank God, you didn't c— call him. Vincent has no intention of letting either of us l— live, no matter what he says. We'll never be safe from h— him."

"Vincent won't live out the night. Don't worry about him." Furious over her continuing terror, Dan bit his lip on the things he wanted to say. Telling her what he had planned for Vincent for scaring her this badly wouldn't help her.

When her breathing had slowed, and the sobbing stopped, she used her shirt to wipe her face. She pulled back to frame his face with her hands and kissed him before speaking.

"No, you can't kill him." She pressed her lips to his when he started to speak. Lips millimeters from his, she continued, "Not because murder is wrong, that wouldn't be murder but self-defense, but because his men would hunt us down.

"Then I'll kill all of them."

A half laugh greeted that.

"Don't. I couldn't bear it if anything happened to you and these guys are trained killers. Gino is a real marksman, not just a thug who waves a gun around."

"Angel, I can—"

She interrupted him. "Besides, if you have the ring Candice stole, we don't need to kill him. Don Pedro will do it for us."

"What ring?"

"The ring Candice stole from his safe deposit box. Do you have it?"

"Sorry, Angel, I don't know what you're talking about."

She bit her lip and sat back. Again, she wiped her face with her shirt before taking it off and blowing her nose in it. Dan's gaze strayed from the door to his wife's naked breasts. A fading bruise on right breast caused his eyes to narrow. He cleared his throat and forced his gaze back to the door. She didn't notice, too busy rubbing her eyes.

"Damn, I'd hoped you had it. Don Pedro would've killed him for sure." She twisted her bottom lip. "Maybe he still would if we tell him, but without proof, I don't know..."

Dan glanced at her, then back at the door. "What's so important about this ring?"

She leaned against him again, running her hands

under his shirt as she kissed his neck. He stifled a groan and kissed her. Before he knew it, he had her under him on the closet floor, kissing her passionately, his palm cupping her left breast, rubbing the nipple with his thumb. Both her hands fumbled with his belt as she made a soft mewing sound that went right to his groin.

"Oh, God, we can't," he murmured as she slid the zipper of his jeans down.

"Please? I promise Gino won't come in. I missed you so much." While she spoke, she ran her fingers over the hard length of him, her thumb caressing the head of his penis.

"Mmm." The throaty sound of desire she made when he kissed her breast made his cock throb in her hand, and she repeated the noise.

"You sure no one will come in?" Dan's gaze went to the half-open closet door as his hands roamed her body. A need beyond desire possessed him.

"They never have before."

Dan pulled his hoody off, removing the coat and the t-shirt under it while she shimmied out of her pants and underwear. The bruise on her hip caused his throat to tighten, and he scanned her body with dread, afraid to see what other bruises she might have. Fading bruises on her arms and neck were clear handprints.

To his relief, her thighs and legs were clear of bruising. She was trying to push his pants down as he sucked her nipple into his mouth and gave up when they got stuck on his knees and pushed him over instead. A deep groan escaped her as she slid onto him.

He gasped and bucked hard, seating himself as deeply as he could. The familiar feel of her body reassured him. Tense muscles relaxed. The tight look of her shoulders eased as her body softened.

Eyes closed and head tipped back, her inner muscles clenched him tight. Her hands braced on his shoulders as she leaned forward, a curtain of silky blond hair brushing his chest. Eyes intent on his, she began moving slowly.

"More than anything on Earth, I love you. Without you, life would have no meaning for me." She began moving faster. "Let's get married, really married."

"Yes," he groaned in a harsh whisper.

A breath of a giggle escaped her. "Is that for marriage or this?" she moved faster, circling her hips and rocking between thrusts.

"Both. Don't stop." Dan's voice cracked.

"Give me babies, Dan. Let's be a family.

"Oh God, yes." Love and lust, fear and relief, mingled. He wanted to possess her, to own her soul as she owned his.

She stopped whispering and began panting.

A shudder rippled her skin as she came, and he missed the sound of her yelling out for him, resenting the need to be quiet. Her muscles clenched him tightly as her body relaxed. The strength of her orgasm triggered his. Deep and hot he spurted, wishing he could make her pregnant right now.

"As soon as we're home, you're getting that birth control implant out," he said.

"Ahh," She fell forward onto his chest while her hips jerked against him.

"Angel. We can have any kind of wedding you want,

but I'm already your husband. No one and nothing can change that. Can we go now?"

Her long hair covered his cheek as she shook her head. "I need to feel you near me a few minutes."

The delicate caress of her breath on his neck soothed him and he relaxed, holding her tenderly now. Her hands roamed his body. Fingers threaded through his hair, she kissed him again, resting her lips against his, breathing his air. No one had ever needed him so much, been so desperate for his touch. Overwhelmed with gratitude that she was here, safe in his arms, he closed his eyes and prayed, thanking God and promising to be a good husband.

"Angel, I want you to get on the first flight to California. Tom will meet you and stay with you."

She sat and stared down at him, biting her bottom lip. "I'll do whatever you say, but maybe we can get his own men to take him out for us? Vincent had me checking his books, and I found lots of issues. Some of his top men are stealing from him. If we tell them he knows..."

A scared, nervous expression on her face, she twisted her fingers together, staring at them. "Joe Conti might do it when he finds out Carmin Nunzio killed Candice on Vincent's orders."

Dan sat and pulled her to his side, running his fingers through her hair. "Can we prove it?"

"Legally? No, but I probably have enough detail to convince Joe."

"No, we aren't doing that. You're going nowhere near these men. I'll handle it and make sure no one is left who wants to harm you."

"Or you!"

"Or me," he agreed and kissed her brow. The trembling of her hands and escalating breathing alarmed him.

"We should call the police and let them handle everything. We c— can go into witness protection and—"

"Angel, we aren't living our lives staring over our shoulders. Our children will be safe from the moment of their conception."

She bit her lip and looked miserable.

"You never did tell me what Vincent wants from us."

Before she spoke, she took a few deep breaths and wiped her eyes hard. "Candice stole a ring from his safe deposit box. Vincent's father killed Don Pedro's father thirty years ago and kept the ring as a souvenir. Candice planned to blackmail him, but he scared her, and she decided to sell it to Don Pedro instead. Two birds with one stone. Don Pedro would kill the Palgrino family and Candice not only gets to keep the money and jewels she stole worry free but gets whatever Don Pedro pays. Vincent thinks he'd pay a lot. For years, a three-million-dollar reward has gone unclaimed for information on Don Pedro's father. No one knows what happened to him, he just vanished."

"Do you know?"

Angie began to shake, and tears fell across her cheeks. "Vincent is going to kill me and make me vanish too."

Instantly sorry he'd asked, he tightened his grasp on her. "Never! I swear it."

"Dan, there's so many of them and just us. We need to disappear." The tears escalated again until she was taking hitching breaths and clinging to him.

"Okay, here's what we're going to do. First, we get you out of here. Then I'll go talk to Don Pedro—"

"I'm going wi— with you."

"No, you're staying with Tom and maybe sending out warnings to Vincent's crooked business associates if they promise to leave you alone. Hell, you can send the information to Joe too. When the police find the dead body in our apartment, tell the truth, just not all of it. We don't know who took you only that they wanted something Candice stole."

"So where was I?"

"Make up an anonymous room and masked men. I'll say I called the number and they traded you for money."

"Bu— but, Vincent might ge— get, away and he'll come and ta— take, me again and give m— me to Gino."

Her whisper became shrill. The sobbing stutter nearly broke his heart. A wave of furious anger made his hands clench, inadvertently pulling her hair.

"That he won't. Don Pedro gets one week to handle it, or I do. Calm down, Angel. Gino won't ever touch you again. Trust me, okay?" He kissed her temple and ran his hands over her soft skin until she stopped crying and breathed easier. The effort to hide his distress and offer her comfort when he wanted to go kill this Gino guy right now made his palms sweat.

"Get dressed, Angel. Put on the darkest clothes you have and shoes you can run in. Dress warm." Dan glanced around the closet. "Whose clothes are these?"

"Candice's. When she left him, Vincent destroyed his room searching for the ring but saved some of her clothes. The guards are still searching his house, but he doesn't think she left it here. They've been finding things taped all over though."

"Taped all over?"

"Yeah, seems one of her favorite hiding places is taping things to the bottoms of lights and drawers and stuff." Angie grabbed a thin, silk dress and wrapped it around her shoulders. "I can never get warm here. How will we get out of here?"

"I can pick this lock." Dan grabbed an armful of clothing and surrounded her, rubbing her arms and back.

"The door is alarmed. If that alarm goes off, Gino will come kill us."

"Just Gino?"

"Believe me. He's enough." A shudder shook her. "More men will probably show for an alarm though. Four men are usually with Vincent, and there are two with his father plus the nurse. And hell, for all I know the housekeeper is a killer too. And that's just the ones I'm sure of. There could be a hundred more I don't know about." She began to shake and breath as if she couldn't catch her breath.

"Can you call Gino in here?"

"I'm n— not a—allowed t— to spea— k to h— him. If I d— do, he c— calls Vin— Vincent."

Sobbing again, her wide, terrified eyes stared at him.

"But he'll come in at eight?"

She nodded and gathered her hair, wrapping it into a bun while staring at the door, an expression of deep fear on her face. Then she seemed to remember Dan was there and hugged him, shaking in his arms, letting her hair fall around her shoulders.

Dan lowered his head and rested his cheek on her hair. "I swear to God; he won't touch you ever again."

Her body relaxed against him as her breathing slowed. Dan wiped her face with a dress he grabbed from the floor. She cried for a minute before grabbing the dress from him and blowing her nose again. Still sounding choked up and terrified the stutter was gone when she spoke.

"He never did anything to me. Not really. I mean he just holds me, but he wants too and..." she trailed off as another shudder traveled over her. Lips pressed over his heart she took deep breaths.

"And you can't call him for any reason?"

"I'm allowed to ask to use the bathroom or a computer while I'm working with him. That's it."

"Okay, once you're dressed, bang on the door and tell him your toilet is broken and overflowing."

"Can't we call for help?"

Angel, if we call for help and he turns up dead, we're going to be suspects. Yes, the police can get us out of here, but I guarantee they don't arrest Vincent or at least not for long and then he'll be free to hunt us down."

TWENTY-FIVE

———— ◆ ————

IF SHIT GOES DOWN, IT'S GOING TO BE MASSIVE

IN THE end, they did it her way. Dan called Tom.

"Morty, I swear to fucking God, if you don't answer the goddamned phone again—"

"I have her, and she's fine." Dan kissed Angie's temple. "I'm calling the police to get us out of here."

"Where's here?"

"Vincent's goddamned house."

"JT sent Lee and Keith to New York in case this was Joe and not Vincent. He's seriously pissed. You have some serious explaining to do. How come we never heard about any of this shit?" Before Dan could answer, Tom continued, "JT, Squirrel, Ronny, and I are outside."

"Outside Vincent's house?"

"No outside Disney Land. Yes, his fucking house. We can take this place like it *was* Disney Land," Tom said eagerly.

"Angie is worried I'll go to jail. The dead body in our apartment and all will lead the police to here."

"So, what are we doing?"

"Call Commander Darmin and report. I'll call the police here, but if it goes to shit, be prepared to back me up."

"Easier to just take these fuckers out," Tom grumbled.

Dan bit back a snort of laughter. "Got to go. We only have until eight a.m."

"What happens at eight?"

"A man named Gino opens the door, and I kill him."

"Right. Morty, we hear gun shots— we're coming in."

"Thanks, man."

"De nada."

Dan hung up and called 911.

"911, what's your emergency?"

Dan almost laughed.

"This is Petty Officer First-Class Daniel Barstow. My wife has been kidnapped and is being detained at the Palgrino estate, the home of Vincent Palgrino. I've broken into the house and am locked in a bedroom with her. Second-floor fourth room on the front right. Any minute now armed men will try to remove us from this room. I'm armed. Do *not* send a lone patrolman. My wife, Angelina, has been held here for weeks and the information she possesses is dangerous for Mr. Palgrino. Dangerous enough he'd kill a police officer if he thought he could get away with it."

"Excuse me, sir, did you say kidnapped?" the operator said incredulously.

232

Dan didn't bother repeating himself, he hung up and called the FBI. He repeated his story to the woman who answered and was put on hold. Four minutes later a gruff voice came on the line.

"Mr. Barstow, this is Special Agent in Charge Stanley Wisniewski. You say you're being held against your will, but you have a phone?"

"No, my wife was being held. I broke in. I have a phone and a gun. If I open the door where she's being held, an alarm will sound bringing armed men to her location with orders to kill her."

"And you know this how?"

"She told me."

"Sir, I hesitate to say this, but–"

"No, my wife didn't come here willingly. There's a dead body in my apartment that proves it. My wife, Angelina Morrow Barstow, is an agent of the IRS. While kept here, she's been forced to go over Mr. Vincent Palgrino's books and has found many, many, crimes. Serious crimes, including tax fraud. Every moment she's here, the danger she's in worsens. To get her out safely, without a firefight, requires backup. At eight a.m., when the door opens to bring her from the room, that fight will start. Am I clear?"

"Sir, am I hearing you correctly? At eight this morning you plan on shooting up Mr. Palgrino's home?"

"Damn straight. You have that long to get us out peacefully. If you tell him I'm here, he'll try to kill Angelina. I'm sure of that. So that firefight might start earlier."

Stanley covered the mouthpiece of his phone with one hand and snapped his fingers. When his colleagues glanced at him, he gestured for silence and pressed speaker phone. "Okay, remain calm and stay on the line. You say there's a dead man in your apartment?"

Dan gave him his address, his military ID number, and his commander's number. On hold once more, he turned to Angie and shrugged. Dressed now in black slacks, a black sweater, and a dark-purple silk shirt, she sat on the floor beside him, leaning hard into his side, biting a thumbnail. A fine tremor rippled over her in continuous waves. The pulse in her neck beat visibly fast. Dan was worried he was literally scaring her to death.

"Don't worry, Angel. Whether they come or not you'll get out safe. Half my squad is outside. Nothing will happen to either of us."

She nodded, but her eyes stayed huge, and she began biting her other thumbnail.

Stan turned to his partner George who was already calling the base in California. "Find out everything you can about this guy." Stan beckoned to the woman at the next desk. "Deidra, call precinct thirty-three and tell them to wait for us. They are *not* to engage until we arrive. If this is for real, this is huge. I'm excited on so many levels I don't know where to start."

Deidra snickered as she began dialing. "Tax fraud, kidnapping, murder, if this is for real, we got him for sure this time. But don't get your hopes up, it's probably some schmuck whose wife is diddling the big guy and fed her husband a line of bull."

George placed a hand over the receiver, his skeptical gaze darting between them. "Don't count your chickens." He removed it and turned slightly away, speaking into the phone. "Yes, I'm sure of that ID and..." George began nodding and jotting notes. "Have him call me back immediately at this number. "Stan, ask Mr. Barstow if his teammates are with him."

Stan rose an eyebrow and unmuted his phone. "Mr. Barstow, are any of your teammates with you?"

"Chief Warrant Officer Jefferson Thomas Ford, Petty Officer Second-Class Thomas Moran, Petty Officer Third-Class Enrique Sanquine, and Petty Officer Third-Class Ronald Mitland are outside the house."

"Yes, thank you. Hold, please.

"Four of his friends—"

George snorted. "Not his friends, his team. Well, I'm sure they're his friends too, but that's irrelevant. That's SEAL Team Nine. If shit goes down, it's going to be massive."

Stan hesitated and cleared his throat. Eyes bright, he leaned forward, one hand clenched around his phone. "So, we think he isn't a lone nut, and this is for real?"

George laughed and gave him a thumbs-up as he answered his ringing phone. Stan turned bright eyes to Deidra.

She gave him two thumbs-up as she spoke on the phone.

Two hours later, Dan and Angie had spoken to the FBI at length and were prepared for them to enter. Dan covered Angie with a towel in the claw foot tub in the bathroom and kissed her white cheek.

"Ten more minutes and we walk out the front door," he said in as a reassuring a voice as he could.

"Please, stay with me." Her fist locked onto his black hoody. "Gino is a very dangerous man. You're a sailor, a soldier, but he's a killer. Please, Dan. I couldn't bear it if anything happened to you."

"Nothing's going to happen to me. I've had training. Stay here."

He pried her fingers from his shirt and kissed her cold lips. For sure his wife wasn't cut out for this. The flutter of the pulse in her throat worried him. Rapid and shallow she panted, and a cold sweat dotted her brow.

"I'll be fine," he repeated as he closed the door.

With no lock or movable furniture in the room, the closed door was the best he could do. He expected Gino to come through the door as soon as the police made their presence known.

He took a light from the dresser and plugged it in by the window, closed his eyes, and flicked it on and off twice. In the dark, he stood to the left of the window and peered out. A quick flash of light on the edge of the lawn by a planting of decorative birch trees reassured him.

SWAT was already over the wall. The light in the bathroom went out, and an alarm sounded.

The power to the house had been cut. The light came on a moment later as emergency generators kicked in. Sirens shrilled. Emergency vehicles pulled up to the gate. Flashing lights strobed, illuminating the room in streaks of red and blue.

Dan ignored it, his attention on the door. Crouched on one knee in the corner of the room, to the left of the doorway, he waited for Gino to appear. He didn't have long to wait. The same man who'd escorted Angie into the room earlier, wearing boxer shorts and a gun belt, opened the door. A garrote dangled from his hand.

Gina looked excited, and his boxers revealed he was aroused.

"Drop the weapon and get on the floor right now," Dan yelled.

Gino dropped his hand to his gun belt as he turned. Dan didn't hesitate, he took two quick shots to the center of mass and one to Gino's head as he started to fall. The body crashed to the ground.

Angie screamed, the sound muffled by the walls.

"I'm fine!" Dan hollered.

A loud crash in the distance announced police entry. Men yelled downstairs. Someone ran by the doorway to Angie's room but didn't stop. Booted feet approached at a run.

"Police, Mr. Barstow," someone yelled as another man yelled, "Clear" and doors up and down the hall banged open.

Dan shifted his stance and crouched beside the dresser, gun extended in two hands. "Hold your badge out as you come through this door," he said.

A man's arm, encased in black armor and black gloves, held out a police badge.

"Come in slowly and keep your hands where I can see them."

The police officer entered the room with one hand up, the other holding out his badge, which dangled from a black chain around his neck. A bulletproof vest with the word police stenciled in white across the front and back reassured Dan.

The officer wore typical SWAT gear, armor, radio, and gun. Dan put the gun he carried on the ground in front of his feet and straightened.

The officer keyed his radio on with his chin and

ordered backup to his location.

"My wife is in the bathroom. Can I go to her?"

"Yes." The officer gestured with one hand, the other now resting on the gun at his waist.

"Angie, it's me, Angel. The police are here, and everything's okay," Dan said as he opened the door.

The officer followed him to the door. Angie threw herself into his arms, her entire body shaking.

"Calm down before you give yourself a heart attack," Dan said.

Her voice quavered when she said, "I heard shots. Did he shoot at you?"

"No, I shot at him. Stay here and let the officers handle everything." Dan turned to the officer. We need a medic here."

"No, I'm okay."

"Angel, sweetie, you're not okay. Take deep breaths and try to relax." Dan turned to the officer. Can we get a blanket?"

A female officer appeared a minute later with a blanket from the bed. Other officers conferred in low voices in the bedroom. Dan wrapped his wife in the blanket and rubbed her arms. Two paramedics entered the bathroom and took Angie's vitals.

The medic said, "Mrs. Barstow, your pulse is a bit high and your temperature a bit low. Can I give you an IV for the shock? Fluids will help.

"I'm fine," Angie repeated as Dan said, "Yes, help her."

He turned to his wife. "Let them help you. I'll feel better once I know you're okay."

Angie nodded and licked her lips. The blanket slipped to her waist as she held an arm out for the paramedic. Dan pulled the blanket up and leaned against her back, hoping his body heat would help her.

"Ang, any minute more officers will be here, and they're going to bring us to the station. My Commander, Darmin, will be getting us a lawyer. Be patient, and this will get straightened out. Don't worry when they separate us. They have to do that. Answer honestly and you'll be okay."

Angie nodded jerkily after everything he said. They'd discussed this already, and she knew not to mention the ring or what it signified.

The paramedic glanced at Dan and shook his head. "Keep the IV bag over her head. I recommend she let us take her to a hospital."

Dan nodded as Angie said, "No," and clutched Dan's arm.

Dan said, "If you need medical help, we'll get you help. My friends will stay with you and guard you. Gino is dead."

A violent tremor shook her.

"He came to kill me?"

"Yes, but he didn't. Not even close. And you never have to worry about him again."

"Gino was only one of his men." She stopped speaking and pressed her lips together.

An angry flush heated Dan's cheeks as he lowered his head and kissed her temple. Eyes closed, he hugged her, not knowing how to offer comfort. "Remember, don't leave the police station or hospital with anyone except me or one of my teammates. Tom will take you to his place and give you my old room. Don't go anywhere without them."

"Dan... Are you sure about that? They could get

killed. Vincent has a bunch of dangerous men at his disposal."

The police officer bit back a sharp bark of laughter. Angie turned to him in consternation.

"Sorry, Mrs. Barstow, but if his team can't keep you safe, no one can," the officer said.

Angie rubbed her temple with her free hand. "They're soldiers, but Vincent's men are trained killers. Not the same thing at all."

The officer pursed his lips, narrowed his eyes, and glanced at Dan. As he opened his mouth, Dan shook his head. The officer hesitated.

"Angel, we never talked about what I actually do for the Navy. Believe me when I say they trained me well in more than just how to handle a boat. Later, when you're calmer, and we have time, I'll tell you all about it. Take my word for it that my friends can keep you safe."

The officer laughed, hiding it behind a closed fist and a fake cough.

Dan sighed and rolled his eyes. "We just got married and haven't known each other that long."

"Mmm hmm." The officer made a non-committal noise. Before he could say anything, two more officers entered followed by four men in suits. One of the men held his hand out to Dan.

"I'm Special Agent in Charge Stan Wisniewski; we spoke on the phone. This must be your wife?"

Angie held out her hand, and they shook. "Angelina Barstow."

"Mrs. Barstow, my partner has logged on the computer with the passwords you provided and asked me to tell you thank you. We've been after the Palgrino family for years. The information you've supplied has made a real difference."

The paramedic took Angie's vitals again while Stan spoke and nodded reassuringly to Dan. "Your wife's doing much better. Heart rate and temperature are right where they should be. Keep her warm, give her plenty of fluids, and avoid stress." The paramedic turned to Angie. "Mrs. Barstow, I recommend you speak with a doctor as soon as you can. We can't force you to go the hospital, but you need medical attention."

Dan snorted.

Stan winced and turned to the paramedic. "Is it safe to question her?"

"Yes. If she gets upset, stop and let her rest. Keep it short. Mrs. Barstow, if you experience shortness of breath or tingling or pain in your arms and legs call at once for an ambulance."

"Is she okay?" Dan ran a hand over his wife's hair, lifting the heavy mass and spreading it out over the blanket. With gentle fingers, he separated the strands, combing it with his hands until it slipped smoothly through his fingers.

"Yep, in a day or so she'll be good as new. Finish this IV and keep her warm and hydrated. I don't expect her to have any problems, but if they do crop up, don't hesitate to call."

Stan waited until the paramedic removed the empty IV bag, and then escorted them from the house. Dan glanced back as he got into the back of a police cruiser.

Red and blue lights lit the night. Yellow light illuminated the windows on all three stories.

Uniformed and suited men and women rushed around. Outside the gate, news vans shone spotlights onto the house as reporters interviewed police officers or stood alone making broad gestures at the house.

This was going to be a nightmare, Dan thought as they drove away. One he hoped they could get out of without their names being mentioned. Dan's position on a SEAL team should get him some anonymity. His work required discretion. To protect against mob reprisal, the police should keep Angelina's name out of the paper. He hoped.

TWENTY-SIX

---◆---

SPIRALING OUT OF CONTROL

BLACK coffee sat untasted beside Dan's elbow, growing cold. His tired gaze took in the crowd around the table with exasperation. Five FBI agents, four police officers, and two lawyers talked over each other, arguing their opinions. Worry over his wife's condition kept him on edge.

The gathered people showed no signs of breaking up for the evening even though they'd been in this room for thirteen hours now.

Finally, Dan cleared his throat and stood. "My lawyer has my contact information. I've told you everything I know." He held up a hand as an officer began to speak. "Yes, I realize breaking and entering charges can be brought, but as far as I'm aware none have been. Meanwhile, my wife is in the hospital, and I need to go to her."

Dan's lawyer stood and followed him to the hallway.

"Mr. Barstow, I don't anticipate charges being brought, but that doesn't mean there won't be if they feel it's in their best interest."

Dan grunted.

"The number of dead bodies piling up around you is daunting. While I'm aware you only killed one of them, still... try not to have any more, shall we?"

Dan grunted again as he ran a hand through his hair. "No promises. Vincent comes looking for war, he'll find it."

"Witness protection—"

"No!" Dan cut him off sharply. "Angie and I did nothing wrong, and we aren't running. I'll keep my wife safe."

"If you change your mind, the FBI will see to it."

Dan offered his hand, and the two men shook.

"Keep me informed on the state of the case, please," Dan asked.

"I will, and you keep me informed of your whereabouts."

Dan winced as he zipped the red nylon jacket. "I'm off to the hospital."

His lawyer nodded and returned to the conference room.

A taxi took Dan to the hospital. Outside the elevator, Squirrel leaned against the wall, an unopened magazine in his hand. "Lee and Keith are headed back from New York and will meet us at home. JT is in the room with her." He handed Dan the magazine. Dan nodded his thanks as he slipped the pistol from between the pages into his pocket.

Squirrel tapped two fingers on his left thigh,

indicating he was packing. He used the same two fingers to salute Dan.

Dan handed him the magazine and headed to Angie's room. Outside the door, a police officer sat in a metal chair. He rose when Dan approached.

"Mr. Barstow," he said as he nodded a greeting. "You're, ahh, friend is with her. The agents have left but wish to speak to her again when she's up to it."

Dan's lips tightened. All he'd been told was his wife had been brought to the hospital because of a severe panic attack. Finding her admitted worried him. "As soon as she's up to it," Dan spoke over his shoulder as he brushed past the officer.

The hospital room was dim and quiet, low hums and beeps from the monitors the only sound.

"Dan," JT whispered as he moved from the corner where he'd been standing. "Angie is sedated. Keep your voice down."

"What happened?" Dan leaned over his wife and smoothed her hair.

"A panic attack so bad she lost consciousness, so the police called for an ambulance. The doctors want to get her blood pressure down before they discharge her. She's severely dehydrated and a bit undernourished, but nothing a few days of food and rest won't cure."

JT laid a hand on Dan's arm. "The panic, well, they can give her valium or something, but send her to a therapist."

Tears filled Dan's eyes as he leaned down to kiss her brow. "What set it off?" Shoulders tight, Dan turned to face JT, dreading his answer.

"An officer showed her a picture of your apartment."

Dan sagged in relief. "Benny." Angry now, he paced the small room. "And Tiger. Goddamn, the bastards. She has nothing they want."

"Charlene offered to come sit with her." JT stretched and cracked his knuckles. "My wife had a hard time with what we do at first too. She might be able to help her."

"Yeah, thanks." Dan paused by the windows and peeked behind the drawn blinds. Streetlights illuminated the parking lot, which appeared deserted. "Tell Char I said thank you. I'm getting Angie back on base as soon as I can though, so tell her to wait there."

"Dan, Angie is really upset she killed a man. Self-defense or not, she doesn't have the coping skills for that. Get her help. The base doctors know how to deal with post-traumatic stress. Don't let her put it off."

"I'll take care of her."

JT began to speak then hesitated. Worry lined his voice when he finally said, "Some things we can't help the people we love deal with. As much as we might like too, sometimes love isn't enough. Get her professional help, Dan."

"Did she speak of her time there?" Dan turned away and faced the closed windows.

"Yes. Nothing truly terrible happened, but the fear of it happening really injured her. For one of us, being confined for a few weeks like that would've been a walk in the park. Your Angie is very sensitive. Just talking about thinking you were dead had her crying. Don't think because nothing physical happened she wasn't hurt or that the injuries aren't serious."

"Oh, thank God." Dan sagged, resting his palms on the windowsill. "Yeah, I know she was harmed

246

regardless of whether it was physical or not. The marks on her body, I thought...

"No. she claims no one except Gino touched her. He got grabby a few times, but nothing more than that. She's very afraid of him."

"He's dead." Dan's voice dripped with savage satisfaction.

"His body is dead." JT sighed hard. "The world has become a scary place for your wife. A very scary place. Most people never realize it, or if they do, it happens slowly. Forced to face it all once is overwhelming her."

"I'll get her help." Dan gave JT a quick hug. "Thanks for looking out for us."

"Always. All in, all the time." JT slapped Dan on the shoulder. "Don't leave her until Tom gets here."

"Thanks."

———————•◆•———————

JT nodded and left the room, closing the door quietly behind himself. He passed Squirrel without acknowledging him.

Behind his sunglasses, Squirrel narrowed-eyed gaze followed a man in a business suit. Work roughened hands, and an athletic stride clashed with the man's clothing. Magazine tucked under his arm, Squirrel stood and stretched. He turned the ball cap on his head backward and followed, picking up his gait as the man ahead of him paused the slightest amount before Angie's hospital room door.

Squirrel took out his cell and snapped a crappy picture of the back of the man's head.

The man ahead took out his cell and paused to make a call. Still walking fast, Squirrel passed his target while pretending to fumble with headphones. Careful to keep a swagger in his step, he entered the next open doorway.

"Sorry I'm late. I was waiting for the old man to leave," Squirrel said loudly in a fake whiny voice. "Oh, for crap's sake, the asshole gave me the wrong room number. Sorry, man."

Without giving the surprised patient in the bed time to react, Squirrel exited the room and took a picture of his targets face as he hit his number three speed dial. One foot balanced behind him on the wall beside the door, Squirrel slouched backward as his target passed. Still speaking on his cell, the man in the suit glanced at Squirrel, his gaze traveling over the long, messy brown hair and unruly beard with no sign of alarm or recognition.

JT answered on the first ring.

"Exiting the fourth floor now. Elevator six, picture inc." Squirrel hung up and hit the send button for the picture he'd taken.

He removed the fake beard as he slipped his cell phone into his pocket. Beard and phone tucked away, Squirrel scraped back his long hair with both hands and secured it in a tight ponytail. More than once not sporting the same regulation crew cut the other members of his team wore had come in handy.

Beside Angie's door once again, Squirrel opened the magazine and sat in the nurse's cubicle with his sneakered feet propped up on a desk.

JT called him five minutes later. "I'm on his ass. He's headed uptown. He our guy?"

"Well, I can't prove it in court, but if I were a betting man. I caught the word 'guard' as I passed him and the word 'tonight' as he passed me."

"Right. Let's see where this fucker goes. Send the pic to the team. He shows up again, he's treated as a hostile.

"Copy that." Squirrel opened his email app and in less than a minute had forwarded the picture to all sixteen of his platoon members. The seven men in his squad texted him back within moments. Darmin would forward the picture to the other one hundred and twelve men on his team. If this man showed his faced on the base in California, his team would notice.

The nurse at the desk offered to bring him a coffee. Squirrel declined but thanked her. A heavyset man carrying a black coat hurried down the hall. Again, Squirrel followed. The man entered a room two doors down from Angie. Squirrel eavesdropped outside the door until he was certain the man and the patient were acquainted.

Back at the nurse's desk, he removed his sunglasses, placing them on top of his head and sat behind the desk with a stack of folders before him.

Eyes alert to anyone approaching, he followed everyone who walked past Angie's room, making sure they all had a legitimate reason to be on this floor.

———————— • ◆ • ————————

DAN read the text from Squirrel as he kicked off his boots and laid down beside his wife. Careful of the IV in her hand, he eased his arm under Angie's shoulder, settling her against his chest. Within minutes he was asleep. Her slight weight across his chest was deeply comforting.

He woke when Tom entered. Tom nodded a

greeting, dropped Dan's duffle bag by the bed, and settled himself in the corner of the room. Dan closed his eyes and went back to sleep, sure of his safety with his team present. Tom had guarded his back countless times in much more dangerous situations.

The nurse woke him when she entered to check on Angie. Pale-gray morning light crept through the window blinds, revealing the lines of strain on Angie's face even in her sleep. With practiced professionalism and a kind smile, the nurse performed her checks as Angie began to stir. Dan kissed his wife's forehead and sat in a chair beside her.

The nurse entered information into the clipboard at the foot of the bed. "Your wife is doing very well. While I can't say for sure, I believe the doctor will discharge her this morning." She smiled at Dan and nodded at Tom who remained in the corner of the room.

Angie rubbed her eyes, then sat abruptly, relaxing when she spotted Dan.

"How you doing, Angel?" Dan leaned forward and smoothed her hair.

"Fine. Embarrassed. Can we go?" Lips clenched tight in her pale, pinched face Angie sat, letting her feet dangle from the side of the bed.

Dan lifted the blanket and wrapped her. She hadn't seemed to realize Tom was in the room. The hospital gown she wore gaped in the back, giving Tom a great view of her bruised hip and side. "As soon as the doctor okays it."

"I'm okay now." Tears filled her eyes. Heels of her hands pressed against her face muffled her voice when she spoke. "The pictures shocked me. I killed a man, Dan. How did this happen to me? I was a good person.

Now I'm surrounded by violent men who want to hurt me. I don't even recognize myself."

Dan sat beside her and put an arm around her, pulling her close.

"His blood covered me. The man I killed. The sound he made... those sensations will haunt me. And I got Tiger killed for nothing." A shudder traveled her. Two gasping breaths later, she pushed away and straightened. "I need a shower."

"Ang, nothing those men did was your fault. Nothing! Tiger's death wasn't you. Benny deserved what he got. You have a right to defend yourself."

Without acknowledging him, she hopped off the bed and pulled the pole holding the IV behind her to the bathroom.

Dan turned to Tom. "Damn..."

Tom winced and leaned his head against the wall.

"Thanks for bringing my kit," Dan said as he grabbed his duffle bag.

He rummaged through it and removed a clean pair of jeans, and a white t-shirt followed by a faded blue sweatshirt. The roll of duct tape he carried fell out and bounced across the floor. Dan picked it up and hefted it in his hand, a thoughtful expression on his face.

He dumped the entire contents of the bag onto the hospital bed and sorted through it. Clean clothes he put aside, separate from his clean uniforms. Dirty clothes he added to the mesh bag. A pair of sweatpants and matching gray sweatshirt he set apart before repacking the entire bag. His clothes would swim on Angie, but she might prefer them to Candice's castoffs.

"Ronny can pick something up for her to wear."

Tom nodded toward the sweats in Dan's hand. "Shall I call him?"

"Yeah, thanks." Dan told Tom Angie's sizes for clothes and shoes. "Find us a ride back as soon as you can. If we can fly back, that would be great. I want her on base ASAP."

Tom took his phone from his pocket. "I'll do what I can, but she has no ID or anything, so a plane might be out." He stepped outside the door to make his calls. Dan knocked on the bathroom door.

"Ang, want a pair of my sweats?"

"Yes, but give me a minute, please."

Forehead resting against the door, Dan sighed. The closed door between them was a physical pain. She was shutting him out, and he didn't know how to help her or gap the distance. He stood outside the door for ten minutes. When she finally cracked the door and asked for the clothes, his voice broke when he spoke.

"Ang, please don't shut me out. Let me help you. I'm so sorry about all of this."

Without speaking, she took the clothes he offered and closed the door again.

"I'm okay with you needing time alone or space or whatever, but you're pushing me away. Please..." He gasped in relief as she opened the door. The relief died at the sight of her face.

"I love you so much, Dan, but I'm going to get you killed. Too much violence surrounds me. These are really bad people willing to do anything to get what they want." Fists clenched in the black hoody he still wore, the sleeves of his sweatshirt covered her hands, she turned her face to his. "We need to disappear."

"No, I can protect you."

Tears filled her eyes as she dropped her hands. "Then I need to leave you, so you'll be safe. Bad men will come. We both know it. I'll get you killed." Both hands rose to cover her face as she spun away. Her hair had soaked the back of her sweatshirt.

Dan grabbed her by the shoulder and tried to pull her hands away from her face. Icy cold, her hands were clenched tight, so tight he'd hurt her if he forced them down. He released them, pulling her into his embrace, rubbing his hands over her damp back.

She began to cry deep wrenching sobs. Dan scooped her up into his arms and carried her to the bed where he sat and held her.

"We'll work it out and stay together. It's forever for us, Angel."

Face buried in his neck now, the crying slowed. "You'll come with me?"

"I promise, we'll be together."

Dan missed her softness. Tense and hunched, she clung to him. Every muscle in her body felt tight. *Her blood pressure was probably through the roof again,* he thought ruefully as he stroked her wet hair.

The nurse returned a few minutes later followed by a doctor.

"I'm Doctor Schwartz."

A portly older man wearing a blue suit covered by a doctor's white coat offered his hand to Dan. Dan shook the man's hand as Angie stood and clenched her hands together.

Doctor Schwartz turned to Angie. "How are you feeling this morning, Mrs. Barstow?"

"Fine, thank you. Can I be released?"

"Yes, Nurse Ingram has your discharge papers and

a prescription for Valium. I want you to see your doctor when you return home. High blood pressure is nothing to take lightly. Eat, drink, and rest. Avoid stress." The doctor sighed. "I realize you have a lot going on, and stress can't be avoided completely, which is why I'm giving you a prescription for the Valium. Take one if things start spiraling out of control. You can take up to three tablets in a twenty-four-hour period. The pills act fast and should help keep you calm. I'm prescribing enough for two weeks, which should be enough time for you to meet with your primary care physician and find a psychiatrist."

Soft and bitter, Angie said, "You think I'm crazy?"

"Not at all. I think the stress of the situation you find yourself in is affecting your health. The calmer you are, the better, so take a pill when anxiety begins to overwhelm you. In a few days, once your body recovers more with food, water, and rest, I'm hoping the pills won't be needed. But don't put off the doctor's visit even if you feel better."

"I'll see that she goes," Dan said, ignoring the annoyed glance from Angie.

The doctor performed a quick exam and signed the discharge papers. "If you have any problems, call me."

"If the police let me, I'm taking her home today," Dan said.

"Then call your GP or take her to the emergency room. The pills will help, but they aren't a magic cure. Mrs. Barstow, if you have trouble catching your breath or feel faint or dizzy call for help. Don't forget to buy the blood pressure monitor and check your pressure at least once a day, preferably at the same time every day, and make a note of it to show your doctor. There are medications that can lower blood pressure, but I don't think they'll be necessary once you're more hydrated and if we can get your stress under control."

"Thanks, doc." Dan offered his hand as Angie murmured, "Thank you."

Tom entered the room as the doctor exited. The nurse gave Angie a pen to sign her release papers and went over the doctor's instructions with her again. Angie assured her she had no questions.

Dan took the papers. "Where can I get this prescription filled?"

The nurse smiled. "There's a pharmacy downstairs. I'll call, and it'll be waiting for you."

Tom turned to the nurse. "Our friend will be here within an hour with clothes for her. Can we wait here?"

"Sure. The cafeteria is open. Shall I bring you some breakfast?"

"You've been very kind," Angie said before Tom could answer. "We can get it but thank you."

The nurse nodded, patted her hand, and left.

"She shouldn't be anywhere near me," Angie said bitterly. "None of you should be. When Vincent's men come, you're all going to be hurt."

Tom snorted. "Vincent is busy, too busy to worry about you. The charges you pressed are the least of his worries. The IRS has him neck deep in agents. Even the police officers are subdued. Nobody wants to draw their attention."

Angie rubbed her eyes with both hands.

"I'll get us breakfast." Tom paused at the door and gave Dan a hard glance. "Don't worry about us, Ang. We can handle whatever Vincent throws our way."

TWENTY-SEVEN

WHAT'S REAL

THE CLOSER they got to Charlene's house, the tenser Angie became. By the time they arrived, tears sparkled in her lashes.

"No. I'm not going in there."

The shrillness of her voice startled Dan.

"Char doesn't mind—"

"No! Look at this place! I have no business bringing my evil here!"

Dan glanced out the window at the quiet, middle-class neighborhood. Children played in driveways while soccer moms jogged on the sidewalks, calling greetings to each other and the children. Peaceful citizens going about their daily lives.

Tom stopped the car and JT exited, headed into the house as Angie pushed Dan's reaching hands away, her voice growing louder and shriller as she demanded they go somewhere else.

Charlene ran from the house, dragging a blanket, and pushed Dan aside as he tried to reason with his wife.

"Tom, take us to your house," Charlene said as she turned to Squirrel. "Get in front. I'm riding in back with Angie." Sure she would be obeyed, she slid into the backseat and placed the blanket around Angie's shoulders. "Now, what's the problem, Ang?"

"Char, I appreciate you wanting to help me, but no one can help. These men who want to kill me are dangerous. And sick. God, what kind of person brings this trouble to their friends? You and JT have been so good to me, and I know the guys think because their soldiers they can handle this, but that macho bullshit will get them killed."

Angie took a deep trembling breath. "They're sailors, electronic specialists, not professional hitmen. I'm going to get them killed. I'm going to get you all killed." Tears trailed down her cheeks as she leaned forward, hiding her face in her hands, muffling her voice. "I should've made Gino shoot me. At least then you'd all be safe. This ends when I die, and I'm such a coward—"

"Stop! Never say that again! Never!" Furious, Dan shook her shoulder. He fumbled in his pocket for the pill bottle and tried to hand her a pill. "Here, take this. You'll feel better."

Angie slapped the pill from his hand. "Pills won't change the truth."

"Take the goddamned pill," Dan shouted.

"I'm going to get you killed!" Angie shouted back. "How can I live with that, Dan? I can't! I'd rather die now before you die trying to protect me from these men."

Charlene laid a hand on Angie's shoulder. "Both of you calm down. Dan can handle these men. JT can handle these men. He'll eat them for breakfast. Hell, they'll just be a light snack."

"Char," Dan said warningly.

"No, enough. She's worried as hell. Tell her the truth."

"Char!" Dan glared at Charlene.

"The truth?" Angie said, sounding confused.

"I mean it, Char." Dan's voice shook with a mix of anger and worry.

"Dan, you're a fool." Charlene took Angie's hands. "Dan is a Navy SEAL," she said the last words loudly over Dan's heated, "Stop!"

"What?" Angie drew her hands away and turned to Dan, a puzzled expression on her face.

"Charlene, I swear to God...." Dan trailed off as his wife's expression changed to a mix of terrified anger. "This is why we didn't tell her, Char. The idea scares her."

"You're a Navy SEAL? Like you see on TV?" Still sounding disbelieving, Angie turned to Squirrel. "You too?"

"Yes, ma'am. SEAL team nine at your service."

"Dan?" She smothered deep gasping breaths in her clenched fists as she hunched away from him.

"I'm not a bad person, Angel. Damn it, Charlene! This is no time to add to her stress." Dan handed Angie another pill. "Please take this. The pulse in your neck is pounding, and I'm worried about your blood pressure.

She snatched the pill and swallowed it dry. "How could you lie to me like that? Damn it, Dan, I was so worried and all this time... Jesus, everything is a lie." Angie turned to Charlene. "What's real? Are you really a teacher and my friend?" Angie yanked her arm away from Dan when he laid his hand on it.

"I'm exactly who I said I was," Charlene said calmly as she put an arm around Angie. "Nothing we told you is untrue."

Angie snorted and bit back a sob. "Patrols? Perimeter checks? What were they really doing? And don't give me any classified bullshit!"

"Patrols and perimeter checks," Charlene said as she squeezed her shoulder as Angie began to pull away. "Underwater. The mines in the water need to be checked and sometimes replaced or removed. Boats that come too close need to be searched. Ronny needed training and its good practice for them."

"Practice?"

"Sure, in the real world they don't have a map of the minefield. The bad guys don't announce their presence."

"The bad guys," Angie repeated faintly.

"For them, Gitmo is a vacation."

"A vacation," Angie parroted in a dull voice.

Dan wanted to plead with her and beg, but the presence of his teammates inhibited him. She still sounded angry to him. Angry and disbelieving.

"I'm not a violent, bad person, Angel. I'm a trained professional. I never lied, I just didn't tell everything..." Dan's hands clenched as she glared at him, the glare melting to an expression of lost betrayal.

She slumped back in the seat as if exhausted.

"Okay, it was a lie," he said. "But I was worried you'd hate me. Three years, Angel. I swear I'll quit."

Angie said nothing. No one in the car spoke for the remainder of the ride.

At Tom's apartment, he opened the door and let them in.

Dull and lifeless, Angie turned to Tom. "Is there somewhere I can take a nap?"

"Dan's room is available. Help yourself." Tom gestured to the hallway. "Second door on the right."

Angie thanked him in a subdued voice and left, trailing the blanket behind her.

"Damn it, Charlene," Dan said in a furious whisper when the door closed behind Angie. "If she leaves me... Goddamn it. I wanted time to ease her into it."

"Don't blame me for this mess you made," Charlene snapped as she sat at the kitchen island. "Let her worry about real things, not imaginary ones. Trust works both ways, Dan. You want her to trust you can look out for yourself and her, but you don't trust her to love you enough to stay with you if she knows who you really are."

"Violent men terrify her. You saw her. She thinks that's me."

Charlene pointed to the stool beside her. "Sit. Leave her alone to process this information. Accept that you made a mistake and she'll be angry. Don't try to manipulate her. Let her be angry."

"You had no right," Dan insisted as he sat.

"Yes, I did. She's my friend. Angie doesn't exist in a vacuum where only you get to interact with her. The worry she has of bringing violence into our lives is real and justified. My life, Dan. My child, husband, and home. I have every right to tell her truths and who better? Do you think it was easy for me to love a man who does such a dangerous job?"

Charlene's voice rose. "Do you think I don't care when he leaves on missions and I don't know where he is or when he'll be back only that he's called out to do dangerous work? You men love your work and assume because we don't complain we're okay with it. Nothing could be further from the truth. I'm counting the days until he retires. Every time he leaves, I pray and cry and curse. Every time! But JT isn't a tame sort of person, and I knew that when I married him. I accept who he is even though who he is causes me both pain and joy. What you've done to Angie is unfair. Hiding your true nature from her, not letting her make an informed decision, tricking her into loving you... well, I'm surprised at you."

"Fuck!" Dan leapt to his feet and spun away. "I know it's wrong, but I want her so much.

"Only in truth will you really have her," Charlene said.

"I fucking know that, but I thought I could ease her into the truth. Not shock her with it. And I'm willing to quit to be whatever she needs. Jesus, Char, now I won't get the chance to make her love me."

"I already love you, stupid."

Dan whirled. Angie stood by the bedroom door, a furious glower on her face.

"I'm angry on so many levels I don't know where to start," she said.

Dan nodded, his mouth dry.

"How could you not tell me you can handle those type of men—"

261

"I did. I told you I had training."

"Jesus, Dan. I thought you meant basic training. Not specialized training in killing people.

Dan winced.

"That's not what we do," Tom said unexpectedly. "Well, we do kill people, but it's not like we're assassins. We're sent in to rescue hostages or infiltrate for information. Sometimes we're backup for other teams who are attacking. But we aren't murderers. We don't go with the intention of killing people. Yes, sometimes we attack, but only after negotiations have failed and no other options remain. The training we received is the best in the world, and we're very good at our jobs. This," —Tom gestured around the apartment with one hand —"Protecting an innocent bystander from armed men is exactly what we do."

Angie's shoulders relaxed as she took a deep breath.

"I could still get you killed," she said.

Tom put an arm around her shoulder and led her into the kitchen while speaking, "Not you. Don't take on other people's crimes. If I get killed overseas, it isn't Darmin's fault, or JT's, or Uncle Sam's, it's the bad guys, or my own if I made a mistake. Dan has a lot of misplaced guilt over Juan. I miss Juan. He was a good man. But it was Juan's mistake that got him killed, not Dan's or mine or anyone else's."

"This is my mistake," Angie said in a voice that shook.

"No. Vincent caused this. He made so many mistakes the mind boggles. I admit you're over your head here, but we can help you. Listen to us and follow directions and all of us can get out of this alive.

If someone gets killed, it still won't be your fault."

"I hear what you're saying, Tom, and appreciate it, but I still feel guilty. Vincent's men are thugs, but they can shoot. I saw Gino shoot a quarter out of the air."

Tom shrugged. "I've seen Dan shoot a man five hundred yards away with a handgun while running. Believe me, that's much harder to do. We don't call him *Muerte Segura* for nothing. In my entire life I've never seen a better shot, and I've seen some of the best-trained men in the world shoot."

"Can you teach me?"

"Yes. Any of us could teach you to use a gun safely, but there's a lot more to it than that. Knowing when to pull a gun and being willing to use it are just as important."

Angie sagged, and tears sprang to her eyes. "Yeah, probably pointless to show me. I don't think I could kill someone again."

Squirrel slapped his hand on the counter. "The fucker had it coming. Don't be stupid. If it's a bad guy or you, use the gun. Are you going to let someone come in here and kill Charlene? Or would you grab the gun we keep in the drawer here and shoot them?"

"Shoot them, but I'd hate doing it," Angie said.

"None of us like it, but we do what needs to be done. And you owe it the people who love you to protect yourself in the same way you'd someone else."

Blond hair swung and covered her face as Angie nodded. Her shoulders began to shake. Dan realized she was crying.

"Aww hell, sorry, Ang. I didn't mean to upset you." Squirrel reached over and patted her head, his large hand awkward in its gentleness.

Dan gathered her close and led her to his old room. When the door shut behind them, she collapsed in a heap, crying as if her heart were breaking. Dan sat beside her, saying nothing, rubbing her back.

When the tears slowed, she kissed him, then stood on shaky legs. "I need a bathroom."

"First door on the right."

Dan lay on the bed with his arms behind his head. She returned to him a few minutes later with red, swollen eyes and cheeks damp from washing. He sat when she entered. Unmoving inside the doorway she twisted her hands together.

"I love you," she whispered.

Dan's heart thudded hard. She'd said it sadly.

"I love you too. More than anything. I'm sorry I didn't tell you sooner."

"Me too." Eyes on the ground at her feet, she put her hands in her pockets.

The jeans Squirrel had bought her were a few sizes too big and bagged around her narrow hips. None of the clothes except the sneakers fit her. The weight she'd lost over the last two weeks would take time to replace. She was no longer delicate, but fragile. The hesitant way she moved and spoke, the tense shoulders and curled posture, all spoke of deep fear and unhappiness.

"Do you forgive me?" Dan rose and held out his hand. He almost fell to his knees when she nodded and took his hand.

"I hate this. I want it over with. Last month our life was so perfect." Cold hands ran under his t-shirt along his spine. Her hands heated him as if they were red hot.

"Have patience and soon it'll be back to normal," he said.

"No. Our lives will never be normal. We'll always be looking over our shoulder."

Dan drew back and kissed her lips. The brief contact fanning the flames her touch ignited. "True. But not because of Vincent. My job brings threats with it. Even if I quit today, those threats will remain forever. For the rest of my life, I'll need to take safety precautions. Charlene is right, and it was unfair of me to drag you into it."

Angie leaned on him, stroking his back. For minutes, they stood together before she spoke.

"I heard everything Charlene said. She's a really strong woman. I want what she has— the normalcy of her life. If she can do it, we can too. No more secrets. Total trust. If you say you can keep us safe, I'll believe you."

"I swear it on Juan Barstow's head."

Angie laughed, then sighed as she pulled him down for a kiss. The kiss escalated to caressing hands and gasping breaths. But to his dismay, Angie pulled away from him.

TWENTY-EIGHT

HYSTERICAL

ANG?"

Dan laid a light hand on her hunched shoulder. The overhead light revealed an expression of deep sadness when she turned.

"I feel like a fake as if nothing is real. Maybe it's the pills, but it feels like you're someone else. When the doctor called me Mrs. Barstow, it felt phony, as if I were lying." A sob caught in her throat. "I don't need Tiger to tell me I'm fooling myself here, Dan. Because I want you so much, I'm taking shortcuts and doing things I know are wrong."

"No." Dan's soft denial went unheeded as she turned away.

"Your friends are helping me because they think I'm your wife, and I'm not."

"Yes. You are. I have a paper that says so."

His joke was met with a bitter snort.

"Paper." Low and harsh her voice cracked. "How pathetic am I? Well, I won't do it. Go tell them who I really am. Not the woman you married, but the substitute you got stuck with when the first choice died."

Deeply alarmed now, Dan rose and blocked the door, afraid she'd bolt. "Ang, they know the entire story. I think the pills are affecting you badly. Can you come lay down with me, please? Let's take a nap and talk when we wake. You're my first choice, my only choice, never doubt it." To his relief, she took his hand and let him lead her to the bed.

"Sleep, Angel. When you wake, we can decide where we're getting married." For the first time, he noticed the ring he'd given her was gone. Afraid to upset her, he didn't ask where it went. He settled her on his bed and covered her with Charlene's blanket.

"When Gino comes for me, will you kill him?"

Dan frowned and felt her forehead. "Gino is already dead."

A laugh greeted that. "Dead, sure, but so many wait to take his place." She turned her face to the wall and pulled the blanket up to her chin. "Vincent's cronies and guards all laughed when he dragged me downstairs naked. No one lifted a hand to stop him. I thought he was going to rape me right there on the floor in front of them and they would take turns until I died. I was covered in Benny's blood— maybe I deserved it."

"Stop, Ang. Try not to think about it. The pills are hurting you. Rest please."

Dan sat beside her and stroked her hair.

"No." She slapped his hand away furiously and drew the cover over her head. "Don't touch my hair like him. God, I hate my hair." In a sudden flurry of blankets, she leaped from the bed. "I can cut it off now. Then he won't want me so much." The unconscious grunting noise she made as she struggled with his duffle bag scared him.

"Tomorrow, if you want a haircut, Charlene will take you. Whatever you want, okay?" He spoke in as soothing and calm a voice as he could manage as he took the bag from her.

"That man was so twisted up inside with hate for me."

At first, Dan didn't know who she was speaking about. As she repeated the foul words she'd been called in a dull monotone, his worry escalated. He was almost relieved when scared bewilderment replaced the lifeless quality of her voice.

"Benny blamed me for Vincent cutting his tongue. And I had nothing to do with him or his lies." Tears trickled unheeded down her cheeks from glassy horrified eyes.

Caught up in the memories, her unseeing gaze fixed on the distance. "The sound he made when he spoke wasn't human. His split tongue made him sound like a snake. A screaming, crazy snake. If Gino hadn't pulled him off, he would've killed me right then. I got to your knife, but I honestly don't remember stabbing him. Just his crazy yelling, calling me a lying bitch and the threats..." Head turned away, she covered her face with her hands as if trying to block the memory.

"Nobody's ever hated me before, and I killed him. I remember the blood. So much blood and Gino..."

She trailed off into silence.

Crouched before her with his hands on her knees, Dan waited for her to speak. When it became clear she wasn't going to finish, Dan cleared his throat.

"Nothing you tell me will change how I feel for you. Nothing you did or was done to you will change how much I love you. We'll get you help. Someone you can talk with, but you can tell me anything without fear."

Bright teary eyes stared into his. Filled with disgust and fear, her voice quaked when she spoke.

"Gino masturbated on me, and I was too afraid to try to fight him or run. He told me all the things he was going to do to me when Vincent was through with me with the biggest knife I've ever seen in his hand." Her voice cracked, and she covered her face again. "All the different places he was going to use his knife. Every word excited him more. It was as if he thought the idea of him cutting me excited me too. In his head, terror and excitement are the same."

A red flushed climbed her cheeks. "He kneeled on my arms, his cock in my face, and told me how good it was going to be as he came in my hair. It made him really angry I turned from him. He almost broke my neck trying to make me face him as he came. The entire time, I'm covered in blood still clutching the knife. So stupid, why didn't I drop it? When I wouldn't drop the knife, he killed Tiger. Oh God, I got Tiger killed for nothing."

A sob turned to hysterical crying as Dan gathered her close. Incoherent now, she mumbled Tiger's name and apologies over-and-over as Dan patted her back and kept telling her it wasn't her fault. Gradually, the crying slowed, replaced by sniffles.

"Thank you for coming for me. I was so afraid, Dan.
All his rules and Gino hoping I would forget and
speak. His hands on me at every opportunity and I'm
not allowed to say no or anything. Vincent made me
eat with them, the entire time knowing if I threw up
Gino would have me right there on the table."

"Gino is dead. Your safe now, remember?"

She continued babbling as if she hadn't heard him.
"I hated that maid. She could've helped me instead of
smiling and serving me eggs. Eggs she knew I wouldn't
be able to keep down. Vomit burned in my throat and
mouth, and I would sweat all the way back to my room
until I could puke in private so Gino wouldn't touch
me. He wanted to cut me and hear me scream.

"Why? What did I do to deserve that? Why would
Vincent let him? And the old man was worse, talking
about how he would've treated me when he was young
as if I couldn't hear him. Over breakfast, Dan. Like
asking how did you sleep or what's the weather.
Casually talking about killing me and destroying my
body. Discussing their past crimes and future ones,
every word a nail in my coffin. And I knew they were
going to kill me. They still are, aren't they? Soon, one
of his men will come and take me or kill me here."

"No, sweetheart. We won't let them."

She continued to babble as if she didn't hear him.
"Can I have a gun or ... No, I can't kill again and be
like them. What do I do, Dan? I don't want him to hurt
me or anyone else."

"Gino is dead!" Dan said loudly as he shook her
shoulders.

Wide, dilated eyes met his. Sweat trickled down the
side of her face. "Am I dreaming? Are you real? Is how

I remember things between us right? You're harder than I thought and I'm both happy about that and horrified. A Navy SEAL could take Vincent's guards."

Beseeching him for reassurance, she repeated herself, while her wild eyes scanned his face and her trembling hands clutched his shoulders.

"What we have is the real deal, Ang. The medicine isn't agreeing with you. Please come lay down with me. Your safe here, I promise. Not just me, but every man in my platoon will see to it."

In the bed beside him, she ran her palm over him as if reassuring herself he was there. Whether to assure of his safety or hers, he didn't know. Gradually her hands stilled. As soon as she fell asleep, he rose and snuck from the room. In the kitchen, he read the pill bottle, then called Doctor Schwartz.

After he'd hung up, he turned to Squirrel who sat on the couch with the television on low.

"Can you go pick up a new prescription of Xanax for me? The doc says not to give her anymore Valium, the mood swings can lead to suicidal depression. Try not to give her anything if we can help it."

"No problem." Squirrel rose and headed to the door. "The rest of the squad is outside. Shall I send Keith in?"

"Where's Tom?"

"Taking Charlene home. Ronny is in his room."

Dan rubbed his forehead where a headache throbbed. "We better call a meeting," he said. 'Tell the guys to go home. We got this for now. I really don't see Vincent sending a hitman upstairs here, and there is no line of sight for a sniper. As long as Angie stays in the building, she should be fine."

"Angie is welcome here, but you can't keep her locked up forever," Squirrel said.

"Not forever. I have a plan, but I need a week."

Squirrel nodded, gave him a two-finger salute, and headed out.

Dan returned to his wife, and to his surprise dozed off.

TWENTY-NINE

MAKE A DEAL

WHEN Angie woke, she was calmer. Tom made everyone dinner, and they spoke of trivial things. After dinner, Angie gestured to the dishes.

"Leave it. I'll do them, but can we talk first?"

Surprised, Tom laid the stack of dirty dishes he'd picked up by the sink. "Sure, what's on your mind?"

"No, I mean all of us. What are we going to do?"

"Not that I don't want to tell you, but are you sure you're up for this?"

"Yes, I feel better, less muzzy, more myself."

"Okay." Tom turned to Dan. "Can we meet at Charlene's and talk about what we're going to do?"

Dan took his wife's warm hand in his. "Yeah, call the team."

Forty-five minutes later, thirty-two men had

273

gathered in Charlene's living room. She handed out beer and placed bowls of chips no one touched on the coffee table.

Commander Darmin entered, and his men rose. Since no one was in uniform, nobody saluted, but the respect they bore him was clear.

"Angie, I'm glad Dan found you safe and sound," Darmin said as he gestured his men to sit. "The squad is officially on leave, but I want everyone to carry their beepers and stay close. JT will set a guard rotation. Inside the apartment, you should be perfectly safe, but we need to handle this."

"Angie and I had an idea on how to do that." Dan shifted on the arm of the couch where he sat beside his wife. "She knows who killed Candice and I'm going to call Joe Conti and inform him." Dan reached into his pocket and placed a man's ring on the table. A square-cut ruby in a deeply etched gold setting glittered, catching the light.

"The ring," Angie gasped.

"Yep. Candice duct taped it to the bottom of my duffle bag. Don Pedro's proof. I'm heading to Mexico on a three-a.m. flight."

Angie clutched his knee.

"You're staying here with Tom and planning our wedding. I'd prefer it happened soon like a few days from now, but I'll do whatever you want."

"Dan..." Angie trailed off worriedly.

"I'm going with him," JT said.

"Me too," Squirrel added. "We've got his back, Angie."

"Don Pedro won't do a thing to me," Dan said reassuringly." Admittedly, Vincent's men might try, but they're all busy. I want you to make them even busier. Call Mr. Barnett and tell him what you told me about his taxes. Make a deal with him. He talks the rest of his associates into leaving you alone, and you tell him how to fix his tax problems. You know enough to take them all down; he should be willing to deal."

Darmin snorted as Angie nodded thoughtfully.

"Really? You think he'll back down over tax problems?" Darmin asked dubiously.

"If he doesn't get a handle on his taxes before the IRS files, he won't have a dime and will do serious time. It isn't a problem killing someone can fix," Angie said, sounding relieved. "I need a computer, printer, and new books. And a phone."

"And you can make his problems go away. Legally?" Darmin lifted a brow.

"Yes, if I can get ahead of the other agents." Angie rubbed her eyes. "All my stuff was ruined again. I don't have anything I need."

"I have everything you need," Charlene said.

"No, I can't work here." A hitch in her voice, Angie grabbed Dan's hand hard.

"Don't worry about the stuff." Dan ran a hand over her hair. "Ronny and Keith can go now and buy you whatever you need. Promise me you won't leave the house without clearing it with whoever is on watch."

"I promise," Angie said.

"Make me a list," Ronny said.

Charlene handed her a notepad.

"Can I use your computer for a few minutes?" Angie asked.

"Sure, in the kitchen." Charlene led Angie away.

Darmin waited until they were in the other room

before speaking. "You really think that will work?"

"Can't hurt and it keeps her occupied," Dan said as he glanced into the kitchen.

The two women sat before a built-in desk in the corner of the large room. "Don Pedro will handle Vincent for us; I'm almost positive about that. And it isn't breaking the law to return the ring. Without Vincent to push the issue, why come after her?"

A troubled expression on his face, Darmin shrugged uncomfortably. "Honestly, I think she's in more danger now. You say she knows enough about their bookkeeping to take them all down."

"True, but so will every single IRS agent, killing her won't help them. And the fact that she knows is Vincent's fault."

"Fine, try it." Darmin gestured to Tom. "Stick to her like a tick. Listen to her meetings. If you think they're blowing smoke, we do it the old-fashioned way. I'm arranging to get everyone assigned to Pearl Harbor for three months for SDV training, followed by another tour in Gitmo. So, we have six months to decide if they're sincere or not. Special Agent Stanley Wisniewski promised to keep me informed on what the grapevine is saying about her. If he hears from any of his informants a hit has been issued, we meet again and discuss a more final strategy.

"JT, Squirrel, sidearms and knives only. I'll get you transport to our base in Baja California and arrange for a vehicle. Dan, it's probably best if you go in alone. If it goes to hell, it'll be better to have the two of them outside. Make sure you're clear on code words before you enter."

The men continued to discuss strategy until Angie

returned and handed a paper to Squirrel.

His eyes widened at the list.

Charlene laughed. "I'm coming with you. Angie needs clothes and things that I'll pick out." She kissed her husband. "I should be back before you go, but if I'm not...

"Consider it said, honey." JT kissed her again. "Piece of cake. Don't worry about us."

"Don't get cocky," Charlene said warningly, but she smiled when she said it.

Charlene's confidence in JT seemed to reassure Angie who offered them a tremulous smile. Dan nodded at Charlene gratefully, he owed her a big apology.

The men rose and made their way from the house after kissing Charlene's cheek and receiving assignments from JT.

In minutes it was just JT, Tom, Squirrel, Dan, Angie, and Charlene.

"Dan, we need to go to our apartment before you leave. We can't leave Tiger there like that. Angie's eyes filled with tears. "I can't do that alone..."

Charlene hugged her, tears filling her dark eyes. "No need. JT Junior brought Tiger here and buried him in the backyard. The boys went through the place, and everything that was salvageable is in my garage. There wasn't much left, I'm afraid."

Angie sighed. "Our insurance rates are going to go through the roof." She wiped her eyes. "Tell JT I said thanks."

"No thanks necessary. He liked Tiger. All his life my son has lived with stories of violence and death. That was the first time he's seen it. Tiger's death convinced him to stay in school. And while I'm not happy the cat died, I'm grateful it convinced my son to be a civilian.

"Char." JT took his wife's hand. "Don't get your hopes up that it will last. The first time is hard for everyone. I won't try to talk him into joining, but as you said, it's been his plan for a long time now. After he finishes school, he still might join as an officer."

"Every day he's safe at home is a treasure. So, I'll take what I can get." Charlene kissed JT's cheek and gestured Squirrel to the door. "After you. We'll be back in a few hours."

Tom, Dan, and Angie followed them out.

THIRTY

———◆———

ALL IN, ALL THE TIME

S QUIRREL slammed the man's face into the doorway as he punched him in the kidney. A knee to the back followed as he grabbed the man's neck and hit his face on the door again. The sharp crack of breaking cartilage and a spray of blood was his reward.

The man struggled, striking out with an elbow. Squirrel hit him again, squeezing the man's neck hard and forcing him to the ground. Keith ran up and grabbed the man's hands, pushing them down and back as he knelt on the man's back. In less than three minutes, six men, all dressed in black, appeared and surrounded Squirrel's captive.

"Fuck! What the fuck? Get off me!" The man on the ground cursed and pulled at his bonds before lying still, panting on the ground. "I'm gonna sue your ass."

Squirrel punched him twice. The first time on the side of the head, the second in the kidney. The man wisely quieted.

A quick pat down revealed a gun, a knife, and a thin piece of wire. Ronny zip-tied the man's wrists as Squirrel examined the man's wallet.

"So, Harvey, long way from Chicago, aren't you? Funny thing about us Californians, we can spot your kind a mile away, and we fucking hate tourists."

More men dressed in black clothing showed up.

Squirrel pulled Harvey upright into a sitting position. Harvey's angry gaze traveled the surrounding men as he wiped his dripping nose on his shoulder.

Commander Darmin arrived with the MP's. The black-clad men faded into the night.

"Ah, nice catch, Squirrel." Darmin tipped the man's head back, shining his flashlight on him. "Same guy who tried to visit in the hospital." Darmin prodded Harvey with his toe. "As you can see, we take security pretty seriously around here. Make sure you tell whoever sent you that next time there won't be any survivors."

Darmin straightened and gestured to the two MP's who stood back waiting. "Throw the book at him and make sure you check for outstandings."

"Me?" Harvey huffed as the MP's pulled him to his feet. "I was assaulted and want to press charges."

Squirrel grinned. "Glad to assist. Charge away, I can't wait to find out all about you. This"— a contemptuous grin on his face, Squirrel gestured at Harvey's bloody nose—"is nothing. Wait until you see what Taxes does. Angie will be calling her friends at the bureau right now with your name. Everyone you know will be receiving a visit from one of her friends very soon."

Squirrel stepped back and grinned as the man paled. The MP's pushed Harvey into the car then asked Squirrel to sit. Commander Darmin accompanied Squirrel to the police station. Black-clad men lined the route. By the time they reached the station, over two hundred men had gathered, crowding the parking lot and lining the front stairs. The MP's exchanged amused glances as they hauled their captive out. Squirrel and Commander Darmin followed.

The men straightened to attention as Darmin passed. A low murmur of 'war' grew as the MP's mounted the steps. By the time they entered the building, the sibilant whisper had risen to a growling shout. Darmin halted before the door. Without turning, he straightened, and the sound died away. In moments, the men had vanished back into the night.

Inside, Darmin rapped his knuckles on the booking desk and leaned into Harvey's face. "Tell your boss my men are willing and anxious to go to war. Another incident, no matter how small, will start tourist season in Chicago. Am I clear?"

Harvey nodded his head fractionally. Darmin slapped Squirrel's shoulder and headed off to speak to the captain.

An hour later, Darmin escorted Squirrel into his apartment. Dressed in black combat gear and carrying rifles, Ronny and Dan greeted him at the door.

Dan gave Squirrel a quick hug. "Angie slept through it. What do we know?"

Commander Darmin rubbed his chin. "As messages

go, ours was pretty clear. Vincent might have some tough men, but we have more. Let that set in a day or so. Your wife can hold her meeting with Barnett. A full platoon will escort her to reinforce the message. I'm having more and more faith in your plan. Don't go off on your own, we're handling this in house."

"Yes, sir." Dan saluted.

Darmin snorted. "Get some sleep. You leave in less than four hours and need to be sharp. No one is getting past our boys. All in, all the time." Darmin slapped Dan on the shoulder and left.

Dan turned to Squirrel. "Thanks, man; I owe ya one. Is he pressing charges?"

"Nope. Said he tripped and fell." Squirrel grinned and punched Dan's arm as he passed him, heading for his room.

The door to the bedroom closed with a soft click. Angie stirred under the mound of blankets.

"Getting ready to go?" Her voice was soft and sleep groggy, sounding sad and nervous.

"Soon, but we have time yet." Dan hesitated then said," Squirrel caught a trespasser."

She straightened in alarm, clutching the blankets to her chest as her gaze darted about the room.

"Nothing to be worried about. The man didn't even make it to the door. " He told her what happened, and she nodded thoughtfully. "Should I call in favors and get him audited?"

"Yep, him and everyone connected to him. I think you'll be surprised at how willing to help your former coworkers will be. The IRS will want it clear taking an agent to force them to help cover up tax fraud is frowned upon. We aren't alone in this, Angel."

"Two hundred men showed up?" She sounded impressed and embarrassed.

"Angel, we're a team. What effects one of us effects all. The safety of our families while we're away is paramount. The men are taking this very seriously. You were kidnapped right off base. That's a threat we can't let stand. It demands a response. The team is willing to wait and let us try to handle it, but make no mistake, even if I died in a plane crash tomorrow and you got hit by a car, Vincent will still be handled."

"Promise you'll come back to me."

"Cross my heart." Dan dropped his clothes on the floor and climbed under the blankets with her. Still wearing his sweat suit, she snuggled against his side.

"Did you mean it, about starting our family soon?"

"Angel, if you didn't have that implant we would've started our family last night."

The body snuggled against his relaxed.

"Everything I've ever said to you, I've meant. I can't wait for us to have kids. Lots of kids. A big, noisy, close family. "

She sat, bracing herself with both hands against his shoulders. "When I see my doctor this week, I'm asking him to remove the implant."

Dan made a small aroused sound and pulled her down for a kiss, sliding his hands under her sweatshirt. Not sure if she was ready after the fiasco of drug-induced paranoia, he went slow, letting her set the pace.

The nipple under his thumb hardened as her kiss deepened. Blond hair caught in a ponytail brushed his chest. Pale moonlight illuminated her breasts, making his breath catch, as she sat and flung the sweatshirt onto the floor.

"I want you," she murmured as her hands trailed over him. "This might be the last time we ever make love."

"No, don't think like that." Dismayed, Dan framed her face with his hands and kissed her lips. Too dark to see her expression, he had to go by body language. Pliant against him, she didn't seem afraid. He reached over and turned the bedside lamp on, revealing her expression.

She appeared calm and not unhappy as she shrugged. "It's true. Life is dangerous and unpredictable. Anything could happen. More so for us. I don't think I'll ever be able to make love to you again without thinking it might be the last time. I need memories, Dan. Memories to sustain me until I die of old age."

Dan closed his eyes. For a moment, he let himself imagine life without her, that all he had were memories. A groan escaped him, and he clutched her tight. "No, we need more time. There are so many things we've still never done together. We have to go camping and hiking and make love in a green meadow and in snow over our heads inside an igloo we make ourselves. I want to see steam form on your skin in a hot spring and cover you with whipped cream." Dan's voice deepened. "I want to see you nurse our first child and feel the weight of your breasts. Promise me we can do all those things."

Eyes bright with unshed tears, she nodded. "Firelight and our copper tub. I want to do that so many times. And the ocean. Let's rent a sailboat and spend a day naked in the water."

"Make up sex, birthday sex, and Valentine's day sex." Dan grinned and tweaked her ponytail. "Drunk sex and sleepy sex. And in my truck, both the front seat and the bed. And during a drive-in movie."

She giggled. "Every room in our house and our backyard."

"Ahh, on the washer and the dryer. Here in my bed while we need to be quiet because the house is full of people."

Warm breath misted on his skin as she kissed his lips lightly. The sweatpants joined the shirt on the floor. Astride him, she arched her back and sighed hard, her hips making small circles, she began breathing harder.

"No let me," she said as Dan began to thrust hard.

Dan stopped moving, fighting the urge to surge against her. The soft sounds she made as her hips rocked faster made it difficult to hold still.

"Ang," he hissed. Without intent, he thrust. Tight warmth enveloped him. Her muscles squeezed as she groaned. Unable to stop himself, he thrust again. In seconds, he was pounding hard. The slap of flesh-on-flesh was loud in the room.

At the moment, Dan didn't care that Ronny's room was behind his headboard. "Jesus," he moaned when she came and collapsed on his chest. He continued to thrust as she screamed into the pillow beside his head. A minute later he came too and couldn't help the loud the groan that escaped him.

"Guess we need to try that one again," he said.

She giggled and blushed.

THIRTY-ONE

———◆———

TAXES

A SHARPENED pencil laid precisely along the edge of a thick green folder. Angie straightened, took a deep breath, and grabbed her phone. Tom sat across from her at the small kitchen table. Ronny stood at the counter making coffee.

"This is Angelina Barstow from the IRS. May I speak with Mr. Barnett, please. Yes, tell him it's with regards to discrepancies in form 1139 on his loss carrybacks. No, I'm afraid I can't call back. Any unhandled admissions get passed to my supervisor, and an agent will be sent to personally— yes, I can hold a moment." Angie rolled her eyes at Tom who snorted.

She grinned. "Works every time. No one wants an IRS agent on their doorstep." Her attention sharpened as she picked up the pencil and hit speakerphone.

286

"Thank you for taking my call, Mr. Barnett. As I'm sure your aware, Mr. Palgrino was arrested two days ago. What you may not be aware of was he was in the process of an internal investigation regarding his finances and had copies of his books on the premises, both sets of them." The tip of the pencil followed a line on the page in front of her. "This call is in the nature of mutual help."

"I'm sorry, but who did you say you were?" the man on the phone asked in a gruff voice.

"Mrs. Angelina Barstow, the IRS agent your boss kidnapped and had going through his books."

"So, this isn't an official call then?" he sounded annoyed now.

"I assure you I work for the IRS in the tax frauds department. The head of the Washington department. I'm very, very, good at my job. In less than a week agents will be knocking on your door with warrants."

"And your calling to inform me why?"

"Let's speak bluntly here." Angie took a deep breath. "Mr. Palgrino will be out of the picture, either in jail or dead. Neither of those things are my fault, and I want that clear to his business associates."

"Dead? Are you threatening me?" Mr. Barnett sounded amazed now.

"Absolutely not. As I stated earlier, this call is about mutual help. Mr. Dentin will assume control of the company. His finances checked out. While I'm aware of his money laundering scheme in Panama, there's no solid proof."

"How are you aware?"

"Misters Palgrino's spoke quite freely in front of me. But the point is, I'm sure a meeting of your compatriots will be called to discuss the state of your businesses. Quite a few of your associates will be doing time for tax fraud. A fact I had nothing to do with. I need a man in my corner. Don Pedro will likely act over the death of his father. While I can't say what he'll do, it seems probable that Mr. Palgrino won't live long in jail."

"I see." The line was silent a moment before Mr. Barnett spoke. "And why would I help you?"

"Because I'm going to help you. I'm going to give you information that will cement your position as number one among your fellows. I'm going to tell you how to avoid jail time for tax fraud. Then, I'm going to tell you which of your associates is stealing and how. The last thing I'll tell you is which of your associates has no chance of avoiding jail time, serious jail time. If you choose, you may warn them in time to flee or disappear, but before I tell you anything at all, I want assurances that neither my husband nor I will be held accountable for Mr. Palgrino's actions."

Mr. Barnett snorted. "And you'll take my word, I suppose."

"Honestly, I don't think it will be that hard for you to convince your people to leave me alone. I had nothing to do with anything that happened except to be there. Candice stole my identity and got me involved, and believe me, I want nothing to do with any of this. So yes, I'll take your word, but I'm not stupid, and my position as an IRS agent gives me leverage."

"So, if I don't comply, you'll what, sic your friends on me?"

Angie bit back a sharp bark of laughter. "I have resources," she said noncommittally.

"Resources." Mr. Barnett sniffed, then cleared his throat. "Fine, I'll help you, and you help me, and then we're quits."

Angie's shoulder slumped. "Thank you, Mr. Barnett."

"Oh, don't thank me. I'm aware this bargain helps me— more than helps me. I have resources as well, and I agree it won't be hard to get my, um, associates to leave you alone. Your husband's position alone will prove convincing. His reputation proceeds him. Muerte Segura had dealings with associates in Nicaragua. Vincent should've known better than to mess with death and taxes. No one escapes those."

Tom slapped a hand over his mouth, his eyes dancing with mirth. Angie stabbed the mute button as Ronny burst into laughter, which he quickly stifled and gave her a small apologetic shrug. She unmuted the phone.

"Our business should be concluded in person at your earliest convenience. Bring your accountant and business manager. Not Mr. Namon, as he's stealing from you. In fact, if I were you, I wouldn't tell any of your associates until we speak as most might act precipitously."

Mr. Barnett chuckled. "Advice duly noted. Where shall we meet?"

"When you arrive, call me, and I'll come to your hotel. My husband's co-workers will be accompanying me. Once they assure themselves of my safety, they'll leave us alone to speak."

"Fine, I look forward to our meeting."

"I look forward to having this behind me."

Mr. Barnett's laugh cut off abruptly as he hung up.

Angie touched the disconnect button and rotated her shoulders. "Well?"

Tom burst into laughter as he stood. "Death and taxes. Jesus, he isn't wrong. Remind me not to get on the wrong side of you." He slapped her shoulder lightly. "You'll be fine. Give him a way to save face, and he'll let you alone. Meanwhile, stay inside and with us. Have you heard from Dan?"

Angie wrapped her arms around herself and shivered. "No. Not since he landed."

"They'll be fine. JT and Squirrel will take good care of him."

Elbows on the table, Angie rested her head in her hands. "This plan only works if Vincent is dead. What if Don Pedro doesn't believe him, or what if he believes but does nothing?"

Ronny pushed a cup of coffee and a donut to her as he said, "Vincent has so many men after him now I'll be amazed if he lives out the week. His own men are going to want his hide when they find out he turned them over to the feds unwittingly or not."

Tom and Ronny exchanged dismayed glances over her bowed head.

"No matter what happens we'll keep you safe, Angie," Tom said as he sat in the chair beside her.

She lifted her face from her hands and smiled wanly. "You'll try, but there are a lot of bad men."

Tom put an arm around her and winked "True, nothing is certain except death and taxes."

She laughed and grabbed the donut.

THIRTY-TWO

◆

I'm Not Trying to Help You Break the Law

TWENTY-FIVE men dressed identically in black cargo pants, black t-shirts, dark-blue ball caps with the word Navy emblazoned in white across the SEAL trident, with black sunglasses shading their eyes, surrounded Angie as she headed into the Hilton Hotel. Dressed in a blue suit with low, black pumps, Angie was dwarfed by the men surrounding her.

Tom towered over her on her left. He carried a portable printer and a small stack of books. In her right hand, she held a briefcase. Heads swiveled in the lobby as everyone watched them enter the elevators. Loud whispers cut off as the door closed. Angie glanced at Tom, an anxious expression on her face.

Tom smiled, a bright flash of white in his dark face. "We got this. Do what we talked about, and you'll be fine."

She nodded and clutched the handle of the briefcase tighter.

The men exited the elevator, and Ronny knocked on the door of room three-hundred-twelve. A tall, thin man wearing an Armani suit answered. His gaze traveled the crowded hallway, settling on Angie.

"Ahh, Mrs. Barstow, welcome. I'm Mr. Barnett." He stepped back and gestured behind him "Mr. Thorn and Mr. Gotlieb my lawyer and accountant." He nodded to three men in dark suits who stood in the corners of the room. "My other, ahh, associates will wait in the hallway with your, um, friends."

The SEALS surrounded Angie as Mr. Barnett's bodyguards exited the room.

Ronny patted down the three men remaining and stepped back. "I'll be texting Mrs. Barstow every five minutes. If she doesn't answer with the correct code, we'll be coming in," Ronny said as he took position beside the door.

"Noted," Mr. Barnett said dryly as he turned away.

Tom followed Angie inside and placed the printer and books on the small conference table in the corner of the room. After he'd pulled her seat out, he retreated to the farthest corner where he stood at ease.

Angie opened her briefcase and passed a sheaf of stapled printouts to Mr. Barnett. "Sign and file these forms by nine a.m. tomorrow. Attach a check for at least twenty-five percent of the penalty. Your lawyer can file a request for acquittal, but the most you can hope for is a reduced fee."

Mr. Barnett's eyebrow lifted as his gaze traveled the papers. "That's quite a hefty sum."

"It's a pittance compared to what you've neglected

to pay. The idea is to preempt charges. Once charges are filed, the case for you will become extreme. Between back payments, penalties, and fees, you'll lose everything. Tax fraud of this extent will get you ten years, minimum, but more likely twenty-six years in prison. Yes, you're going to have to pay, but not nearly as much this way. No accountant on Earth can make the tax laws go away. Once the IRS realizes you misfiled, payment will be due. The trick is to claim it was a mistake, not fraud. If you beat the agents, it can be claimed it was a mistake. The moment they file it becomes fraud. My helping you is entirely legal. Nothing I'm going to tell you to do is illegal. This is the legal way to avoid jail. Nothing will let you avoid payment."

"And they file tomorrow?"

"No, they file in three days, but you don't want them to file, you want to beat them. The IRS must receive that payment *before* they file."

"Three days? It will take that long for the mail to get there, never mind someone opening and reading it."

"Not with my help. Courier the letter directly to my friend tonight, and she'll enter the information in the morning. Without my help, you don't have a prayer of beating the charges. Please keep in mind that none of this is my fault. I didn't sic the IRS on you, Vincent did. Every time he forced me to use my password on the IRS mainframe it put my search into their records. His bookkeeping, spelling out the connections, is what will bring your house of cards down."

Mr. Barnett handed the papers to his accountant. His lawyer read them over his shoulder.

Angie licked her lips and continued, her voice firm.

"Vincent has copies of every company he's connected to on his hard drive. The feds will be putting the puzzle together, and when they do, the connection between Drint Industries and Hiffen Corp will become clear. I estimate three months before the IRS realizes every company that did business with Drint was laundering money. Drint only produced enough actual product to fill maybe one company's orders, ergo the others are lying. To stay out of jail, you need to be that company."

"How am I supposed to do that?" Mr. Barnett asked doubtfully. His eyes glittered angrily.

Angie tapped her pencil against the paper before her, her gaze darting to Tom. The sight of him steadied her, and she continued with confidence.

"Have boxes of those office supplies on your shelves and desks. When the inspector comes, make sure you can show physical evidence. Drint only bought enough supplies to produce orders for one company. I have no idea if they actually made anything or not, but if they did, and it's sitting like props on their shelves, go get it. Everyone who can't offer proof of actual purchases will be screwed, but the company with the items will be fine."

Mr. Barnett nodded thoughtfully and leaned back in his seat. "I see."

Angie passed over a manila envelope. "These are the companies I'm sure will be nailed for money laundering. The IRS would've noticed this eventually. Vincent just sped things up. The supplies they buy in no way match their output. Not to mention the repeated use of social security numbers on sure to be fictitious employees. I didn't have time to ascertain who in your chain of companies uses each business to launder, but the IRS will have agents unraveling the knots as we speak. If you do business with any of them, make sure you have proof of items received. Physical proof. The only other option, and I'm unsure this would work, would be to file police reports right now claiming you never received the items."

Angie straightened and folded her hands before her. "Look, I'm not trying to help you break the law. If you've been laundering money with any of those companies, the IRS will find out and inform the feds. I'm here to clear up your tax issues. Pay the tax or do the time."

Angie handed over another form. "Make a copy if you want to follow along," she said to the accountant. The printer whirred to life as Angie pointed to the first line. "This is going to take a while. Line 2a, use the amount of the gross after non-itemized deductions."

In the corner, Tom leaned against the wall as Angie went through each tax form line-by-line while the accountant Mr. Barnett had brought frantically scribbled notes.

Three hours later, she reached into her briefcase and withdrew another thick sheaf of papers. "Look these over while I use the bathroom." She tapped a quick text into her phone. Tom took her elbow and helped her rise. The two walked to the bathroom as Angie stretched and rotated her neck.

"Mr. Thorn's head is spinning. Barnett seems to be happy with you though," Tom said as he glanced over his shoulder. Before he let Angie into the bathroom, he searched it, then waited outside the door for her. "Don't drink the water," he reminded her as water ran in the sink. He texted Ronny.

When Angie emerged, he escorted her back to the table and reseated her. "My colleague will be knocking in a moment with water and food for Mrs. Barstow. If you'd like refreshments, they'd be glad to pick some up," Tom said.

"Yes, fine, sandwiches and coffee or soda would be appreciated." Mr. Barnett stood and stretched.

Fifteen minutes later, Ronnie delivered food while Angie went over forms in a quiet voice.

Night had fallen, and Tom escorted Angie to the bathroom twice more before she'd covered everything with Mr. Barnett.

Finally, she closed her briefcase. "I believe I've kept my side of the bargain."

Mr. Barnett leaned back in his chair and idly tapped a pencil on the form before him. "You have and thank you. I would offer you a job..." His gaze landed on Tom who'd stayed motionless in the corner the entire time." But I think you're content where you are." He reached into his pocket and removed a dark-blue ring box, which he slid across the table to her. "This is yours. I'll make it crystal clear you have nothing we want and had nothing to do with anything that follows. If you ever find yourself in need of a job, call me."

She reached a trembling hand for the ring box.

Tom beat her to it. "You can have it after we examine it, Ang."

She nodded and rose, straightening her blazer and smoothing her skirt.

In the hallway, the men who'd accompanied her remained in the same positions they'd taken when she'd entered. Mr. Barnett's guards sat against the wall; one slept.

Mr. Barnett's hard gaze followed the men as they escorted her to the elevator and he prodded his sleeping guard with his foot. "Make it clear to everyone that we don't want to mess with them. She has nothing we want, and none of this was her fault. If I find out anyone comes here; they'll deal with me before I turn them over to them. Am I clear?"

The man nodded.

Angie glanced back as the elevator closed. Her shoulders sagged as the door dinged. By the time it reached the bottom floor, Tom held her arm, half supporting her weight.

"You did great, Ang. Tough as nails. You scared me with talk of fines and fees, never mind the jail time. No one is going to mess with Taxes. Once Vincent is handled, you're home free."

"I need a shower. It feels like I've been swimming in filth. That man is a crook and just as bad as Vincent. I hate that I helped him."

"Well, if it makes you feel better, Dan texted, and he should be meeting with Don Pedro now. Soon, this will all be behind you." Tom gave her shoulder a squeeze.

THIRTY-THREE

LET THE DON DECIDE

A GLANCE in the rear-view mirror revealed Squirrel three cars behind him. Directly behind Dan, a blue Ford Taurus contained two men, both wearing sunglasses. While that in itself wasn't unusual, the pallor of their skins and business suits was. Dan slid his sunglasses to the top of his head and laid a hand over his ear to better hear Squirrel on the ear bud he wore.

"I make two possible contacts directly behind me. Let's see if they're following." Dan read off the license plate number for JT as he took the next left turn.

"Damn, following for sure, and they have back-up," Dan said as he glanced in the mirror again and noted the passenger in the car behind him on a cell phone.

"Head to the rendezvous," JT ordered. "I'm heading back to you. Stay on the route we mapped. We don't engage unless we absolute have to. I've scoped out Don Pedro's place, and he has tight security. If you can reach him, his men can handle resistance. The man owns the entire town from the school to the grocery store. The people here seem happy, and the standard of living is good, nice houses, clean streets, and low police presence. Don Pedro runs a tight ship."

JT turned his motorcycle in the middle of the street and headed back to Don Pedro's estate. A guard house flanked the entrance to a long curving drive. A red tile roof was visible in the distance but lush greenery and the twisting driveway blocked the view of the house. JT pulled his bike to a stop and with hands raised, showing they were empty, he approached the alert guard.

"A friend of mine will be arriving soon with an urgent message for Don Pedro regarding his deceased father. The man responsible for Senior Pedro's disappearance has sent men to stop him. Your security might want to prepare for his arrival."

The guard lifted a radio to his mouth as JT turned. "Sir, your name?"

In clear but accented English, the guard called after him as JT mounted the bike and drove off. Once out of town, he broke the speed limit heading back to meet his men.

"Squirrel, any activity?" Dan asked.

Squirrel had dropped farther back, staying two miles behind Dan. "Nothing suspicious. All traffic is either obeying the laws or appear to be local boys."

"Don't assume they didn't hire local help," JT said. "Dan, if I were planning to stop you, I'd have people waiting about two miles past exit sixteen. There's a long section of twisting road with no homes or business bordered by scraggly pines and cactus trees. I counted three dirt road turnoffs there. It'd be a great spot to make someone disappear permanently. Stop at the gas station before exit twelve. Squirrel, leave the bike there, and you drive. Dan, shoot out one tire the first clear shot you get when you exit. Don't kill anyone."

"Copy that." Dan hesitated. "Sir, these men are sure to be his most loyal guys. Either we end them now or later, but the chances of them not taking revenge are almost nil."

"Yep, but the chances of Don Pedro letting the men who tried to keep the truth from him leave his town alive are almost nil too. Get us clear pics of their faces if you can but is all you need to do is stall them and reach the hacienda."

The back of Dan's neck itched, a tight feeling that warned of danger behind him. His face set in hard lines, he glanced in the mirror again. He wanted these men dead. Dead and buried, unable to harm or scare his wife. Squirrel sped passed him, weaving in and out of the light traffic. The men behind him didn't seem to take any interest in him. With his messy brown hair and dusty old motorcycle, Squirrel appeared to be a native.

Dan pulled into the gas station. He rested a hand on his pistol, the other clutched the wheel. The blue Taurus followed him in and parked as far away as they could. Dan exited the Jeep and stretched. From the corner of his eye, he saw Squirrel approach as he headed to the Taurus.

"Dan," Squirrel said sharply.

Dan grinned but didn't turn. "Keep your panties on. I'm just getting a good picture."

"Fuck," Squirrel mumbled as he glanced around the parking lot.

The gas station sported a convenience slash liquor store and did a brisk business. The parking lot on the left of the building was mostly full. He reached behind and unsnapped his holster, making sure it was securely clipped into his jeans, then loosened the knife in the sheath before following Dan, trying to look as if he wasn't.

Dan headed straight to the two men with his hands open and at his side. The two men in the car appeared tense. Sunglasses followed Dan's every move. The passenger exited the car and leaned against the hood. The car blocked the view of his body, leaving only the upper part of his chest and face visible. Both hands remained out of sight. Dan halted five feet away.

"Plan on following me all the way to Don Pedro's?"

"Don't know what you're talking about, Mac." The passenger turned his head, scanning the parking lot.

Dan snickered and reached into his front pocket. The passenger tensed. Cell phone in his hand now, Dan pointed at the ring on the hand holding the phone. "Call the boss and tell him I have the ring. Don Pedro will have the ring in an hour or so. If Vincent wants to chat about this, I'm staying one night at Rainforest Motel right outside town, room thirty-two." A grin on his face, Dan snapped the picture, turned and sauntered away.

"What the fuck was that?" Squirrel glanced back as he got in the driver's seat.

"He's on the phone, right?"

"Yeah...."

"I didn't want anyone to miss this party. Let them come to me."

Squirrel sighed.

Dan gestured with his thumb at the blue Taurus following them again. "If these fuckers miss the party because of a flat tire I want to be sure everyone can recognize them if they show up on base." As he spoke, he forwarded the picture to his teammates.

The sparse traffic lightened even more the further east they went.

"Ten miles until our exit," Squirrel said.

Rolling hills covered with dense vegetation surrounded them. Civilization had fallen behind twenty miles ago.

"Copy that," JT replied.

Dan climbed into the back of the jeep. By the time Squirrel pulled off the exit, Dan was burning with impatience. The Taurus followed. The back window of the jeep was plastic. At the end of the exit ramp, Dan had it unzipped. "Hang back a second. When they take this corner, I'll stop them here."

"Roger that." Squirrel brought the jeep to a stop on the sharp curve of the exit. The following men might be surprised they hadn't driven on.

The driver of the Taurus slammed on the brakes, and a gun appeared in his hand as Dan shot out the right front tire. Squirrel laughed as he drove away, followed by gunfire.

Dan returned fire, aiming high with no intent to hit them, just keep their heads down and aim off. The car followed for fifty feet before pulling to the side. Both men bailed out and opened fire. Too far away to present a threat, Dan climbed back into the front seat and reloaded.

"Well, that was fun." Squirrel grinned at Dan.

Dan rolled his eyes, then laughed, and slapped Squirrel's shoulder. "Let's see what other fun awaits us."

The grin on Squirrel's face grew. "I always have the best time with you."

Dan chuckled.

———————◆———————

JT caught up with them a mile down the road and motioned Squirrel to pull over. "Two pickup trucks with five to six men each are about four miles down the road beside the first turn off. I expect they'll block the road and demand you accompany them. They appear to be local boys— hired help. While we could take them, I hate to bring them into our war."

"Locals huh?" Dan said thoughtfully. "Maybe we can inform them we're on our way to speak to the don?"

JT removed his blue ball cap and scratched his head. "A big risk. Hell, for all I know just showing your face is a death sentence. If we're trying that, I better go speak to them."

"Fuck, no! Char will have my balls if I let anything happen to you. This is my problem. I'll handle it."

"Gimme the bike," Squirrel said as he exited the jeep. "Do this like Mogadishu."

Dan bit his lip. "Twelve men with you as a hostage? Not great odds for you. Mogadishu was a mistake we made right, not a plan we want to reproduce. I have a better idea. Give me the bike. Roll the windows of the

303

jeep down, and JT drives slow. Play loud music, and they'll likely let you by thinking they have the wrong guys. I'll leave the bike and hike around them, and you pick me up.

JT tossed the bike key in his hand, a thoughtful expression on his face. "And if they don't?"

Dan snatched the keys in mid-air. "Then we Mogadishu their asses."

JT got in the driver's seat. Squirrel pulled his hair into a tight ponytail and laid his gun under his thigh. "Have enough bullets?"

Dan tapped his back pocket. "Two full extra clips and a full load, but I only need twelve."

JT snorted and pulled away.

Dan let them get half a mile away before following. He had no intention of letting them try to pass.

"After this curve," JT warned.

Dan hit the gas and flew by them, going sixty-five miles an hour on the rutted dirt road. A haze of dirt filled the air as he sped past. Before him, two trucks with men holding rifles spread out across the road. When they saw him coming, the men began running to get behind the trucks.

His hand squeezing the throttle hard, Dan leaned into the bike, trying to present as small a target as possible, aiming the bike at the gap between the trucks. Behind him, the jeep came barreling down the road with the horn blaring.

"Morty, damn it, this wasn't the plan!" JT yelled in his headset.

Men hunkered behind the trucks less than half a mile way now. A few chose to stand behind the trees beside the road. One man stood in the road gesturing, unable to hear him, his meaning was clear— halt, or we'll shoot.

Wind whistled by Dan's ears as the sharp report of gunfire began. A moving target at three hundred feet was hard to hit, but he'd be close in seconds. He slammed on the brake and swung the bike into a controlled sideways skid, sending up clouds of dust. When he judged the bike was slow enough, he let it go and tucked and rolled. A hundred and fifty feet away, he sprang to his feet and headed into the brush beside the road as he grabbed the gun from his waistband.

Behind him, the jeep screeched to a halt, and JT and Squirrel both began shooting.

Dan ignored it, intent on his target— a man in the trees to the left of the red truck. The cloud of dust was settling. Men yelled in Spanish. Dan grinned, they hadn't seen him roll away in the dust; he had a few seconds. JT and Squirrel kept the attention of the majority of the men. Shots were fired on the bike. The sharp pings of bullets impacting metal muffled the sound of a man yelling for them to cease fire. Dan's gaze traveled the men as he ran.

He lifted his gun and shot, intentionally shooting the dirt by the feet of the man who aimed at him.

The man screamed, "There he is!" and opened fire right as someone else hit the gas tank of the bike.

A brilliant flash of light was followed by a loud whoomph. Hot air ruffled Dan's hair. Men screamed and yelled as pieces of burning motorcycle flew through the air.

Dan reached his target. The man saw him coming and lifted his gun right as Dan arrived. Dan dropped his gun and grabbed the man's arm. He twisted hard, and the gun dropped from the man's hand. A big man, the loss of his gun wasn't enough of a deterrent. A meaty fist connected with a solid hit to Dan's jaw.

Dan grunted and jabbed at the man's kidney. He grabbed the descending fist and turned into the punch, using his assailant's momentum to throw him. A loud oof as the man hit the ground made Dan wince.

He followed him down, grabbing his arms and using his knee to turn him. One arm around the man's neck, the other pulled him tight to his body, using him as a human shield.

The men around him realized he was in their midst but couldn't take a shot. Most of Dan's body was safely tucked behind his target. In moments, quiet descended. The jeep engine and small pops and pings from the still burning bike were the only noise.

Dan inched backward, tightening his hold as the man tensed.

"Stay still, and we all leave here alive. I need to speak with Don Pedro, and believe me, he's going to be mad as hell you delayed me."

The men began talking and yelling questions.

Dan rose his voice. "Me and my friend here are going to take this truck!" His back to the front tire of the red truck, Dan released his captive enough to stand. "Have you been paid enough to go to war with the don?"

His words caused confusion and more yelling. While they were deciding, Dan fumbled for the door handle. Sweat trickled down the side of his face and made his palms slippery.

"Look, what could it hurt to let me go there. I'm unarmed, and he has guards. Let the don decide," Dan said in Spanish as he slid into the truck. A glance over his shoulder showed men aiming rifles at him, but they didn't look angry, they appeared confused.

"Dan!" JT yelled.

"Don't shoot!" Dan shouted back. "These nice gentlemen are going to let me go speak to the don." A glance behind him now showed the men aiming at the jeep. "Nobody needs to get hurt here. Let the don sort it out. You kill me, and my message goes undelivered, and he sure as shit is going to be furious."

The man Dan held twisted in his grasp as he spoke, "Manny, he could've killed me. Take him to the boss. If he's lying, we can always kill him later."

Dan snorted a laugh. "Gee, thanks."

The man he held relaxed. Dan released him, letting him move away.

"I'll take him." He gestured with his chin for Dan to enter the truck.

"Amiro, you sure, man?" Manny stood with his gun pointed at Dan.

Amiro glanced at Dan and nodded.

"Fine, get in the truck." Manny turned and called out four names. The men he called climbed into the back of the truck.

"I'm telling my team to stand down," Dan said as he lifted a hand to the earbud clipped to his ear. "Mission accomplished, sir. I have an escort to the don."

Amiro glanced at Dan as he turned the truck into the road. "Who are you? You don't sound or look like cartel."

Dan laughed. "Is that what Vincent said? We were drug agents?"

"Yep, warned us a new crew was moving in and

sending a hitman for the don. We like the status quo around here. The don is a fair man. A good man, doing his best for all of us. You can tell your boss there's no chance in hell any of us will work for him. Go somewhere else. There's plenty of towns that would be happy for the income. Us— we make money the old-fashioned way. We work for it."

"Despite what you've been told, my visit has nothing to do with drugs." Dan lifted his hand and rubbed the ring on his finger.

Amiro glanced over and swerved as he grabbed Dan's hand.

"My visit has to do with justice," Dan continued.

"Where did you get that? Jesus!" Amiro crossed himself and rapped on the window separating the cab from the bed of the truck. Manny stuck his head in. "Call ahead, he has the Senior's ring," Amiro said.

Manny grabbed Dan's hand, his eyes wide.

"You're a dead man if you had anything to do with this." He dropped Dan's hand. "Amiro, if this fucker is involved with Senior's death, we're in deep shit if we bring him to the hacienda."

"Call, tell him we're coming and what happened." He turned to Dan. " What's your name?"

"Petty Officer First-Class Daniel Barstow. SEAL team nine. The don and I have some things to discuss. In person."

The rest of the ride passed in silence.

THIRTY-FOUR

—◆—

CRIME IS PUNISHED HARSHLY

THE TRUCK slowed as it approached the gate to Don Pedro's home. Armed men lined the driveway. Two police cars with lights on were parked beside the entrance. Dan held his empty hands out and offered no resistance as Manny pulled him from the cab.

One of the police officers searched him. "He's clean," he said as he dropped the two clips and Dan's knife in the dirt at his feet. The officer gestured to a man wearing a private guards uniform. "Timon will take you inside to speak with Don Pedro—"

A shot interrupted him. The officer gasped and slumped, falling to his knees, only Dan's grip keeping him from falling face first. The men surrounding him yelled commands and raced toward the sound of the shot. A group of men converged on Dan as another shot whistled over his right shoulder. Dan dropped to the ground.

Timon grabbed his shoulder. "Come!"

Dan jumped to his feet and followed. More shots sounded as the two men ran down the driveway. Behind them, men yelled as the sharp bark of rifles mixed with the whine of smaller calibers. The distinct roar of a fifty-caliber joined the mix, and a man screamed.

Dan grinned, Squirrel was using his gun.

Five new men appeared, all wearing the same uniform as Timon.

"Get him to the don," Timon gasped, clutching a hand to his shoulder. The white of his uniform turned red under his hand. "Go!" he snapped and waved away the man who came to him. "A flesh wound— I'm fine. Stay with him and guard the don."

Sirens of both police and ambulance sounded faintly from the distance as the men hustled Dan through the covered portico and into the house.

Thick cement walls deadened the sounds from outside, the coolness inside was refreshing after the scorching heat of the Mexican midday sun.

Dan brushed at his filthy clothing, then straightened his shoulders. Blood covered the front of his white shirt. Nothing except new clothing and a shower would make him presentable, so he gave up.

An older man, still straight-backed with thick, black hair greeted him. Only the wrinkled visage gave his age away. His step was still firm.

"I'm Don Pedro. The news you bring must be of utmost importance to precipitate this level of violence. I haven't seen the like since I was a child in this house."

Dan bowed slightly. Two fingers twisted the ring from his hand. On his palm, the ruby sparkled. Don Pedro's eyes narrowed as he reached for it. Eyes bright with unshed tears, Don Pedro lifted his gaze from the close examination he gave the ring.

"Where did you get it?"

"My wife."

The don gestured him to a seat. A young woman in a maid uniform appeared and poured tall glasses of lemonade. A white Persian cat followed her in and jumped into the don's lap. A bead of sweat trickled down the side of the girl's face as she handed Dan the glass.

"I didn't catch your name, Miss." Dan placed the untasted glass on a marble-topped table beside him.

The girl's gaze darted from Dan to the don. She licked her lips before replying in a voice barely above a whisper. "Miranda."

"Hello, Miranda. You look warm. Why don't you sit and have a sip of lemonade with us?"

The don paused with the glass halfway to his mouth. His eyes narrowed as the girl wrung her hands together, her gaze darting between the two men.

"No thank you, sir. It wouldn't be proper." A blush settled into red patches high on her cheekbones.

"I insist, Miranda," the don said.

Dan gave her a shark smile as he handed her his glass.

The glass shattered at his feet, cool liquid soaking his jeans.

"Sorry, sir. How clumsy of me." Crouched before Dan, Miranda avoided the don's gaze as she dabbed at the lemonade on the tile floor with her apron and shaking hands.

"Leave it." The don rose his voice, "Hernando. See Miranda to the kitchen. Make sure she waits there for me. We can talk about this later."

The girl bit back a sob.

The don's eyes hardened. "And bring me something to take samples of my drink and the mess on the floor. And you better take a sample from everything in the refrigerator prepared since yesterday. Send Jefferies to the children. Ensure they have no food or drink and keep them in the safe room until I'm finished here."

Every word the don spoke caused Hernando's eyes to widen. "Very good, sir. Come with me." He gestured Miranda to follow him.

She glanced back and stopped beside the door. "Sir, I'm sorry, sir. No one else knew... please. It was only his glass."

The don waved one hand. "Later, Miranda. You'll have an opportunity to explain yourself."

Tears trailed across the girl's cheek, and she fell to the floor sobbing." Please, sir. My parents..."

A harsh jerk of the don's head, and Hernando grabbed the girl by the arm and dragged her from the room. The sound of crying faded into the distance.

"How did you know?" One eyebrow lifted, the don gestured with his chin to the mess at Dan's feet.

"Candice, the woman who stole the ring from Vincent Palgrino, must have called here to set up an appointment. Whoever she spoke to obviously set her up. Ergo, someone here didn't want you to have that ring. I'm betting you'll find Miranda was bribed and it wasn't personal. No one's help is so efficient they bring the boss lemonade as shots are being fired on the grounds. She seemed like a likely suspect. I doubt she's in it alone."

The don lifted a hand and gestured for him to continue.

"I assume Candice looked up your number and called the house. The maid answers and asked to what the call is regarding. To fool Candice, she then must have had a male counterpart pretend to be you. The meet is set. Candice recognized Benny and Carlos and ran. They chased. I don't think they scared her as much as realizing whoever was on the phone sold her out. She was more freaked out when I arrived at the hotel then when I found her running from them."

"And where is Candice now?"

"Dead. Murdered right in front of me."

The don leaned back in his chair and crossed one leg over his knee. "Tell me everything."

Dan told his story. "Now my wife is in danger and our home destroyed. Through no fault of her own, your family troubles have crossed the border and threatened her."

Don Pedro sipped his drink. A tall, thin woman with clear caramel skin entered the room and rose a manicured hand to remove her sunglasses. Silver hoop earrings caught the light, shimmering in her long black hair caught up in an elaborate braid that hung over her shoulder.

"Papa, Timon, Officer Ortiz, Roberto, and Miguel have been shot, but not fatally."

The click of her high heels against the tile was loud in the silence as she crossed the room. The woman leaned down and kissed the top of Don Pedro's head.

"Doctor Santiago is with them now. The children are in the safe room. *La policia* would like to come speak with you. Four men have been killed and six apprehended." Dark and sultry, her voice sounded musical despite the harsh, clipped way she spat the sentences.

She turned her startling amber eyes onto Dan. "What trouble have you brought to my home?"

"Trouble from the past, I'm afraid." Dan rose and inclined his head. He gestured to the front of his blood-soaked clothes. "Excuse my appearance. Bringing word to your father was more difficult than I anticipated."

"And yet here you are."

The annoyed tone of her voice made Dan hide a grin.

"Isabelle, enough. He is an honored guest." Don Pedro handed her the ring.

A deep inhalation was followed by a short, sharp cry as her hand clenched around the ring. "You bring word of my grandfather's disappearance?"

"I'm sorry, ma'am. Your grandfather was murdered. His body disposed of somewhere between Seco and Wilberth within a mile of the road. Vincent Senior claimed he dragged him for twenty minutes through the brush before he left him. He said he was thirty minutes outside of town. I'm sorry I have no clearer description."

A soft cry from Isabelle became tears that she rubbed from her cheeks with an angry gesture.

A brisk knock on the door was followed by two men entering. Dressed as guards, they bowed slightly. "The perimeter is secure. All parties await your convenience."

Another Persian cat sauntered past them, tail swaying, giving it a jaunty air. The cat headed straight to Dan, leaped into his lap, and began sniffing the dried blood on the front of his shirt. Dan frowned at the cat, suddenly angry that these people had a home and safety when his angel had neither.

"You don't like cats, Mr. Barstow?" the don asked.

Isabelle stiffened at her father's words and rose from the arm of her father's chair to remove the cat from Dan's lap.

"I like them fine." He rubbed behind the cat's ear until it purred. "My wife's cat was killed in front of her to terrorize her into revealing the location of the ring, which she didn't know."

Isabelle grabbed the cat from Dan and laid it against her shoulder where it purred even louder. "Martin, send Leticia for Mischief. Tell her I want them all accounted for."

The smaller man on the left bowed and retreated. The bigger man inclined his head again and closed the door with himself outside it.

Dan cleared his throat as the don sipped his lemonade again. "Should you be doing that?"

Isabelle frowned and turned to her father. "What?

"Miranda attempted to poison our guest," Don Pedro said.

"In the lemonade?"

The don nodded as he took another sip. Isabelle returned to his side and kissed the hair on his head again, then leaned against his chair. The cat in the don's lap rubbed against her hip. One hand absently petted it as she took the glass from her father's hand

and sipped.

"You're awful sure she told the truth." Dan's skeptical gaze followed the glass.

"Yes. We have no murderers. Any woman in the village could safely walk the streets at any time here. Crime is punished harshly."

"Unto the third generation," Isabelle murmured between sips.

Dan pursed his lips and tilted his head as he watched them sip the drink. "And yet, your maid tried to kill me. Never mind the twenty men who held me up on the road."

"Such a shame; I really liked her parents." A soft clink followed that as Isabelle placed the glass on the table beside her.

Dan frowned. "Her parents had nothing to do with anything." He sighed. "Never mind. None of my business. Keep in mind I wasn't harmed and am a stranger here. That should count for something when passing judgment. I guess I better meet with the police and get this over with."

The don waved a hand in the air. "No need. I'll handle it. Martin will see you safely delivered to the airport."

"I can't leave quite yet. I issued an invitation to two men in Vincent's employee to meet me tonight in my room at the Rainforest Motel."

The don's eyes darkened and his lips tightened. "Martin will see to that as well. Thank you for visiting me. Assure your wife that the Palgrino's will be a threat to no one." Don Pedro snapped his fingers and the door opened. "Return everything Mr. Barstow had on him when he arrived. Replace his soiled clothing and take him anywhere he wishes. He is to be treated with the utmost courtesy. Any request he makes, honor at once."

The man at the door nodded and closed the door again. The don stood and offered his hand. "My father was a good man. The estate he inherited from his father included enterprises in which he didn't wish to continue. An honest man, he had to do things which troubled him to make this a safe and prosperous place to live. You'll think us lawless and cruel, but here in Mexico if we don't police ourselves, we become fair game for criminals and dictators.

"The law here is harsh but just and applied equally to all. We're not murderers and thugs, but strong men who will protect our own. Your wife, Angelina, is now under my protection. Harm to her will result in the law being carried out. My men will see that the Palgrino men are informed. If anyone troubles her, contact me at once."

Dan shook his hand.

Isabelle rose from the arm of the chair. "Family is very important to us. The words of my father will be honored."

Dan nodded as the door opened again. An older woman with graying hair and a tear-streaked face entered the room. She gave Dan a nervous glance and sidled passed him as if he would bite.

"Mistress, the cats are all accounted for and in with the children. Shall I take Mischief and Trouble?"

"Yes, keep them locked in until this situation is handled." The two women left together, carrying the cats.

Martin handed Dan a bag and led him to a

bathroom, saying, "The motorcycle will be replaced and returned. The abandoned jeep as well."

Martin turned away as Dan entered the bathroom. His cell phone and earpiece and all his weaponry where inside the bag alongside clean clothes in his size.

Dan called JT. "Where are you?"

"The scrub, about thirty yards from the house. Do you need extraction?"

"Marzipan," Dan offered the code word to inform them he was speaking freely with no duress. "No, I'm fine and being treated well. The don was grateful and put Angelina under his protection. While he never said the Palgrino's will be killed, he made it clear crime is dealt with harshly here. Martin tells me the jeep is out of commission but will be fixed and returned."

"Shot to Hell," Squirrel said cheerfully. "We could use a ride back."

"I trust him, but not that much," JT said. "Squirrel and I will meet you on base. Let's not put all our eggs in one basket. And, Morty, stay alert. Sometimes people decide making problems disappear is easier than dealing with them."

"Roger that." Dan hung up, stripped off his clothes, and jumped in the shower.

Twenty minutes later he was headed down the road in a limousine with tinted windows. Six pick-up trucks surrounded them. No sign of the altercation on the road remained. The motorcycle was gone with no trace of fire or wreckage left behind.

THIRTY-FIVE

◆

AS FAR FROM OKAY AS A PERSON COULD BE

ANGIE answered the phone on the first ring.

"You're okay?" She sounded choked up as if she might cry at any minute.

Dan winced and rubbed his forehead. "Great. It went well. I'll fill you in when I get home, which should be in a few hours. JT, Squirrel, and I are just waiting for our flight out. How did the meeting with Barnett go?"

"He seemed sincere, but those men lie easier than they breathe. Ronny and Tom don't let me out of their sight. Armed men patrol around the apartment twenty-four-seven. I haven't been outside in days. This is terrifying, Dan."

"Have patience, Angel. We leave for Hawaii in two days. The base there will be safer while things shake down here."

"I don't feel safe. I feel hunted and alone."

The soft words nearly broke his heart. "As long as I live, you'll never be alone. Even when I'm not with you physically, I'm there mentally."

"Tom is teaching me to shoot."

Dan winced again. "Great," he lied. "How's the wedding plans coming?" To his dismay, she began to cry. "Never mind, sweetheart, we can talk when I get home. I miss you like crazy." Dan bit his lip as she muted her end of the phone. Everything he wanted to ask or say might make her tears worse. "Just a few more hours, okay?"

"Yeah, I'm okay." The lie was clear. She was as far from okay as a person could be.

Stumped for a safe topic of conversation, Dan hesitated.

"Call me as soon as you arrive," she said.

"I promise."

She hung up.

Dan lowered his phone, his expression troubled. Angie had nothing in her life that wasn't scary, no job, friends, hobbies, home, nothing. She needed things to do that didn't upset her. Normal activities to look forward to. Not shooting guns or worrying about criminal's tax forms or replacing her possessions again. He'd hoped planning their wedding would distract her. The fact that it made her cry really worried him.

He called Tom. "We're heading back. Angie sounds really upset. How'd the meeting go?"

"Fine. She handled Barnett like a pro. She spends most of her time in your room with the door closed seriously depressed. Char comes by, but Angie won't visit; she's afraid to let her be close. She thinks armed men are coming for her any second. Agent Wisniewski met with her this morning. Without being asked, she told him about her meeting with Barnett. The agent left angry. I think Angie might be worried she'll be arrested now."

"I'll call him. Thanks for the heads-up. Oh boy," Dan muttered as he called agent Wisniewski.

Stan answered on the third ring, "Mr. Barstow, my colleagues and I were just talking about you. Have a nice vacation in Mexico?"

"Yes, I visited a friend, but I'm heading home now."

"Did you know your wife planned to speak with Mr. Barnett?"

"Yes, it was my idea. None of this is her fault. She wants it clear to everyone involved that she had nothing to do with any of it."

"Well, word on the street is to stay out of California. Since Angie spoke to Barnett, there've been three shootings. And that's in less than twenty-four hours. I expect there are disappearances we'll never hear of. While I understand why she did it, I wish she'd trusted us to keep her safe. We were so close to cleaning up that entire crew."

"The cost is too high. If she were your wife..."

Stan sighed. "I do understand; I just don't like it. Can I expect her to testify or will she suffer amnesia?"

"Oh, she'll testify to everything she told you. Believe me, we want Vincent and his cronies behind bars a long time."

"The DA has ruled the killing of Gino self-defense. No charges will be filed. Vincent hasn't pressed charge yet for breaking and entering. His lawyer is arguing

Angelina was there willingly. No jury on Earth will believe that though. Witness protection is still being offered."

"Thanks, but I can keep her safe."

"I hope so. Our case rests on her testimony. The IRS will be filing charges, but I want them to do hard time. Palgrino senior is in the hospital claiming he knew nothing, playing the dementia card. The bastard will get away with everything."

"Trust in karma," Dan said.

"And Mexicans with grudges?"

Dan laughed and hung up.

———— ◆ ————

A group of fresh cadets ran around his apartment chanting a cadence. Men in both civilian and uniform clothing loitered around the apartment building. Dan recognized three men from his team although not his squad. All three nodded and gave him a two-finger salute. Angie was well protected whether she realized it or not.

She greeted him with a loud happy, "Dan!" Bright-blue eyes ringed with dark circles met his. Her obvious happiness to see him relieved him.

He kissed her still gaunt cheek. "God, I missed you." Angie still in his arms, he bumped fists with Tom and Ronny. "Thanks, guys. I'm starving. What's to eat?"

Squirrel pushed past him, headed for the bathroom. "Dibs on the shower. Order a lot, I could eat a horse."

"Char invited us all for dinner," Tom called after him.

"Is that a good idea?" Angie drew back from him,

her eyes worried.

"Better than good. It's fantastic. Wait until you try her lasagna," Tom said as he tweaked her ponytail.

"No, I mean...." She trailed off, looking anxious.

Tom patted her on the shoulder. "I know what you meant. I promise you'll be safe. We'll all be safe. The team knows where we're going. Believe me, they hope someone tries something; they're itching for a fight. No one will though."

Dan glanced at Angie's troubled face and said, "Bring us back lasagna. My wife and I could use some alone time."

Angie gave him a grateful smile as Tom laughed. "Sure."

Squirrel exited the bathroom, wearing nothing except a towel around his hips. Angie's gaze followed him into his bedroom.

Dan cleared his throat. "Standing right here."

She blushed and laughed. "Can't blame a girl for looking."

Tom chuckled and called after his roommate, "Squirrel, hurry up. I'm starving too. Meet you in the car."

"Help me wash up?" Dan asked invitingly.

Angie grinned and followed him to the bathroom.

"In ten minutes we can be as loud as we want too, "Dan whispered as he closed the door.

"Are we going to be loud?" Angie began removing her clothing.

"I don't know about you, but I'm going to be." Dan's clothes fell to the floor of the bathroom. The shine in his wife's eyes excited him. Her admiring gaze excited him even more. Her hand on his hip made him groan.

A soft laugh greeted that. "A few more minutes," she whispered.

Dan pulled the elastic from her hair and ran his hands through it. One hand cupped her breast, his thumb circling the hardening nipple as the other tangled in her hair, pulling her head back. She arched into the caress, moaning softly. His lips on her other breast made her groan louder.

"Yes, just like that," he said as his hand dropped lower.

When she was panting, stifling her groans in his shoulder, he picked her up and slid her onto his erection. Her warmth encasing him made him call her name. Arms and legs around his body, her hair blanketing him, she drew him as close as she could.

For minutes, they kissed as he held her. Finally, she wiggled to be put down. When her feet hit the floor, she turned, bending slightly and bracing her hands on the sink.

"Hard," she said in a low voice, meeting his eyes in the mirror. A gasp fogged the mirror as he surged inside her. In seconds, she was grunting as she pressed back against him, meeting his thrusts, each one harder than the last.

The slap of flesh-on-flesh was loud in the tiled room. The feel of her wet tightness was so good, so perfect, he closed his eyes to savor it. He was so caught up in the feel of her, he was speaking for a minute before he realized he was saying it aloud. A continuous chant of, "Yes, fuck yes," growing louder as her hips pushed harder against him and her grunts became one long uhhh. Liquid trailed across his balls as she came and screamed his name.

He continued to pound hard, holding her by the hips now, her body supported by the sink. His thighs were wet with her come as she screamed a high-pitched hoarse cry, and still he pounded. Legs shaking, she stilled, unable to support herself, his hands keeping her from falling. Each thrust caused another spurt of wetness to add to the loud squishing noise he made. When he came, he cried out and jerked his hips in an uncontrollable spasm.

Dan lowered her to the floor, laying her on top of their discarded clothing. The hard tips of her breasts beckoned him. Skin salty from perspiration hardened even more under his caressing tongue. Kneeling between her legs, he used two fingers inside her while his thumb brushed her clit. Another squirting orgasm made her body shudder. She tasted of the sea, salty and fresh, like life itself. He took his time savoring her taste, long slow licks as she panted, trying to catch her breath.

"Turn around so I can reach you," she moaned as he continued to lick her.

Her mouth on his balls filled him with heat. In a minute, she had him fully erect. Every swirl of his tongue she mimicked. Soon he was rock hard, the sensations of her lips on his cock distracting him until his mouth stilled and he groaned as she sucked him.

Not able to concentrate, he laid back on the floor as his hips began to buck. The excited sounds she made as she sucked him deep made him sweat. On the edge of orgasm, she teased him, licking the tip of his penis then down the shaft before resuming taking him as deep as she could.

When he came, he spurted in long continuous jets.

More than the physical act of love exited him, her response made his orgasms so much stronger.

Exhausted, he closed his eyes as she dropped to his chest, panting hard.

"Tomorrow I get the birth control implant removed," she said.

Her soft words cause him to groan and his hips to buck. The thought of making her pregnant aroused him. Even though his body was sated, he craved her, wanted to be inside her, to hear her pant and gasp.

"I can wait though if now isn't a good time. A baby is so fragile— and permanent," she continued unhappily.

"Now is the best time. We're living now. I'll do anything I have to, to keep us safe. And we're already permanent. Let's have as many kids as we can afford." He stroked her hair. "About the wedding." Her body tensed under his hand. "I expected you to have it all planned, but if you'd rather, I can do it, or we could do it together?"

Hot tears trickled to his chest, although she made no other sign of distress. "I don't want to marry you in secret in a dark room somewhere as if we're ashamed, but churches have so many windows, and they're all in the middle of public streets, how could we be safe in one? Every person we invite would be a security risk. Anyone could find out when and where we would be."

"Can we compromise? How about a beach wedding?"

She balanced on an elbow and examined his face. "A beach wedding?"

"Lots of people have them. Let's have a destination wedding on a Hawaiian beach. A nice secluded beach that's both safe and beautiful. "I bet I can plan one within a week."

Eyes alight, her laughter eased his soul.

"I love you."

I love you too," he said.

THIRTY-SIX

---◆---

WE'RE THE REAL DEAL

OLY crap, what happened to you?" Charlene stepped back from the doorway. A hand raised to cover her mouth, her expression was caught between worry and mirth.

JT scowled and brushed passed her, heading toward the bathroom. A livid black eye and cut along his forehead matched a swollen lower lip. Dried blood flaked off his skin. Tom followed, dabbing a wad of blood-soaked napkins to his forearm.

"We caught a demon," JT said over his shoulder.

Angie joined Charlene at the door, peering past her. Squirrel and Dan stood on the doorstep. Squirrel laughed and rubbed his thigh. A skinned knee peeked from the new hole in his jeans, and dried blood dotted his cheek.

"A demon?" Angie's voice caught.

"A kitten. A harmless little fur ball. What a bunch of sissies you guys are," Ronny said as he pushed past Dan, laughing as he flopped onto the couch.

Squirrel grabbed Angie's shoulder and Charlene's arm and pulled them back. "JT might be right. I've had easier captures of armed men. That kitten might be possessed by a devil."

Charlene glanced at the bathroom door. "A kitten did that?"

Ronny laughed louder. "JT jumped into a dumpster where we thought we had it cornered and the lid fell on him. Situational awareness— it's a thing. You might want to look it up. They teach us new guys that right in basic. See, I don't have a scratch on me." He snickered as JT exited the bathroom growling.

Charlene pulled away from Squirrel and examined her husband at close range. A laugh she failed to stop with the hands pressed against her mouth burst from her lips in a peel of giggles. "Oh God, we need a picture of this." Her nose wrinkled as she stepped closer. "After you shower. What the hell was in the dumpster?"

A low growl built to a ripping snarl as Dan passed them, heading to the kitchen.

Squirrel grabbed Charlene's arm again as she turned to follow. "Stay back. Well back. That fiend needs a bath. I helped capture it, but you're on your own there, pal. I value my life too much."

Angie stared after Dan, an expression of amused disbelief on her face. The snarl turned to hisses punctuated by savage growls. All six of them crowded the kitchen doorway. Dan stood at the sink holding a five-ounce ball of matted orange fur that twisted and flailed its body trying to escape. Held with two fingers by its scruff, its efforts redoubled as its paws touched the water.

Angie clapped a hand to her mouth as Charlene laughed louder.

"I thought it was a cat, a big one by the noise it's making." Charlene's gaze traveled Tom's scratched arms and JT's bruises. "It's not even a pound. Wait here, I need a picture." Still laughing, Charlene ran to her bedroom, returning a moment later with her cell phone.

"Hey, Ronny, make yourself useful. Go get us some supplies," Dan called as he fought with the cat, forcing it into the warm water.

"Sure." Ronny winked at Angie. "Holy water, a bible, maybe a priest. What else you think you'll need? Maybe another squad of SEALs in case it gets loose?"

"Go!" JT growled as he grabbed a bag of frozen peas from the freezer and slapped them over his eye.

Still snickering, Ronny left.

JT stood back, glaring at Dan. "Let's save the kitten. Angie will love it," he said in a sarcastic voice. "That isn't a kitten, it's a demon in fur. We chased it for over an hour in an alleyway not much bigger than this room. You never saw such a wily animal."

The women burst into laughter as JT continued describing the capture.

Thirty minutes later, Dan rubbed a towel across the still growling cat's head. Copper eyes glared from the wet fur and tiny white fangs glinted menacingly. Snug against his side wrapped in a towel, the cat's claws were neutralized. Dan grinned ruefully at Angie.

"It seemed like a good idea at the time. I meant him

to be a wedding present, but..." he trailed off as the cat's growl rose in pitch.

"Maybe I can tame him," Angie said doubtfully.

She took a can of tuna from the cabinet and poured a small bowl of milk.

"Let him go in our room."

Released from the towel, the cat arched its back and hissed. It ran under the bed, but reappeared a moment later, nose twitching and squinting at the tuna Angie slid closer. Still growling, it crawled on its stomach to the plate and began to eat. It ate every last piece before disappearing under the bed again. A low growl announced it still wasn't happy.

Angie grinned at Dan. "He's perfect. I love him already."

Dan rolled his eyes. "I think I have fleas. I need a shower. Call the vet and make an appointment. We can probably trick into a box with more tuna."

"Why didn't you do that to begin with?"

"Don't you start," Dan said over his shoulder as he left the room.

Angie's laughter followed him out. A grin on his face, Dan hopped into the shower. He couldn't wait for the wedding tomorrow.

———————◆———————

Dan's wedding day dawned with a magnificent sunrise, which he was able to view at his leisure as he dressed in his best uniform. At ten this morning a boat would take them to a private island where he and Angie would exchange vows.

He'd arranged a surprise reception following the ceremony at a restaurant right near the base. Angie thought the ceremony would end the day. He planned to celebrate all night.

The kitten sat in Angie's lap as she watched him dress. On the floor in the corner of their room, she'd enticed the kitten to her with more fresh fish. Dan could see it was just a matter of time before the cat adored her too.

The cat scurried away as he approached.

"Don't be late," he said as he kissed her brow and offered her a hand to stand. She laughed and pushed him toward the door.

At ten of ten, she emerged from their room, radiant in a simple silk dress. Charlene had helped her arrange her hair into an intricately braided bun and was still patting at it as they left the room.

Outside the house, men had gathered, wearing their dress uniforms. The smile fell from Angie's face as a commotion grew outside the door, ending in JT yelling for someone to halt and drop the box.

"Stay here." Cursing to himself, Dan peered through the peephole on the front door, then opened it a crack.

Why today of all days when he wanted Angie relaxed and happy. A wall of men stood between him and the outside. His eyes widened as he peered over their shoulders.

"Martin?"

Martin, Don Pedro's servant, glanced to the doorway but kept his arms raised. "Mr. Barstow, my employer has sent me with wedding gifts. If I might approach?"

"Let him through," Dan said.

JT followed Martin onto the porch and handed him

the box. "He's clean." A grin creased his face. Widening when Dan took the box.

"Might I speak to your wife?" Martin asked.

Dan stepped back and gestured toward the door. Tom, Squirrel, Ronny, and JT followed him in and spread out around the room.

"Ma'am, I've been tasked with delivering this to you personally, a gift from Isabelle Pedro. She instructed me to tell you that Seraphim is dear to her and she wouldn't entrust her where she had the slightest doubt of her safety."

Martin handed the box to Angie who opened it and cooed.

"Dan, look! Isn't she beautiful?"

A small, fluffy ball of white was offered for his inspection. A soft musical purr and glinting blue eyes greeted him.

"The cat is purebred and worth a fortune," Martin said. "Ms. Isabelle chooses recipients quite carefully. She really does love this cat. That she entrusts it to your care means she believes it will be safe with you." He handed Angie an envelope. "A letter from the don expressing his thanks and best wishes for a long and happy married life."

Martin bowed and backed away, returning to the limousine that had brought him.

Dan took the letter from his wife's hand. His eyebrows rose at the check for three million dollars.

"We can certainly afford as many kids as we want now...." He handed her the check.

"Dan, we can't accept this."

"Let's worry about it later. Right now, I'm going to marry you. And we're going to live happily ever after."

"With our angels and demons?" A beautiful smile erased her worried expression.

Dan laughed as he took the fluffy ball of white from her hand. "Angel, we're the real deal. Anything life throws at us we can take."

Eyes full of promise, she took his hand.

THE END

About the Author

---◆---

C. M. Conney lives and works on the family farm in New England alongside her husband and two grown children. She loves animals and owns more than she'd like to admit. Most days, when she isn't baking or planting, she spends her time writing. An avid reader since childhood, she appreciates work in all genres and likes to mix it up a bit in her own work.

---◆---

Her other books include, *Take the Shot, Ms. Denali,*

The Enemy at Home and Moon Caught

If you enjoyed meeting Seal Team Nine,
their saga continues in—

TAKE THE SHOT

———— ◆ ————

A -ST9- THRILLER

RONNY MITLAND, a spotter for Navy SEAL team
nine, wants Cameron Howard. And he isn't the only
one. Al-Jadr, an emerging terrorist group, also want
her to complete the computer programming on a
surveillance device they've stolen.

Unfortunately, Ronny's wife and job are getting in
the way of his pursuit. Before he can explain his
friends with benefits arrangement with his wife,
Cameron is kidnapped by Al-Jadr operatives.

His team has chased the leader of Al-Jadr to the
hills of Pakistan. Now he needs to decide what kind of
man he is. Will he take the shot, even if it puts him on
the wrong side of the law?